"Harbison dazzles in her latest. . . . Absolutely first-rate."
—*Publishers Weekly* (starred review) on
When in Doubt, Add Butter

"Sure to appeal to fans of Jennifer Weiner, Jane Green, and Emily Giffin. It's a tasty dish of light, escapist reading."
—Examiner.com on *When in Doubt, Add Butter*

"As slick and enjoyable as a brand-new tube of lip gloss."
—*People* on *Hope in a Jar*

"Enough heart . . . for beach readers and foot fetishists alike!"
—*Entertainment Weekly* on *Shoe Addicts Anonymous*

"I would happily recommend *Shoe Addicts Anonymous* to anyone who loves shoes . . . or smart, funny, realistic women enjoying each other's friendship and the happiest of happy endings."
—Jennifer Weiner on *Shoe Addicts Anonymous*

the

COOKBOOK CLUB

Also by Beth Harbison

SHOE ADDICTS SERIES
Shoe Addicts Anonymous
Secrets of a Shoe Addict
A Shoe Addict's Christmas

STAND-ALONE NOVELS
Hope in a Jar
Thin, Rich, Pretty
Always Something There to Remind Me
When in Doubt, Add Butter
Chose the Wrong Guy, Gave Him the Wrong Finger
Driving with the Top Down
Head Over Heels
A Girl Like Her
If I Could Turn Back Time
One Less Problem Without You
Every Time You Go Away

the

COOKBOOK
CLUB

a novel of food and friendship

beth harbison

WILLIAM MORROW
An Imprint of HarperCollins*Publishers*

P.S.™ is a trademark of HarperCollins Publishers.

THE COOKBOOK CLUB. Copyright © 2020 by Beth Harbison. All rights reserved. Printed in the United States of America. No part of this book may be used or reproduced in any manner whatsoever without written permission except in the case of brief quotations embodied in critical articles and reviews. For information, address HarperCollins Publishers, 195 Broadway, New York, NY 10007.

HarperCollins books may be purchased for educational, business, or sales promotional use. For information, please email the Special Markets Department at SPsales@harpercollins.com.

FIRST EDITION

Designed by Diahann Sturge
Title page spread, part opener, and notepad images © BrAt82 / Shutterstock, Inc.
Meeting notes illustrations © Istry Istry / Shutterstock, Inc.

Library of Congress Cataloging-in-Publication Data has been applied for.

ISBN 978-0-06-295862-4

20 21 22 23 24   LSC   10 9 8 7 6 5 4 3 2 1

To Lucia Macro, for guiding this project and all of the fun and flavor that went into it, and to Annelise Robey, for so much support in getting it together and out into the world. I propose wine and fondue to celebrate as soon as possible.

June

CHAPTER ONE

MARGO

Margo Brinker always thought summer would never end. It always felt like an annual celebration that thankfully stayed alive long day after long day, and warm night after warm night. And DC was the best place for it. Every year, spring would vanish with an explosion of cherry blossoms that let forth the confetti of silky little pink petals, giving way to the joys of summer.

Farmer's markets popped up on every roadside. Vendors sold fresh, shining fruits, vegetables and herbs, wine from family vineyards, and handed over warm loaves of bread. Anyone with enough money and nothing to do on a Sunday morning would peruse the tents, trying slices of crisp peaches and bites of juicy smoked sausage, and fill their fisherman net bags with weekly wares.

Of all the summer months, Margo liked June the best. The sun-drunk beginning, when the days were long, long, long with the promise that summer would last forever. Sleeping late, waking only to catch the best tanning hours. It was the time when the last school year felt like a lifetime ago, and there were ages to go until the next one. Weekend cookouts smelled like the backyard—basil, tomatoes on the vine, and freshly cut grass. That familiar backyard scent was then smoked by the rich addition of burgers, hot dogs, and buttered buns sizzling over charcoal.

So there was nothing to complain about on this June 11, when it was unseasonably mild enough to have the kitchen windows cast open. No need for the air conditioner.

She was playing housewife. No matter how legit she tried to feel, she always felt like she was playing house. No matter that she'd been married for ten years—which she googled and found out was the tin anniversary. It felt like someone else's life when she stood in her kitchen, surrounded by her own appliances, and made dinner for her husband. The dog was in the living room, the fence had finally been repaired, and she had an opinion on air-filter brand. The dishwasher was running, the sound of the washer and dryer rumbled from the laundry room (at the corner of the yard it smelled like dryer sheets under the vent), and she was dicing farmer's market veggies for a salad for Calvin.

Calvin was having a weight crisis.

It was impossible to count how many times in the last decade that Calvin had had what he perceived to be a weight emergency. But then, if it wasn't weight, it was the fear that his higher-end-of-*normal* cholesterol levels were dangerous. Or that sugars were going to age him prematurely. He'd just read an article about activated charcoal and how it could save your life. He'd just read an article about activated charcoal and how it might kill you.

There was a twenty-gallon Rubbermaid in the garage filled with Calvin's retired, preemptive lifesavers. Things that, if they worked, would presumably give him the gift of immortality. Ergonomic keyboards. Ridiculous-looking orthopedically correct shoes (Margo said they were high heels designed by Dr. Seuss; Calvin said she didn't understand the human body). Running suits to increase sweat but that made him look like a stand-in for Mister Fantastic. This Rubbermaid stood beside a personal sauna and a machine that vibrated the fat away—this one Margo had genuinely thought was a joke. "Wasn't that the same machine used for comic relief in *Mad Men*?"

She used to think it was cute. When they'd first gotten together, little more than kids themselves, they'd run together, tried meditating together, then hung it all up and eaten together, enjoying a lot of wine before toppling into bed.

Maybe it was the wine that had made him so pleasant. He didn't drink it much anymore. Something about clear liquors being less fattening.

They hadn't had a real meal together in years. Those late, boozy nights with sloppy cheeseburgers and too many appetizers were long gone. No longer would they get pasta and wine by the bottle, telling their Sicilian server not to judge them for how much cheese they wanted ground over their gnocchi and carbonara. They would drink beer and share those plasticky nachos and watch awful bands cover extremely good bands.

Their indulgence might kill them one day, but wasn't it worth it? That had been her opinion. She'd never really considered what would happen once the indulgence was gone.

Margo, luckily, was always up for whatever challenge made her days more interesting. She was constantly trying to make dupes for whatever she—or he—was really in the mood for. Egg white huevos rancheros, turkey meat loaf, chicken chili, and on one disastrous Thanksgiving, Tofurkey. Nutritional yeast weakly filled the big shoes of good Parmesan. Lettuce did the minimum to live up to the utility purpose of a tortilla while textured vegetable protein tried pitifully to be taco meat.

It would have felt like a stupid waste of mealtime if her mother hadn't been interested in getting the recipes to make for Margo's dad, whose cholesterol—unlike Calvin's—was legitimately high. Last year he'd had a heart attack. And though he seemed for all the world to be okay now, both Margo and her mom lived in constant fear of it happening again.

Which was how Margo had ended up starting a tiny YouTube channel as June's Cleaver so she could send instructional videos to her mom, inspired by *Leave It to Beaver*.

Anyway, her mom got a kick out of it, and since, when it began, she was the one and only subscriber, that was all that mattered.

Now she had thirty-six whole subscribers because her mother had passed the word along to friends in her retirement community, so Margo felt she had a small responsibility to them, even though they were living a better life than everyone else she knew. While most people Margo's age were exhausted, her mom's friends were taking pottery wheel classes and getting together to drink boxed chardonnay and make her healthy salads.

It wasn't going to become a cash cow, but it was a fun hobby, and Calvin kept saying Margo could take tax deductions for their food bills. Something about allowing a loss for three out of five years for a "hobby" business.

That was Calvin these days—always looking for ways to capitalize by characterizing Margo and the things that defined her as a "loss."

She set everything up in place on the counter, turned on the camera, and started talking.

"Hey! Okay, guys, so since this is healthy, it's—by definition—boring, so we need to add flavor and punch wherever we can. I sprinkle chopped egg whites with cayenne for a little extra zing." She chopped the egg whites and added the cayenne with a flourish. "You can also chop a brazil nut and add it for both texture and valuable selenium, which is good for the heart *and* cancer prevention. That's what I've heard anyway. As you know, I'm not a doctor or medical professional so always consult with your physician before making any radical changes." She felt stupid saying it, but her father had insisted she work it into every video.

"I'm adding red bell peppers today too. They're a real super-food, nutritionally. I like them raw, but if you prefer them roasted, pop them on your gas burner or under the broiler for a few minutes to bring out that sweet meatiness. If that description didn't jar you, you're not paying attention or you're falling asleep." She smiled at the camera, then went to adjust its position to show the pepper she was blistering on the burner. "Turn it with tongs, never your hands, because that will hurt like hell, be*lieve* me, and it gets hotter than you think, faster than you think. Rotate it until it's as cooked as you like it. I prefer these blackened peaks, but leaving the grooves red and raw." She turned it again, then removed it with her tongs and placed it on the wooden butcher block, adjusted the camera, and chopped.

"A little all-purpose seasoning—you know I've recommended this one, called Spike"—she sprinkled some on the chopped red peppers—"and it's ready to add." She added it to the rest, not mentioning that earlier she'd wrestled that pack of Spike out of the dog's mouth and gotten inspired to cook when his breath smelled like pot roast. It was a confusing feeling to get hungry from the dog's breath.

The salad *looked* gorgeous, no doubt about it. And her addition of her own Marilyn Merlot vinaigrette was almost certain to be a hit with her subscribers, but she couldn't wait to add a little ranch dressing to it for actual flavor. You can only do so much.

Her phone dinged and she wiped her hands on a dishcloth and picked it up. Calvin.

Going to be in a hurry tonight, heat up one of my dinners.

His "dinners." She called them his Mean Cuisine. They came in a sad box, and a sadder microwavable tray with film.

It was good that he was trying to stay healthy. She appreciated that. She just wished he was a *little* more fun in the process.

The really bad part was that somehow she was beginning to get used to eating this blah prepackaged food herself. It wasn't like she was going to rip the plastic off his dinner and plop it on his plate then set about making Florentine stuffed manicotti for one. In fact, she'd recently eaten a bite of something real, and found herself thinking, blasphemously, that it had too much . . . too much . . . what was it . . .

Flavor.

For ten years she'd been searching for the middle ground in almost every area of her life so she could settle into something that, if it wasn't happiness per se, would at least resemble contentment.

Meanwhile, she was a well-oiled machine, producing everything on a timetable, as requested and predicted. Calvin would be home about six, eat his dinner, leave his dishes, and go do whatever it was he was so eager to do after dinner.

At 7:00 P.M., she'd get some appetizers out of the refrigerator that she'd prepped and wrapped in the morning, then heat them up for her book club meeting at seven-thirty.

Calvin might not be her dream man anymore, but he was her husband. They had a life. They had come up with a rhythm. Ever since she'd turned thirty, the years seemed to flow so quickly. Sometimes it was disconcerting, but most of the time it was just . . . life, which was what most of her friends seemed to have as well.

Life with Calvin.

Yes, maybe without him she might finally live in London. She never would or could with him, he couldn't find good in the rain or the cold and he "couldn't understand the damn accent." She could live on some little street, have a local pub . . .

She could do whatever she wanted, whenever she wanted. Follow some ridiculous decorating trend in the house without his observation. But they had been together since they got married at twenty-three; life without him was unthinkable.

She so envied the girls a decade behind her who had Pinterest at their fingertips.

She couldn't imagine what it must feel like to be twenty-two now. She imagined the optimism that must be felt by a girl that young who could imagine a bachelorette's studio. Gilded mirrors. Etsy prints. No husband's-great-aunt's afghan—just a lush, warm, faux-fur blanket.

Her kitchen—she couldn't even think about that. In a perfect world, she'd have special, collected pieces. Those beautiful wineglasses she wanted from Crate&Barrel. That French-looking ceramic rolling pin from Anthropologie. Special pinch bowls into which she could happily toss a handful of freshly chopped mirepoix.

She could have art up that she liked. She could have a big closet that didn't make a man ask why she had so many clothes she never wore—and she wouldn't have to answer that the problem wasn't how many clothes she had but how few outings and events.

She would be happy with less money, less space, less everything. It gave her such a thrill to imagine the stack of Condé Nast magazines she could artfully arrange beside rose-gold coasters. Drinking rosé alone in a living room, binge-watching whatever show she wanted . . .

Margo snapped out of it, realizing the twenty-three-year-old full of hope had just morphed into a more hopeful and independent version of herself.

But the moment Margo's mind ever started to drift there, she started to think again about paying the bills by finding something she was qualified for. She thought of being alone. She thought of how fleeting the freedom might truly feel. She was just starting to assemble the book club appetizers when Calvin came in, looking unusually buoyant. She smiled at him, a pang of guilt ringing through her. He had to come in looking so happy, right after she'd been having naive fantasies about leaving him and—what, traveling in time to be twenty-two again?

She felt like an idiot.

"Hey there," she said, gathering her camera and tripod and

putting them aside. No question of whether or not she was in the middle of using them.

"Is it ready?"

"In a couple minutes."

He came to the counter, but not to her. "Something smells good."

"Maybe it's the Caesar dressing." She pointed with her elbow at the bottle marked ZERO CALORIE ROMAINE EMPIRE.

He bent over it and sniffed. "Mmm."

And there's your serving, she thought, since, according to the label there was no nutritional difference between smelling it and eating it.

"How was work?" she asked him, putting the little frozen black plastic dish on the counter. It clattered like she'd set a slab of marble on the granite.

"Really good," he said, dipping his finger into the bottle and tasting the dressing. "Really, *really* good."

He didn't elaborate immediately, so she had to nudge him. "What? What happened?"

"Well." He smiled the smile of a person who just couldn't help it. "They're promoting me to VP of the San Francisco office."

Margo actually gasped. "Congratulations!" She felt like she'd tripped over an uneven sidewalk. A promotion? San Francisco? How was this the first she was hearing of it?

"Thanks."

Something about that set her into an old mind-set she had chosen long ago to grow out of. She always assumed she was about to be left, and could hear a simple word like "thanks" and take it to mean, "Thank you, because this is my thing, and has no effect on you, and now I'm leaving you for a twenty-two-year-old with an interesting Pinterest presence."

She needed to remember that wasn't how people engaged with each other. Especially married people.

"I had no idea this was even in the works!" She studied his expression, curious as to what was making his jaw muscle twitch behind his smile. "Did you?"

He leveled his hand and tipped it side to side. "I didn't want to say anything in case it didn't work out, but . . ." Then he beamed and shrugged. "It happened. It's a huge change, but meant to be. A brand-new start."

"I'll say."

He wasn't bothering to try to sell her on it.

Did he just expect her to drop everything and go across the country?

She went to the sink and washed her hands, buying a couple of extra moments so she wouldn't sound too sharp. "When were you thinking we'd leave? There's a lot involved in closing up shop here, so to speak."

He hesitated. She froze, eyes locked on the window crank above the faucet.

"That's the tricky part."

"Tricky?" She turned the water off with her forearm and wiped her hands on the towel hanging on the bar in front of the sink. She remembered a restaurant she'd gone to in San Francisco, years before. Delfina? That was it. She'd had delicious sourdough bread there, painted with butter. Fragrant, crisp-on-the-outside Saffron Arancini. Bright fresh salad with real oil and good vinegar and fresh cracked pepper.

She was avoiding it.

There was no denying that the food scene by the bay was on a par with New York City, and though Calvin would probably not join her, she could picture getting carryout for herself now and then.

Maybe even sitting in a nice little café with a book and a sandwich or pasta. And real cheese instead of the no-fat stuff Calvin put on his air-popped popcorn on "special occasions."

He wasn't saying anything bad. That was in her head.

"Yeah." He seemed to be musing to himself. "Tricky."

She fluffed up his salad and handed it over.

"Elaborate."

He took a short breath. "I guess I'm just going to have to be right up front with you. Fast and honest, like Robin says."

A cold finger of dread ran down her spine. "Robin?"

"Yeah, you know Robin, my therapist?"

"Dr. Lang?" Since when did he call her Robin?

He gave a half shrug. "I've been seeing her so long that it seemed silly to keep calling her Dr. Lang."

"Mm. Seeing Robin." Her teeth were gritted hard. She forced them apart.

He nodded. "Yes, seeing my therapist." He squinted and looked at her, and had the nerve to look irritated by her. Like she was being a bit much. "This new job," he said. "The move. Everything. I'm . . . I'm going alone." He took a bite, finally having the guts to look as avoidant as he was being. "Boy, this is good."

This was a man who could find the good in that salad, but not in their marriage? Was she hearing correctly?

"What do you mean you're *going alone*? To find a place to live? While I sell this place? Or . . . ?" She didn't take her eyes off her husband, though his glances were flitting all over the place.

He pressed his lips together and shook his head. "No, it's just me." He closed his eyes for a moment and she just *knew* he was picturing "Robin," who had probably coached him through this conversation, telling him he was entitled to it. "I'm leaving."

The words rang through the acoustics of the kitchen. The echo had been a selling point when they first found the house. Margo had said "I'm *married*!" and listened to the way it bounced off the walls.

"I see," she said now. It was all there was to say.

"Yeah, that *wasn't* so hard. Just out with it and, boom, it's over." This seemed like an aside to himself, rather than to Margo.

The dryer finished its cycle and started its insanely long

jingle. Never had it ever bothered her so much, and it almost always bothered her.

She gave a sharp inhale and shifted her gaze to the salad in front of him. The video she'd posted. An idiot woman makes a salad for the man who is about to divorce her and for her thirty-six geriatric YouTube followers.

Oh, what she'd give for him to have that heart attack he'd been dreading. Right now. Right here. The whole scene played out in rapid motion in her head: him clutching his chest, falling to the floor, trying to choke out the words "Call . . . nine . . . one . . ." while she pretended to not understand his request.

Nine one? I don't understand. Who do you want to call?

"That was . . . *easy?*" she repeated his words. Her mouth felt numb. "Calvin, am I understanding this right? I can't tell because you're being super weird. Have you just said you are actually leaving me? Leaving our marriage? As in, you want a *divorce?*"

He replayed her question in his head, she could tell by the thoughtful look and three short nods before he said, "Yes." Then, as a long afterthought, "I'm sorry. But it's for the best."

The nerve this took was unbelievable. "For *whose* best?" But she knew the answer. Throughout their entire marriage, they'd both done everything possible for *his* best.

"Well . . . *mine* for one." He gave a quick smile, as if he'd said something amusing. "But yours too, you'll see."

She let the wave of rage flow over her flesh, and then she followed his gaze to the salad he clearly wanted to eat. Momentarily, she thought about dumping the whole lot into the trash. But she hated to waste food, even though he didn't deserve to eat it and she didn't have an appetite suddenly. Automatically, she went to the dishwasher and started emptying it, even though it hadn't finished its eternal heated dry yet.

What was she *doing*?

Trying to feel normal, she guessed. There was no way this was really happening. No way.

"And is *Robin* part of your plan?" she asked. "Is *Robin* going with you?"

He scoffed. "She's my therapist! Of course she's not. In fact, she's already referred me to a former colleague who works there, so, really, it's working out perfectly. Meant to be."

That's what she'd thought once. *Meant to be.*

"Eat," she said, shoving his bowl closer as she passed him. "You're going to need your energy."

"For what?" He took a big bite and rolled his eyes in bliss. "You've really gotten so good at this lean stuff."

She gathered her internal strength, vision blurring. "Packing and getting the hell out of here."

He shook his head, chewing. "I don't have to leave right away," he said with a mouthful.

"Oh yes, you do." Seeing how much he was enjoying her food enraged her. It was probably more accurate to say it pulled the pin on the anger that was already tightening deep beneath her disbelief, but whatever caused it, she found herself unable to fight it. "In fact, you've got three seconds to eat whatever else you're going to eat there before you're wearing it."

He looked genuinely shocked. "Margo, this isn't like you!"

"Correction: this isn't like Margo your wife." The flames of fury engulfed her. She couldn't believe this was happening, and that it was happening so . . . so casually. "Let me introduce you to Margo your *ex*-wife."

"Can't we be friends?"

The idea that they could suddenly shift baffled her violently.

"No." She picked up the bowl and dumped the whole thing in his lap, careful to make sure the oily dressing saturated his shirt. She looked him over and clicked her tongue against her teeth. "Get yourself cleaned up, Calvin, honestly, you're a mess. Oh, and you have half an hour to pack what you want and get out. If you don't, I'll call the police. I don't know if they'll be able to *enforce* anything, but I do know that will embarrass you to death, and if there's one thing you hate, it's being embarrassed." She walked out of the room, shaking inside but hoping he couldn't tell from the outside.

"My dinner," he said stupidly, still sitting in the position she'd left him in.

She walked to the sunroom, where she had everything set up for book club, and sat down. It was supposed to start in an hour. Some people had to drive that long, so she couldn't very well cancel at the last minute like this. Somehow she was going to have to see this through.

"I need more than half an hour," he said, as if that was the point. As if that was the point *at all*.

"My book club is coming then. Do you really want to slither out of here in front of them? Because I *promise* you, I will call the police whether they are here or not. In fact, witnesses would probably be good."

His face colored and she knew he was imagining word getting back to his colleagues somehow.

"I'll pack a bag," he conceded. "Then I'll be back for my things."

Book club, formerly an enjoyable enough diversion for Margo, had all at once become a nightmare.

In dreading having to entertain that night, after receiving the blow of news that her entire life was shattering, it hadn't occurred to her that Susi Winslow's husband also worked at Calvin's firm, Cromwell and Covington, and that she might know about the promotion.

She did, despite the fact that it was the biggest firm in the area and the men's paths probably never crossed.

And in a move she obviously thought was a kindness to a humble Margo, she made the announcement the minute everyone sat down with their drinks, going so far as to raise a toast to Calvin—and by extension, Margo—for their good fortune.

"You are going to *love* San Francisco! Summer is an *awesome* time to move there, warm days and cool nights. But, really, the weather is always amazing. We're going to miss you in the book club, but, my God, you are going to have the time of your life!"

Margo didn't know what to say. How to brace the world for the news without coming out with the whole true story right here and now. She couldn't help but be glad he'd gotten out because, for all her bravado, she really didn't want to have this scene in front of everyone.

So she sat there, frozen like one of those goats that goes stiff and falls over when it's scared, half hoping she didn't fall over silently. Half hoping she would. She cleared her throat, trying to buy a little time for an answer.

"You know . . . we've only just talked about it a little bit," she said. "Obviously Calvin is going out there first . . ." There was nothing obvious about that at all, in fact it was weird, but she had long since learned if you said something definitively enough people didn't even bother to think you were lying.

"Well, sure," Marie Bentz muttered, after an awkward moment. "Makes sense."

"And I'm not sure how I feel about leaving this town, honestly. I do love it here." Never mind that an hour ago, for one brief moment, she'd been thinking what she'd give for a whiff of the Saffron Arancini and meatballs at Delfina. Or, right before that, fantasizing like a middle-schooler about the (alternative) life of a grown-up.

"Oh, come *on,*" Susi said, smiling and red-faced as usual. "You'll get over that! How could you *not?*"

Margo tried to put on a smile, but it felt distinctly like the pursed, unyielding lips sewn into a corpse to prevent a reflexive gasp or gape. "We'll see." Desperation manifested as a rabbity heartbeat and tingling fingers and toes. She couldn't have them start in on selling San Francisco to her. "Should we get to the book?"

There was no question that people noticed something was up with her. How could they not? Usually they spent a good long time catching up on each other's lives before diving into the subject matter, and that was when no one had anything going on. That she was pushing ahead now when, ostensibly, she had some tremendous life news, it had to be crystal clear that something was up.

As it continued to be as they continued the discussion and she was mum. Her eyes were filled with tears, so she had to be careful not to blink too hard, lest they spill over her cheeks and become obvious. So she was still as a mannequin, with her painted-on mini-smile and wide, glassy eyes.

Finally, Jody Brooks nudged her, and it was her undoing. "What do you think about the distinction between grief and mourning, Margo?"

And that was all it took. Suddenly the tears she thought she'd held in so well all came out, and when she opened her mouth to speak, instead she took a gasp like a drowning person who'd been under for a minute or so too long. Suddenly she was shuddering and crying and everyone around her—friends, but not *real friends*—stayed in their places, looking absolutely flummoxed.

She tried to remember if she'd ever had a conversation of any consequence with any of them. If she'd ever seen a genuine emotion from anyone or shown one herself. Book club was easy, chatting about a book they'd all read was easy, lunch was easy, shopping was *really* easy. But if they were truly her friends, wouldn't she have told them about Calvin the minute they'd walked in? Looked to them for comfort?

Instead she was just embarrassed beyond belief.

"I'm sorry," she managed.

"What on earth is it, Margo? I had no idea this book would affect you so deeply!"

The book. They thought she was upset about the book. Her ironic laugh morphed into another sob.

"I found it exhilarating," Jody said, and Margo took a minute to think the worst of her for simply echoing the word all the critics had used, which was pasted all over the book.

Margo looked at her, then at Michelle, and Susi, and Cynthia, and Sara. She still thought of Sara as "the new girl," even though she'd joined them around Easter and Margo had even met her at Nordstrom Café for lunch once. They'd talked about shoes. The whole time.

"It's just that . . ." The words surged in Margo's throat before she had time to think about it, much less talk herself out of it. The lie came fast and somehow felt like the only thing that was believable. "I haven't told many people this, but . . . I was married before. When I was young. And he died," she hastened to add, lest her implication wasn't clear enough to shut them up.

"*How?*" Sara asked, tactlessly. Of course she *wanted* to know. They all *wanted* to know. But one of the things about being an adult was realizing that you're not allowed to ask how people died, no matter how hard you wondered.

She pictured Calvin, in a fast slide show of the ways she'd like to murder him right now: strangled, pushed down the stairs, battered to death by his plate, stabbed in the back with one of the steak knives he had told her were too expensive for a birthday gift.

None of those scenarios would work for her dearly departed nameless first husband, however. So she drew all the dignity she could muster around her. "I'd rather not talk about it. Like I said, we were young, it was a long time ago." The more imaginary distance she could put between herself and this lie, the better. "I . . . I thought I could do this, I really did, but it's just too close to the bone still."

"We understand, don't we, girls?" Susi said, but her eyes were nearly wild with the clear intention to quiz Margo on this later. Of the group, Susi and Margo probably were the closest, but that wasn't saying much. About three times a year they added a game of tennis to what was, with everyone else, simply an occasional lunch. That was what constituted friend-ship for them.

How had she let that happen? How had she lived in solitude for so long? Some of her friends were still getting invited to bachelorette parties in Cabo. They felt like teenagers, but they were merely people who had waited to be frozen. Waited until they were themselves.

Some of her old friends hadn't even been married yet—which wouldn't have been worth noting if she wasn't suddenly, *so* suddenly, about to be divorced.

And what would happen if she just opened up to all of these women?

It seemed like there was too much to say all of a sudden; how to explain the past ten years of her marriage realistically, after not complaining in all that time, so they'd understand this sudden end. But it wasn't possible. These weren't the kind of people she had shorthand with. Even now, thinking Margo was grieving over some long-lost love, they all made nervous, short movements, like unsophisticated robots.

"Yes, we understand," said Susi, when the agreement was stilted and minimal.

Everyone present mumbled some form of agreement with Susi and pitched in to clear the dishes or find another tidying task, but Margo insisted she could do it herself. "It will help me focus on something less painful," she said, hoping that was an argument that they couldn't refute. "I'm really sorry."

It was a clumsy, long, apologetic goodbye from everyone, and it took way longer than she would have liked. Finally, everyone left. At least everyone was happy to take home a small box of appetizers. Margo had sprung long ago for a restaurant-size pack of those brown envelope-style to-go boxes.

Either her cooking or her lie was good enough for them to take it, and right now, either felt like a win.

Margo went back to the sunroom and drank every one of their remaining drinks—not even giving a damn about every gross backwash story she'd ever heard—before sitting down next to the fatty artichoke dip she'd initially been careful to park on the table farthest from her seat so as to avoid eating too much. Now it was a free-for-all, and she ripped pieces right off the baguette, rather than using the delicate little serrated knife she'd left out for that purpose.

Her marriage was over.

Her book club was over (it wasn't like she could play the role of widow forever, and she *definitely* couldn't admit she'd lied on top of further confessing her marriage was over).

The champagne was quickly gone.

Her real estate hobby had never really paid that well to begin with, but it certainly wasn't going to earn her enough for a good lawyer, and there was zero guess as to what she might get in alimony as an able-bodied thirty-three-year-old, never mind that she had no marketable skills.

What in the world was she going to do for "fun" now?

CHAPTER TWO

MARGO

Two weeks, four showers, merely four changes of yoga pants, and one talk with a lawyer later, the idea came to her. It appeared from nowhere when she pulled the Shun chef's knife out of its block.

I could just kill myself, Margo thought, always having a flair for the dramatic. *It would be so fast.*

She'd almost majored in drama in college but her parents had convinced her it was a useless major that wouldn't lead to any profitable career options, so she'd settled for taking a few classes as electives and had instead majored in the equally useless, but somehow more respectable, English literature.

Of course she couldn't stab herself. If she were going to kill herself, and she definitely wasn't, she'd find a much less painful way to do it. What she really wanted was for the pain and insult of rejection to go away. The emptiness to be filled. The gaping uncertainty about *everything* suddenly and the way it mixed with the previously unacknowledgeable dissatisfaction that she now *had* to focus on, even though it made her feel terrible too.

The dismantling of her future. From a solid—if frightening—boulder into rocky shards of rubble that blocked her every move.

If she were gone suddenly, there would be no eruption of grief. Just a suburban rumor mill fueled by tap water gossip.

She considered the knife again, strong and solid in her narrow hand. She really should have killed Calvin with it. À la *Chicago*. He had it comin' . . .

That would have solved all of her problems neatly.

She looked at the blade of the eight-inch Shun DM0522 chef's knife she should never have sprung for. It was new—razor sharp, as she got all of her knives sharpened frequently and professionally. Like all those As Seen on TV ads—Margo's knife was sharp enough to cut through an empty Coke can!

Though who'd willingly do that to their blade? (Or their fingers when it came time to pick up the shredded can and throw it out.) The knife shop in town where they sharpened for two bucks an inch.

This knife had cost sixteen bucks to sharpen.

Calvin wasn't worth wasting that sixteen-dollar sharpening on.

No, turns out she wasn't the murder *or* the suicide type.

She was just another divorcing woman, leaving her twenties in the dust behind her, without enough money, without enough self-esteem, and without enough energy to start over.

But she *did* have a superb knife.

And that could take her a reasonable distance toward *some* satisfaction, if not happiness. Culinary satisfaction.

The prospect of eating a huge plate of tender-tough noodles with bright Tuscan tomato and shaved Parmesan was extremely appealing. She literally couldn't imagine the last time she'd made something decadent in this house because she was always so worried about Calvin's needs.

Damn it, it wasn't fair that she'd had to worry about his needs so much when he clearly didn't give a damn about her.

She put down the knife and went to the beautifully organized pantry she took so much pride in.

She was pained deeply and suddenly by the idea of cooking anything for herself. Dicing, kneading, pounding meat—even the aggressive promise of emotional release sounded like too much energy. She'd have to draw too much from an empty well.

The tears were slow to come by now. The ache came. The pain was there all the time. But the satisfaction of tears was growing elusive.

Her eyes blurred on the shelf full of collected spices.

Malnutrition and misery sank her to her feet, and she slammed against the door, then reached for her phone.

Out of habit, she opened Instagram.

She was faced with women her age who had taken a nose-dive into the Mommy-identity, and girls from her past posting fancy cocktails at trendy restaurants.

Speaking of moms.

She tapped the "favorites" button, then "Mom." She held the phone to her ear for one second before hanging up. Good God, she didn't even know what time it was. So instead she went to her cookbook collection to pick out just the right recipe, no matter how much energy it drained from her.

She knew which book she was going to pick. She knew it was always Marcella Hazan's. But she took the time to linger over the spines nevertheless, like she was perusing high school pictures of old friends.

The Enchanted Broccoli Forest. Oh, what a pleasure that was! Mollie Katzen's handwritten and illustrated recipes that recalled some glorious time in upstate New York when a girl with an appetite could work at a funky vegetarian restaurant and jot down some tasty favorites between shifts. That one had the Pumpkin Tureen soup that Margo had made so many times when she first got the book. She loved the cheesy onion soup served from a pumpkin with a hot dash of horseradish and rye croutons. And the Cardamom Coffee Cake, full of butter, real vanilla, and rich brown sugar, said to be a favorite at the restaurant, where Margo loved to imagine the patrons picking up extras to take back to their green, grassy, shady farmhouses dotted along winding country roads.

Linda's Kitchen by Linda McCartney, Paul's first wife, the vegetarian cookbook that had initially spurred her yearlong attempt at vegetarianism (with cheese and eggs, thank you very much) right after college. Margo used to have to drag Calvin into such phases and had finally lured him in by saying that surely anything Paul would eat was good enough for them.

Because of *Linda's Kitchen,* Margo had dived into the world of textured vegetable protein instead of meat, and tons of soups, including a very good watercress, which she never would have tried without Linda's inspiration. It had also inspired her to get a gorgeous, long marble-topped island for prep work. Sometimes she only cooked for the aesthetic pleasure of the gleaming marble topped with rustic pottery containing bright fresh veggies, chopped to perfection.

Then *Bistro Cooking* by Patricia Wells caught her eye, and she took it down. Some pages were stuck together from previous cooking nights, but the one she turned to, the most splattered of all, was the one for Onion Soup au Gratin, the recipe that had taught her the importance of cheese quality. No mozzarella or broken string cheeses with—maybe—a little lacy Swiss thrown on. And definitely none of the "fat-free" cheese that she'd tried in order to give Calvin a rich dish without the cholesterol.

No, for this to be great, you needed a good, aged, nutty Gruyère from what you couldn't help but imagine as the green grassy Alps of Switzerland, where cows grazed lazily under a cheerful children's-book blue sky with puffy white clouds.

Good Gruyère was blocked into rind-covered rounds and aged in caves before being shipped fresh to the USA with a whisper of fairy-tale clouds still lingering over it. There was a cheese shop downtown that sold the best she'd ever had. She'd tried it one afternoon when she was avoiding returning home. A spunky girl in a visor and an apron had perked up as she walked by the counter, saying, "Cheese can change your life!"

The charm of her youthful innocence would have been enough to be cheered by, but the sample she handed out really did it.

The taste was beyond delicious. It was good alone, but it cried out for ham or turkey or a rich beefy broth with deep caramelized onions for soup.

She bought plenty. Asked for the girl's name, fully intending to contact the store and say how helpful she'd been—but as with all things like that, Margo forgot.

And as with most things Margo forgot, she ate cheese instead.

Margo loved best pulling the browned melted cheese off the lip and sides of the bowl after broiling it. It was a hard-earned delicacy like no other.

She made a mental note to revisit that soup, but tonight she needed carbs. Tonight she needed Marcella Hazan. *The Essentials of Classic Italian Cooking*. It sounded dull, right? That's what Margo had thought every time she passed it in her grandparents' kitchen. Until that time she'd desperately needed her grandfather's Bolognese recipe and learned it came straight from the book. It didn't matter; that might be his source, but to her it was still the dish she ate and loved at the long, scarred wood table in her grandparents' modest apartment kitchen, the wood out of place on the ugly linoleum floor, yet perfect when topped with the slightly chipped porcelain plates he brought back from the tiny restaurant he owned, when he could no longer serve on them, and the fresh, bright green salads and crisped, buttery garlic bread that was a must with every meal.

There was no question that if she was going to have one solid comfort meal, it would be one of Marcella's pasta dishes.

Screw Calvin. She was going to do it.

First she set one of her four-quart All-Clad saucepans on the stove. *America's Test Kitchen* had rated them highest once upon a time, and she had been collecting bits and pieces ever since. Most treasured were these beautiful, bright, Skittle-colored lacquered pots.

Next, she took out a head of garlic from the bowl on the green-flecked black countertop she'd once loved passionately. Now it was just a surface, but it was a strong enough surface for her to crash her fist down on the head of garlic and split it into multiple cloves, which could then be easily separated with a knock on the broad side of her favorite knife.

Shun to the rescue again. She smashed eight cloves of garlic and set them aside, knowing whatever she made she wanted it to be rich and garlicky, then swept the bits of papery skin into her hand and threw them in the trash.

Next, she heated the Le Creuset gently on the gas stove. The piece was robin's-egg blue on the outside, cream on the inside, like an old convertible or a young girl's gingham dress and pinafore. The color had seemed so fun and retro when she bought it. Calvin hated it, said without explanation that it was so *like her* to pick that.

When, in fact, it wasn't. In some senseless, unidentifiable way, it had been a compromise. Maybe she'd just gotten so used to thinking that anything she hated equaled something he liked, and vice versa.

In reality, she wanted pretty things. Especially in the kitchen.

She wanted pastel chaos—a cacophony of sweet colors to set ablaze on the gas stove and from which to plume well-spiced aromas.

Who knew how long she'd compromised unnecessarily, but nevertheless, here she was in her stainless and marble kitchen, surrounded by dull-oak cabinets. A spark of color found only where she'd been unable to resist it.

Like this Le Creuset Dutch oven.

When her energy dipped again, she paired her phone with the speaker Calvin was always silencing and put on her retro playlist. Etta James wailed out "Something's Got a Hold on

Me," and Margo shut her eyes and forced herself to give a damn about anything.

Margo tested for the right heat by flicking a speck of water onto the hot surface of the Dutch oven. When it sizzled and evaporated, she put in some pungent olive oil—*not* extra-virgin, nothing around here was—and let it heat until it shimmered.

It wasn't until then that she decided what to make: that thick, meaty Bolognese sauce. It didn't normally call for the garlic, but so what? She happened to have some, and she loved braised garlic in anything. She would eat the soft, tender meat straight off a knife if that was all she had at hand.

She went to the ventilated drawer she'd had installed under the counter, where she kept the root vegetables. She took out two medium yellow onions and one Vidalia. Piece by piece, she cut the ends off, sliced into the brittle skins and pulled them off, dropping them into the trash. She loved onions, but they made such a mess. A subtle one, tiny bits of papery skin on the counter and floor, but a mess nonetheless. When they were all peeled, she set them aside and got the dish sponge so she could clean up all the little flecks of skin that had stuck to the counter and cutting board.

Then she chopped the onion finely and dumped it into the hot pot with a sizzle. A little salt to sweat the vegetables, and within moments the savory aroma was rising into the air. Her appetite pinged in reflexive reaction.

She took carrots and celery out of the fridge and peeled and chopped, stopping every now and then to stir the onion to keep it from sticking. It was getting sweet and translucent, so she tossed the other vegetables in and added a pinch more salt.

Mirepoix. She thought the word to herself, rolling it around in her mind. *Mirepoix, mirepoix, mirepoix.* Cajun "Holy Trinity"—onions, celery, and carrots, diced fine, heated to savory sweet, and left to bring magic to whatever dish they were added into.

No doubt about it, this was going to be great. Almost holy. With a little bread and red wine—body and blood of Christ—she might make up for years of not going to mass.

Either way, they'd go great with the meal.

She dug in the freezer for ground beef and ground pork, found both—of course; she was nothing if not thorough at keeping the kitchen well stocked. She unwrapped the meat. No need to thaw, she just tossed them right in with the cooking mirepoix and stirred, contemplating her life and how many meals she had prepared at this stove, and how many moods had accompanied them.

There were a few standouts—the ricotta she'd finally perfected after watching a ton of YouTube videos. She'd fucked up batch after batch (one burned, one was so thin she ended up with about a quarter cup of cheese curds, one—inexplicably—never set at all and just poured like milk right through the strainer), but finally it had come together, and she'd infused the finished product with garlic and sliced basil and eaten most of it herself before Calvin arrived home and declared it "too rich" and ate his salad without it or the dressing she'd made.

Why did she *miss* him?

She'd just spent two weeks without getting properly dressed, watching everything from *The Sopranos* to *Chopped* and eating through everything in the house from frozen and awful to good and laborious.

And why? Because a selfish, narcissistic jerk had left her life?

Well, kind of, yeah. It's pretty insulting to be dumped by a jerk you fantasized about being without.

You'd think it'd be easier. Good riddance.

But it's not. It's just a different kind of pain.

Really makes you revisit your sense of self-worth. Was he with someone else?

Was he with his therapist?

That was the misery-wound she'd self-inflicted and chose to constantly agitate.

An insane theory that not only had he left her for another woman, but also that the woman was his therapist.

She always pictured her in glasses and tweed, like a *She's All That* plus a PhD.

Did *she* lie in bed next to him every night now, waking every so often to his foghorn farts, her heart pounding so hard she couldn't get back to sleep without an hour or a Benadryl because of the stress that she could not isolate an origin for?

Did he ask her every morning if the bald spot on the crown

of his head was visible (it was) and if the generic Rogaine from Costco was working (it wasn't)? Did she artfully squeeze around the question, like a gazelle in a china shop, reassuring him that he was handsome and charismatic and, apparently, everything a professional therapist could want in a married patient?

Margo stood dazed and lethargic over the stove, methodically turning the blocks of frozen meat over and scraped the cooked bits off, incorporating them into the chopped vegetables. She was getting the milk out of the refrigerator when the phone rang.

She glanced at it. Mom. She set the milk down and lowered the heat.

"Hey, there you are!"

"Yeah, here I am. Sorry, I've been busy."

"What's going on?"

"It was . . ." She scanned her mental file of *lame lies,* pushed aside *dead fictional husband* (Mom knew better), and instead came up with, "Pocket dial."

"So you just never answered again?"

"I—I've been busy. I said. I've been busy." She flipped a chunk of ground beef.

"Oh. Huh. I was kind of hoping you had some big news for me."

"Big news?"

"Maybe little news is more like it."

Margo's brain felt like a stalled car. "I'm not following."

"Baby news."

Ugh. "Not at all," she said. God forbid. When was the last time she and Calvin had had sex? She couldn't even remember. There was no way she could be pregnant. She used to think she wanted kids, though. She had assumed it would happen someday, probably fairly soon.

She wondered if Robin, unfair symbol of Margo's loss, wanted kids.

"Well, never mind," her mom said, "how's everything?"

"I'm just cooking." She picked up the milk and took it to the stove, then poured a good slosh in with the meat.

"Oooh, another video for us?"

"Not this time." Margo stirred the milk as it began to bubble in the hot pot. "How's Sullivan's Island treating you guys?"

"Wonderful, but lordy it gets hot."

"That's the south for you. It's pretty hot here too." At least it had been last she went outside.

An awkward moment passed, then her mother asked, "How is Calvin?"

Margo stirred the sauce. "He's an asshole."

"*What?*"

"Sorry. But he is."

"What's going on?"

She wanted to tell her. She wanted to blurt it all out and get the kind of comfort her mother used to be able to give her when she was a kid and had a nightmare. But she wasn't a kid with a nightmare now, she was an adult with a problem that no one could solve for her.

"I can't get into it right now. It's just so much and I'm so tired. Suffice it to say he's not a great guy."

The only thing she could work up any interest in whatsoever was what was going on right in front of her. The Bolognese. Preparing it, following the tiny steps that moved this one, ultimately inconsequential, yet complete, accomplishment forward.

"I need wine," Margo added, though more to herself than to her mother. Her voice was still strangled with emotion, but she hoped it didn't show.

"Oh, honey, whatever is happening, I really don't know that drinking is the answer. In a mood like this, it might just make you feel worse. You know you already feel worse at night than in the morning."

That was true, though she didn't know if it was real or the power of suggestion. Her mother always told her things would look better in the morning, no matter what was wrong. "I'm not drinking it, I'm making Bolognese." Margo went to the refrigerator and looked for the flaccid bladder bag from a box of chardonnay she'd had a few weeks back.

"You're making Bolognese? No wonder you said it wasn't for June's Cleaver."

"Right? You might as well put a clothespin on Dad's aorta."

Margo turned up the burner. "I'm making this for me." She poured the wine into the Dutch oven and breathed in the bright, citrusy fumes as it sizzled and evaporated. "I've been hungry for years."

"Name me a woman who hasn't been. What we do for men is ridiculous."

"I can't help but feel like a good man wouldn't want a woman to make that sacrifice for him." A good man. Could she still find a good man? She was young, but she was so tired that the idea was overwhelming. "Also I don't do everything I do *for a man.*"

"Don't you?"

Margo balked. "Wow, Mom."

"Well, for a man and everything that comes with a man."

"So kids. Baby news."

"Sure."

"Why were you expecting that? You know I'm not sure if I even want them."

Her mother laughed. "Getting a little late in the game, honey. You know they call it a geriatric pregnancy at this point."

"Mom, I'm fine."

But was she? She didn't know if she wanted them, but if she did . . .

If she calculated how long it might take to meet someone *new,* then to get to know them, hopefully enough to fall in love and maybe get married if they weren't too jaded by the idea, that ate up *years*. Then time spent *trying* to get pregnant . . . she could be lucky or unlucky with that.

The decision was a luxury, before. She used to think she was safely partnered up, but suddenly she wasn't. And that made all the rest of her assumptions about life nothing more than big old question marks.

"Calvin's a good man at heart."

Margo rolled her eyes. "No, Mom. He's really not."

"I don't know what you two fought about but it must have been a whopper."

"Well—"

There was a muffled sound as her mother obviously covered the phone instead of hitting "mute," then she said, "Your father just came in. Do you want to talk to him?"

"Calvin left. *Left* left."

There was a beat. "*What?*"

"Calvin left me. For good. We're getting divorced."

Another pulse of silence, then, obviously to Margo's father, "Not a good time, Charlie. You go on up and I'll be there shortly." She came back clearly. "What happened?" She lowered her voice slightly. "Do you think this is for real?"

"Oh, it's very real. And *nothing* happened. It was sudden."

And then it all came spilling out. The tale of the last two weeks, including the thoughts of homicide-by-Shun, Robin, and her own suicidal ideations—though by admitting them out loud, she recognized them for their melodramatic nature.

"Oh, honey."

"And I told my book club I was once a widow, like a crazy person."

"You told your book club that he . . . died?"

"No, no, of course not. I made up a first husband."

"Oh, of course not, that was silly of me. A first husband? Margo . . ."

"We can unpack what a psychopath I am later. But for right now I just need to freak out because suddenly, I am alone. I don't have Calvin or the life I've been living and I don't even have any real friends. I'm such a mess!" Everything, large and small, was making her cry. She'd almost added the upstairs sink that was draining slowly to her inventory of things that were wrong, but no one would understand unless they were going through it themselves.

"Oh, baby." Something about the pity in her voice made Margo feel even sorrier for herself. "Do you need me to come home?"

It was like when Margo was little and would hurt herself. Somehow she could bear up until she got to her mother's loving arms and then she'd lose it. That she called Maryland *home,* even though they'd moved south ten years ago just made it even more poignant. "I'll be okay. I just need to get through this."

"You need your family."

She went to the pantry and pulled out a twenty-eight-ounce can of Wegmans San Marzano tomatoes. "Honestly, I'm not up for it. I don't want to waste a visit on shock and misery, I'd rather you come when we can both enjoy it. Like in the fall, when we can go antiquing and do all the holiday bazaars." She fished in the drawer for the can opener she needed to replace, found it, and pried the can open.

"Honey, are you sure? I can come twice, you know."

"Dad needs you more than I do."

"Oh, pshh, he wouldn't even notice I was gone."

But they both knew that was a lie. Ol' Charlie was a great orthodontist at work, but at home he was a six-foot toddler who wanted his wife to do everything for him—gee, where had Margo gotten the nurturing gene?—and while he wouldn't say anything if Jane came up to visit, he'd probably just quietly manage to burn his clothes in the dryer and flood the kitchen trying to boil water.

But on top of that, a visit would mean Margo would have to leap right into an energetic life, and she just wasn't up for it. She needed to get out of her rut but not by running six marathons a day. "I don't need anything right this moment, Mom, honest."

"Every once in a while you need to accept help."

She dipped her finger and thumb into the tomatoes and pinched off a piece. It was sweet and perfect, even without any seasoning or cooking at all. How could one strain of tomatoes, grown in one specific region in the world, be so superior to all others? "I promise I'll let you know when I do. I *promise*."

"All right . . ." She didn't sound certain.

"I've got to go now, Mom; I've got stuff to do." Her plans were to sit on the sofa and scarf this stuff down in three hours when it was finally ready. She was going to top it with as much nutty, salty, crystal-pocked Parmigiano Reggiano as she wanted, and she was going to give no fucks.

Then she was going to sleep as late as she damn well pleased tomorrow.

"Enjoy your pasta. And then get your butt out of that house. One thing I know is that moss doesn't grow on a rolling stone and a glum mood can't fester in an active person."

Margo wasn't so sure that was true, but it still made her smile. Momspeak. "I will. I really will."

"I'm calling you tomorrow."

"I'm sure." Margo hung up, paused for a moment, then went back and dumped the tomatoes in the Dutch oven and prepared to simmer for three hours. With nothing better to do, she went to her computer and idly checked Instagram, or, as she'd come to think of it, her only portal to the outside world. Over the past couple of weeks, she'd subscribed to multiple food threads, decorating threads, and a few cute animal threads. If a hashtag had any of about fifty key words, she saw it. And so she saw food porn, fabulous homes, front porches, and cute animals every time she picked up her phone to look.

Her mom was right, she really needed to do more than this. It took no time to go from a sabbatical to an ancient hermit vampire in the imaginations of neighborhood children. She didn't want to be a person who cowered like Nosferatu at the rays of the sun, or even like her neighbor, Mrs. Bach, who drove to the dentist literally three doors down the road from her house.

Good God, maybe Mrs. Bach had been looking at Margo's house, shaking her head thoughtfully and saying, "Lazy, self-pitying cow, won't even go out and get her mail."

With a mental shrug, she returned to Instagram and cooed at a golden retriever slipping down a playground slide, then squinted at a table setting so elaborate she couldn't even figure out how many courses there had to be. But she stopped at the third picture, a gorgeous baking tray of golden buttery-topped tiropetes, with a bowl on the side of bright-colored Greek salad with what appeared to be fresh oregano.

It had popped up because she was following #bethesdafood scene.

The caption, written by BoozyCrocker, said:

BoozyCrocker MUST EAT BUTTER. #TheCookbookClub is now open to new members. Foodies, come join us! Three-drink minimum. No skipping dessert. Meet in Bethesda. DM me. No psychos, no diets. #foodporn #saycheese #cheese #feta #musteatbutter #delicious #whenindoubtaddbutter #bethesdafoodscene

CHAPTER THREE

MARGO

Knocking on the door of the little house on Leland Street was more nerve-racking than walking into a crowded bar looking for a blind date.

Everything in her wanted to turn and run, but she knew enough about anxiety to know that would be feeding a very dangerous monster, and she couldn't possibly afford to do that. The last thing in the world she needed was to become a completely neurotic mess who never left the house.

Before she could even make contact with the door, it swung open and a blond woman exclaimed in surprise, "Oh! Hi! I didn't know you were there!"

Margo's face flamed. Now she felt like a stalker. "I was about to knock."

"Are you Aja?"

Margo felt her face grow even hotter. "No, Margo Everson."

She'd gone back to her maiden name with some optimism. "I DM'd with, um, BoozyCrocker on Instagram?"

"Yes!" She reached her hand out, noticed Margo's hands were full with a bowl of sweet and salty coconut rice, and gave a little wave instead. "Of course! I'm Boozy! Well, Trista Walker. Sorry, I had a fifty-fifty shot and I got it wrong. Come in, come in." She stepped back. "Welcome to Chrissy Teigen *Cravings* night!"

Margo stepped into a compact, chic, industrial-style living room that extended back to a dining room and table at the far end, already getting loaded up with dishes, despite the fact that no one else seemed to have arrived yet. "Should I take this . . ." She nodded toward the table.

"Yup, put it anywhere. What'd you bring?"

"The Sweet and Salty Coconut Rice from the first *Cravings* book."

"Yum! I almost made that, since I did the Shake and Bake Chicken with Hot Honey and the garlic and soy shrimp. That should be great with both of those!"

Margo knew it was Grilled Garlic-Soy Shrimp with a homemade hot sauce, because that was another thing she'd thought about making but dismissed, wary of ending up with an army's worth of shrimp decaying in her fridge if she decided not to come. "You did all that yourself?" This was going to be so sad, all that leftover food.

Trista splayed her arms slightly. "I'm trying to get a good collection of recipes together, so it requires a lot of testing. And leftovers are always a good thing, aren't they?"

Margo smiled. She couldn't help it. She liked Trista. "That's a good way of thinking." She indicated her purse. "I also brought spiced rum. You left the booze options open, so I figured this went with coconut."

Trista gave a laugh. "*Per*fect. I have wine. Ooh, and I have ginger beer and limes we could use! I love this!" There was a knock at the door.

"Aja," Margo suggested with a smile.

Trista nodded. "Got to be. So, make yourself at home and just . . ." She shrugged. "Help yourself to whatever you want." She hurried off to the door.

Margo suspected that Trista had already had a drink or two, owing to her effervescent personality and the light pink hue of her face. But she was very fair, and that might have been her look in general; it had just been a long time since Margo had met anyone who was just *fun*.

Trista came back into the room, followed by a petite girl, maybe midtwenties, with perfect golden-brown skin, chestnut hair with funky copper highlights, and almond-shaped eyes that would keep her looking young forever. She also had both hands on a large green Saran Wrap–covered glass bowl. Fortunately it was a *different* shade of green from Margo's bowl.

"Well," Trista said, "we're all here now. Margo Everson, this is Aja Alexander."

The John Legend soundtrack that was playing swelled.

"You both brought coconut rice!" Trista raised her hands. "I can't *wait* to dig in! I've got to run to the back room but I'll be right back."

Aja made her way straight over to Margo after putting her dish down. She was holding a bottle of water. "Sorry," she said. "I feel like I copied you because you got here with the rice first."

Margo laughed. "You might have started making it first."

"Probably. If you count the dozen batches I burned or otherwise ruined as I was trying to make this one."

"Oh no, really?"

Aja crossed her heart. "I finally had to ask my landlady for help. I'm no cook, so I thought rice would be easy."

Margo *was* a cook and she felt sudden embarrassment at having chosen such a potentially plain dish, not because Aja had said that but because of *why* Aja had said it. "Rice can always burn easily," she said. "It's a weirdly delicate art. And if you get past that hurdle, and make it really well, there's the risk of consumption."

"Consumption is a risk?"

"It is if you eat it all. I ate a ton while I was making it."

Aja nodded, with a smile. "I get that. I can usually take or leave rice, but once I got it right, I was going to town on this stuff! I had to toast extra coconut just to eat it like an animal with my hands while I was cooking. Then again, my eating it all and constantly adding more was probably the only reason I didn't burn the hell out of the coconut too and ruin the dish."

Margo laughed sincerely, picturing this small, pretty thing pigging out on the good half of a half-horrible dish. "So if you don't cook, how did you end up in a cookbook club?" she asked her.

Aja answered without apparent self-consciousness. "I need to *learn* to cook, man, I grew up on Stouffer's frozen lasagna, and that is not impressing anyone these days."

"Please tell me you've tried to pass it off as your own."

"No!" Aja said, but her cheeks turned pink. "But I'm just not into the idea of microwaving a factory-built-and-frozen dinner for three minutes and then sitting down in front of Netflix to binge *Gossip Girl* and obsess over Chuck Bass all over again."

"God, that sounds relaxing."

Aja pursed her lips and nodded. "Granted. But my boyfriend thinks of himself as a lot more cosmopolitan than that, so I'm trying to keep up with the Barefoot Contessa, you know?"

"Dating is the worst," Margo said involuntarily. She regretted it immediately. What an obnoxious, bitter thing to say.

Aja's gaze drifted to her left hand. "Are you married?"

Margo remembered her widow lie but felt no compunction whatsoever to use it. "Not anymore. I guess." She frowned. She wasn't divorced but she was, what? Separated? Legally? So did that make her Not Married? Something made her settle on the truth and let Aja sort it out. "My husband was a jackass and he walked out on me unexpectedly about three weeks ago."

Aja's reaction was to look horrified.

"It's okay," Margo assured her, then smiled. "I mean, he really was a jerk and now he's gone, so all of that is good. I'm just here now because I needed to get out of my house before I went nuts or started adopting a lot of exotic animals."

It had been clear Aja had taken in everything Margo said, but when she got to the part where she said *before I went nuts,* Aja's shoulders had relaxed and she'd begun nodding vigorously. "I so get it. I've had a couple of relationships like that, though they weren't actually marriages, but not much feels better than taking the power position over a bad relationship. When they leave first"—she shook her head—"man, I know that sucks. Particularly when you don't see it coming. Yuck."

Margo would never, ever have said all of that to a veritable stranger, but somehow Aja had a guileless appeal that made it seem perfectly normal coming from her. "Yes," she said quietly. "I think you've defined it." She didn't add that she felt she might spend sleepless hours later thinking about that and trying to assemble it into a rationale for her current state. "So how did you come to join this group?"

Aja was immediately out of the Ex-Zone. "Just coincidence. I was having this craving for beer cheese soup—go figure— and did a search on Insta and boom! There it was. Trista posts a lot of food stuff. I guess you probably noticed that too." She stopped and grimaced. "Am I talking too much? My boyfriend says I always talk too much."

He sounded like a peach. "No, go on!" Admittedly, Margo had lost track of what Aja was saying. "You were hungry . . ."

Aja nodded. "God, *so* hungry. So anyway, I was following her because of her food posts and then she had this group idea and I thought, why not?"

Margo laughed. "That's basically what brought me here too."

Aja nodded and shrugged. "Looks like we're the only ones so far."

"That's okay. Trista seems to have cooked just about everything in the book."

Trista swooped back into the room. "Come eat, come eat! It's only us, so let's have at it!"

Margo went to the table with Aja. She noticed she felt really good. Still a little uncomfortable, admittedly, she wasn't at ease with strangers in general but at least it wasn't a crowd.

When they got to the table, it was easy to recognize some of the dishes just from their pictures in the book. Skillet Broken Lasagna, which smelled of garlic and bright tomato; Fluffy Popovers with Melted Brie and Blackberry Jam (she started eating that the minute she picked it up and could have cried at the sweet, creamy-cheesy contrast to the crisp browned dough). There were also the two versions of the coconut rice, of course, and Trista had placed them next to the platter of gorgeously browned crispy baked chicken with a glass bowl of hot honey, specked with red pepper flakes, next to it, and in front of the beautifully grilled shrimp with serrano brown sugar sauce.

Every dish was worthy of an Instagram picture. Which made sense, since Trista had, as Aja had pointed out, done quite a lot of food porn postings.

There was also Cool Ranch Taco Salad on the table, which Margo had been tempted to make but, as with the shrimp dish, given that she had been ready to bail on the idea of coming right up to the last second, had thought better of, lest she have taco salad for ten that needed to be eaten in two days.

Not that she couldn't have finished all the Doritos that went on top that quickly. But there hadn't been a Dorito in her house since college, and she kind of thought it ought to be a cause for celebration when she finally brought them back over the threshold of Calvin's ex-house.

The Deviled Eggs were there too, thank goodness, and *tons* of them. They were creamy and crunchy and savory, sweet and—thanks to an unexpected pocket of jalapeño—hot, all at the same time. Classic party food. Classic church potluck food too. Whoever made those knew that deviled eggs were almost as compulsively delicious as potato chips with French onion dip. And, arguably, more healthful. Depending on which poison you were okay with and which you were trying to avoid.

There was a gorgeous galaxy-colored ceramic plate of balsamic-glazed brussels sprouts, with, from what Margo remembered of the recipe, crispy bacon crumbles, sour cranberries, walnuts, and blue cheese, which was—Margo tasted it with hope and was not disappointed—creamy Gorgonzola Dolce.

She knew the full lowdown on the dish because, again, she'd been drawn to the recipe when she was perusing the book. If nothing else, she'd discovered some new dishes to try, and God knew she had the time.

Margo was finished with serving rules and tablescapes and which spoon went where. She had her own system now, which was much more realistic than Emily Post's, of making a meal inviting, reassuring, and easily accessed. Take what you want, sit where you will, talk to your favorite guests. Since she was the only guest she'd had so far, it was working well.

But she had never once been part of a Norman Rockwell Thanksgiving with a long rectangular table, set with candles and china and silverware and people who were either too small for the chairs and kept falling off or too old and stiff for the chairs and couldn't get up. Rather, she'd grown up with Thanksgiving being a "perch" holiday, where everyone found a comfy seat in the living room or family room (the dining room was strictly for setting up the buffet) and made conversation with whoever was around. People would come and go, conversations would shift, children would run in, interrupt, and run away.

It was *relaxing.*

So maybe that was why she felt so inexplicably comfortable here and now. In a house in Bethesda, at a tiny party where she still knew no one, but could talk to the two others about the very subject at hand.

The discussion never became formal. Apparently that wasn't the point, which was something of a relief for Margo. It was a potluck where the common interest was a single source for the recipes and then multiple takes on the food. The rum helped, she had to admit, bolster her courage a little, to move along and discuss cooking techniques, recipe glitches, or whatever as she and Trista and Aja sat in the little living room and gorged themselves on every dish.

By the time she was ready to leave, Margo had gone from thinking it was unlikely she'd ever attend again, to thinking about the next book, *The Silver Palate Cookbook,* and how she'd have to do something way more exciting than rice. Maybe even more than one something.

"How long have you been doing this cookbook club?" she asked Trista, then hoped it hadn't sounded sarcastic.

Trista laughed. "This is my first go. Honestly, I wasn't sure *anyone* was going to show. I'm really glad you both did."

"Me too."

Incredibly, little Aja was still eating. "Me too! God, I feel like I have been starving for days. Everything is so good." She looked at Margo. "Your rice is better than mine."

"It's the exact same!"

Aja shrugged.

"I always feel judged when I cook," Margo said, reflecting. "That is, I *did* when I was married." She paused, then gave a dry laugh. "I think it's because I was."

Trista nodded and looked into her eyes. "I used to love cooking for this really crappy boyfriend I had. I might as well have made him an aged rib eye, served it to him with wine, then knelt before him and rubbed his feet while he ate. He liked the food but never had anything nice to say about me behind my back."

"Ugh, I'm sorry. And yet . . . yeah, that sounds familiar."

Trista looked across the room. "I bet every woman has felt the same thing to some degree."

"Sing it, sista," Aja said. "My mom worked when I was a kid, so I had to take care of my little brothers and they never let me forget that my microwaved Stouffer's dinners were not nearly as good as Mom's Prego and shells. They've apologized by now, of course, but I always have this vague feeling that I'm letting people down if I can't give them sustenance. Or comfort. Or whatever basic needs they have."

"I read a great book on it," Margo said, though she hadn't realized what the book was at first when her mother recommended it to her. Everyone saw what a tool Calvin was before she did. "It was about breaking the cycle of trying to control everything in order to stop coddling other people. It was an interesting take."

"I'd like to read that," Trista said.

"I'll text you a link."

"Send it to me too," Aja said. "My number is three-oh-one, *A-S-S, M-A-T-T*."

Trista laughed. "*Ass matt?*"

Aja shrugged. "It doesn't mean anything, but it's easy to re member." She yawned. "Sorry, I've been up since six, so I think I'm going to hit the road. I'm teaching a sunrise yoga class tomorrow at the Om Center."

"That sounds nice," Trista said. "I'm glad you were able to make it tonight."

"You're welcome to join the class." Aja looked from Trista to Margo. "Both of you. Seriously."

"I've got a late night tomorrow," Trista said quickly. "I don't think I could be anywhere by six A.M."

"What is it you do?" Margo asked.

Trista hesitated for a split second before saying, "I was an attorney with Cromwell and Covington."

"Oh my gosh, Carl Covington is on NBC all the time!" Aja said. "He's really cute!"

Trista seemed to wince. "Yeah, I'm not there anymore. Now I'm just closing on a bar down Wisconsin."

"You mean you're *buying* it?" Aja asked. "You're going to own a bar?"

"Yup. Worked there while I was in law school and know it inside out, so when the owner decided he was getting tired of the grind . . ." She shrugged. "That's why I'm trying all these recipes out."

"That's quite a far cry from law," Margo said, impressed. "My ex worked for them and it was pure chaos with all the partners and attorneys. I wish I were brave enough to just up and do something crazy. Not that that's crazy," she hastened to add. "You know what I mean. I hope."

Trista laughed. "I do. Actually, it probably was crazy. Anyway, I started this group as a way of trying out new foods and seeing what people like so I can expand the menu."

Margo nodded. "Very smart."

Trista tapped her forehead. "It's also a way to eat while I'm waiting for profits."

"Good thinking."

"Now that you mention it, this is the best meal I've had in ages," Aja added. "If I could find six more cookbook clubs, I'd never go hungry." She stretched. "Okay, that's it for me for now, though. It was great meeting you guys."

Margo and Trista agreed, and they all stood awkwardly for a moment before Aja added, "I'm going to grab my bowl and go. See you next time!" She headed away.

"I'd better go too," Margo said to Trista. "Thanks so much for being so welcoming."

"It's my pleasure. Like I said, it's helping me out. There's no business more liable to fail than the bar and restaurant biz."

Looking at the tasteful but clearly expensive decor, Margo

really hoped it worked out for her. This neighborhood, once a place where young families lived, had been priced out of the family market and into the wealthy professionals market ages ago.

Then again, if Trista decided to move, Margo would be more than willing to handle the sale.

Oh God, was she becoming that person? So desperate for business that she'd push it on a brand-new friendship? Was the idea of divorce already changing her that way?

Her years with Calvin, being his wife more than her own person, had turned her into a social weirdo.

On the way home, she concluded that it had felt really good to get out and meet completely different people, people who had no preconceived notions about her or her marriage or anything. People who just got together over the love of food.

It just seemed like life didn't need to be more complicated than that. Like maybe it would all be okay.

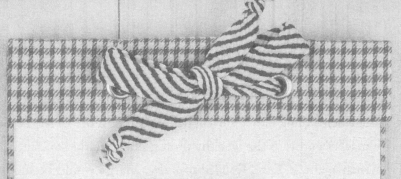

MEETING 1–JUNE
Cravings

COCONUT RICE–Mass appeal, clearly. Add toasted coconut (tableside, if guest prefers).

CHICKEN WITH HOT HONEY–Add hot honey at serving, otherwise too soggy and sticky.
Live and learn.

TACO SALAD–Everyone loves Doritos.

DEVILED EGGS–Excellent, easy appetizer; keep on menu.

*Three members feels lazy but good, removing advertisement for now, as friends needed more than crowd in house. Only other taker was a guy whose pictures were all of bugs. Never answered his DM. Am bad person but mercifully bug-free.

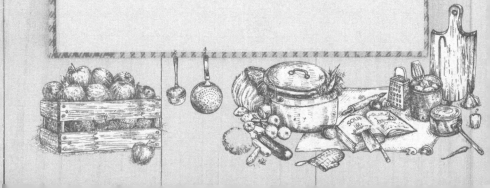

July

CHAPTER FOUR

TRISTA

I'm sorry, that card was declined. Do you want to try another one?"

They were the words Trista dreaded lately, positively feared. When she was working at the law firm, money was never a problem.

For weeks she had been playing credit card roulette every time she made a purchase, but now, standing in the grocery store line with twenty-eight dollars' worth of food and a card that couldn't even cover that, she felt the embarrassment acutely. She'd overspent before the first cookbook club meeting because she'd been so hungry looking through the cookbooks and then went straight to the grocery store. Mistake.

She heard the shuffling feet of the people behind her, people grabbing a few things for dinner and eager to get home. Someone sighed. Everyone had heard, everyone knew what was going on. Their judgment was as thick as the honey she couldn't afford for her Safeway brand tea.

She feigned a carefree laugh—or tried to—and said, "I think they sent a replacement and I put the wrong one in my wallet. You know what? I'll just pay with cash." She dropped the useless card in the cavern of her purse and reached in for the thick pile of one-dollar bills that was held together by a ponytail band. She counted through quickly, recalling, as she often did, the Fun Fact that cash had more fecal matter on it than a public toilet.

She counted out twenty-nine—she'd gotten fast with that—and handed them over. The cashier, a kid of about sixteen with frizzy ginger hair and skin he undoubtedly hated, took the pile and counted through deliberately, holding the fan of cash high enough that everyone would see its suspicious denominations.

Trista's frantic brain, always ready to make up an explanation for any humiliation, was ready with a story about her daughter's Girl Scout cookie money, but she knew that would sound equally bad. Credit card didn't work so she was paying for her packaged Caesar salad, club soda, chicken breasts, Twinkies, and Ragu with her kid's Girl Scout money.

"Oh, hold on." The kid held a bill up to the light. "Never mind, I guess it's real."

Trista felt her face go hot. Like she'd be using a counterfeit *one*?

"It's real," she said, her voice dry. Explaining why she had a bunch of small bills wasn't worth it. No one needed an explanation, they had probably guessed she was a broke-ass stripper already. Her palpable self-consciousness was only making things worse. She just needed to pay and get the hell out of here.

The kid shrugged and put the money in the drawer, counting out the pitiful change.

She took it all, dropped it into her purse—she'd worry about organization later—and started to hurry away when she heard, "Ma'am?"

Automatically, she turned around, though she wasn't, in her opinion, a ma'am. Turned out he was talking to her. He pointed to her bags, still on the counter. "You forgot your stuff."

It didn't seem possible for her face to get any warmer without her skin spontaneously combusting, but somehow it did. She reached for the bags, thanked him, and hurried out of the store, wondering if anyone would believe she had once been an attorney who worked across the street from the White House and was on the fast track toward partner in one of the most established firms in the DC area.

She still worked downtown. Just not quite as close to the White House. And not with the same cushy benefits she'd once enjoyed. Sure, her job was a dream come true, but in the month since she'd taken over the bar, her optimism hadn't been able to translate to any appreciable profits, so stripper should probably be on the list of emergency backups.

She threw the bags into the backseat and got into the car, jerking it into reverse and screaming out of the parking lot. It was after 11:30 A.M.

She was already late.

Thirty-two minutes later, she was running past fetid trash cans, through what felt like a game of Frogger to avoid the rats, to the back door of Babe's Blue Ox, on Wisconsin Avenue north of Georgetown.

She needed to change the name. It wasn't helping business, and she was tired of being asked if she was Babe.

When she'd first started back, after losing her job at the firm, Trista hadn't planned on staying for long. She was just picking up shifts for extra cash until she could clear her name and get another good job with another law firm.

After all that schooling, she'd *never* wanted to return to bartending again, particularly not back here, where she'd worked her way through law school at GW. But one place was as good as another as far as she was concerned, and no matter where she could work, she'd feel like she'd gotten nowhere except very deeply in debt.

Which was basically true.

She'd gotten cocky when she began making money and got a place that was a little more expensive than she could now afford alone. Pottery Barn furniture and kitchen equipment, which had once made her happy and now made her wonder what they'd fetch on eBay and if it would be worth it to sell at a loss while she still literally had them on her credit cards. Probably not.

And it wasn't long until her boss at Babe's mentioned he wanted to sell the place and was willing to finance it if she wanted to take it over. Her first reaction was to be thrilled. Over the moon. Her own place? That was great—that erased all the feelings of failure and replaced them with a sense of *purpose*.

Her next reaction was to hear a parental voice in her head telling her to get a "real" job, not to waste all that schooling and all her great experience. It had to be a parental voice, because she knew as well as anyone who had worked in the restaurant industry—it was a real job. It was a real hard job. And the people who were good at it were really some of the strongest people.

The decision to *just go for it* came after a little research and a lot of going back and forth. She couldn't just start making six figures again—that might never happen, in fact. Restaurants were truly often pro bono endeavors. Something she reminded anyone who complained about pricing at a restaurant when they were out with her.

She talked to a friend in real estate, who projected that the building itself could be worth a fair chunk eventually, since the area was modernizing. She had the kitchen equipment inspected and was delighted to learn that it was in pretty good shape—if it hadn't been, it could have been a money pit.

The sales were the biggest problem. Considering the state of the decor and nonexistent social media presence, she could understand. It was merely outdated. A standard sports bar that made sense in 2009 but no longer worked in the landscape of local IPAs and pre-prohibition-era cocktails with weird and unusual ingredients. The menu didn't make sense when people wanted avocado toast and buffalo cauliflower, and all you had were flavorless french fries that came from a freezer bag.

But now, three and a half weeks after closing, she was already wondering if she'd made a huge mistake.

The people who still came to Babe's were old locals who loved the specialty barbecue sauce, craved the family-recipe apple pie, and who would look merely puzzled at the mention of Snapchat, and students over twenty-one years old, who could get a lot of cheap beer. But she knew the place could be so much more.

Unfortunately, what she considered great menu improvements weren't universally appreciated. She knew she'd have to strike a balance between tried-and-true bar food and the new offerings. That's why she'd gotten the idea for the cookbook club.

Trista went to the main room and got behind the bar and tied an apron around her waist. There was actually a pretty decent crowd this afternoon and so she felt bad for being late, because that had left Tim, the bartender, to handle all this alone before she got there. Better tips for him, but a whole lot more work.

"Miss?" A guy who looked to be in his late twenties raised his hand to get her attention. He sat down at the one empty barstool and held her eyes. He was nice-looking, though a bit typical of the upwardly mobile ilk that came to DC to work their way up in and around politics. Not her type, certainly, but someone's, and that someone was likely to show up tonight, since this was also an area that attracted the yuppie counter-part.

"What can I get you?" she asked him.

"Flying Dog Blood Orange." He took out a credit card. "Can I start a tab?"

"Yup. I'll need your license too."

He reached back into his wallet. "Got to make sure it's me, huh?" He handed it to her. "It is."

She smiled. "Ah, but that's what you'd say if it wasn't, isn't it?" She ran his card and handed it back to him, then put his license in the index box where they kept them until the patron signed off. His name was Brice Kysela, so she dropped it into the *J–L* slot.

Meanwhile, he laughed and nodded his agreement. "You got me. I guess you see a lot of different kinds in this job."

"More than you can even imagine." She went to the tap and

pulled out his draft, having just enough time to slide it over to him before four or five other people summoned her.

The night went like that; every time she got one thing done, a handful of others cropped up. It was frantic, but she liked it that way. Time passed more quickly, and she'd gotten too practiced too long ago to spend any time in the weeds.

Brice was a nice guy, spent most of his time there on his tablet but threw enough cute quips her way to keep things entertaining. She felt like they had a mini-kinship, and toward the end of the evening she started spotting a couple of his beers and even offered him the Buffalo chicken bites appetizer on the condition she could have one. It was her recipe, or rather one she'd found online and modified a bit so that she could call it hers, and it had turned out to be a big hit in the restaurant.

With the new cookbook club, she hoped to come across more unique things she could add to the menu in order to get the restaurant more notice. It did pretty well as it was right now, but a better reputation for food—rather than just a large number of unique beers on tap—would pull in a lot more people.

They had finally kicked all of the garbage beers left in the keg room—though she'd had to incorporate a lot of it into the food. It actually turned out to be a fun new challenge that she sort of kicked ass at.

Tecate was great in the queso dip.

(Expired) Fat Tire was perfect for the onion rings.

The unbelievable amount of bottled Guinness with worn labels still left over from Saint Patrick's Day would have to wait until the weather cooled, but dark beers were fine to wait, though she looked forward to having the space. But once September hit, she'd have tons of items to slip it into.

The food was a slower build, but she was getting there. It was a start that the beer list was getting more unique. She'd always been good at creating good connections with people who might be able to hook her up. Only now instead of exonerating—sometimes painfully guilty—criminals, she was just getting hipsters drunk on the newest release from Burley Oak or Adroit Theory.

The day wore on predictably. Around ten that evening, an older group came in, talking about the dinner they'd just enjoyed at Clyde's. She welcomed this type, they usually tipped well. One of them asked what was on tap, which meant, unlike the frat boys, it wasn't going to be cheap beer all around.

She handed him the preprinted list of what was on tap that week.

"Any recommendations?" he asked. He looked like central casting's version of "midwestern man playing Santa in holiday parade," with pink cheeks, a bulbous nose, a snow-white beard, and short cropped hair. Once upon a time she would have been sure she'd seen him before, but she had been in the business long enough now to know that she'd seen *everyone* before. They weren't the *exact* same people, of course, but they

were all representative of types. Utterly predictable. She could
do a personality profile of just about any stranger she met and
be right 95 percent of the time.

"What do you normally like?"

He gave a self-deprecating laugh. "Coors Light."

She smiled. "Well, we *have* that."

"No, I'm in the big city, I want something a little more interesting than that." He looked over the menu.

"Well, that's a relief."

"How about this Allagash White? Is that good?"

"That's a Belgian wheat beer. Mild. Nice flavor, a hint of
warm spice. I like it. But it's more for Blue Moon drinkers.
How do you feel—"

"Hate Blue Moon."

"Oh, well, see, there you go. You'll like the Victory Prima
Pils. It's a pilsner like Coors Light, only it's . . . you know.
Good." She winked. She'd done it long enough to know who
she could mess with.

He raised his eyebrows and cracked up. "Sold!"

She smiled. "You got it." She turned to go get it, but his objection stopped her.

"Wait, sweetheart, you're not gonna card me?" He looked,
bright eyed, at his table mates to join in the joke. "What, do I
look old or something?"

She'd dealt with this before. "No, you look honest."

The guy to his left—this time central casting's Joseph (as

in Jesus, Mary, and)—slapped his back and crowed at her response. "You thought you had her! She got you good, buddy."

They ended up being a nice group, quiet and generous, tipping an extra twenty in cash when they left, which she appreciated greatly and mentally tabulated toward her electric bill. Boy, times had changed. Not so long ago, she'd been breathing easy for the first time in years, so glad she wasn't ever going to have to count pennies again. Now she was right back where she started. Maybe even worse because of the debt she'd incurred while she was flying so high.

Around 11:30 P.M. a few younger guys came in, reeking of alcohol and privilege. She guessed they were students at Georgetown or American University, and it didn't take five minutes for them to confirm. Georgetown. Prelaw. It was stated in a way that was drenched in arrogance, but they didn't know who they were talking to. She'd known a thousand guys just like them and at the end of the day she knew most of them wouldn't even pass the bar on the first or second try.

In fact, she'd bet a fair percentage would even be too hungover to pass at least one of their finals.

And, of them, probably one would eventually make it to a seat on the Supreme Court.

"I wanna start a tab," a short, dark-haired guy said to her, handing over his license and American Express Platinum card. He knew the routine and he was confident in it. He knew his card wasn't going to be refused. "For me and my friends."

My friends and me, she thought with an inner smirk. Money could buy an education but it couldn't make it stick. "What can I get you?" she asked, dropping his license into the box. Burch Allan Lowe Jr. She could almost picture Burch Allan Lowe Sr., drinking forty-year-old Macallan straight, rather than the kitschy PBR his son and his friends ordered and would undoubtedly overindulge in.

They also ordered food, though, which upped their tab *and* served to soak up a bit of the alcohol they were consuming. She was glad of both of those things, which made her wonder how many years she had *actually* aged in the three years since she'd last tended bar here.

During the few brief moments she had quiet, Trista worked on the infused liquors she loved experimenting with. It wasn't enough to just pull ordinary taps and serve boxed wine and Bubba burgers. She needed to do unique things, she needed to do it *better.* Lavender-Thyme Gin. Adobo Chile Honey Tequila. Espresso Vodka with Vanilla Bean.

Shortly before midnight, Brice asked to close out. At the exact same time, the frat boys also decided to leave. She wasn't so glad to see Brice go, but she was about done with the douchebags, and welcomed the relative quiet to finish her night in peace and get some things done to make the next shift easier.

"I'm really glad you came in," she said to Brice, handing him his charge slip as well as his license. "You were a real calm in the storm."

He put the license into his wallet and said, "That's good to hear, since my fiancée and I are on our way to visit her family in Tulsa tomorrow and they are most definitely *the storm*." He laughed. "Every meeting feels like a test."

Trista was surprised by a vague sense of disappointment at the news he was engaged, but why? She definitely wasn't looking for a boyfriend. It was probably just what she'd said—he was a calm in the storm and her life was a storm.

She wanted calm.

It was about an hour later, when the crowd had dwindled to a few stragglers, last call was out, and she was cleaning up for the night, that Brice came back in.

"Hey there," he said, looking around with something that looked like concern. "I'm back."

Her heart did a tiny trip. "Hey there."

He looked at her expectantly.

Was this the "meet cute" everyone talked about in romantic comedies? Was he back because he had felt a spark and couldn't get her out of his mind? She couldn't say she'd felt the same, exactly, but she was also open to all possibilities. "Another Blood Orange?" she asked.

"Ah, no. My license."

She didn't understand. "I'm sorry?"

He put a license down on the counter. "You gave me the wrong one back."

"I don't understand." She looked at it. Lowe. It said Lowe, not Kysela. And she only remembered Kysela because she wondered what nationality that was. Lowe, though—that one she remembered. She looked in the box, hoping against hope that his ID would be there, but it wasn't. And she wasn't surprised. They'd left at the same time, and she remembered handing them back their cards.

No. She couldn't have.

"Uh, yeah, yep, sure, just hold on one . . . just hold on one sec . . ."

Under the register. In every other alphabetical section. On the ground. She tried, though her heart was in her throat, not to reveal that she was frantically looking. He was on his phone, so she had a moment.

Eventually, it became clear that the truth was as bad as she'd immediately feared. She'd given his ID away to a drunk pre-law dumbass who hadn't noticed the ID was wrong, and even though she'd thought the worst of him all night, somehow she came out the real moron.

"I'm so sorry," she said. "*So* sorry. I must have"—it embarrassed her to even admit such incompetence out loud— "switched your cards when you left." She frantically searched her mind for what to do. Maybe she could call Burch Lowe. She took out her phone to google him, even though he was a student and she was more likely to get his family in—she looked at the license—Alexandria.

"Can you check under the counter again?" Brice asked. "I don't mean to be a pain, but I'm leaving town tomorrow and I *really* need my ID for the airport."

Oh shit. That's right, he said he was going to Tulsa. On a plane. *Tomorrow*. And she'd . . . lost his ID. She checked the box again, lifting all the tabs and shaking them in case, somehow, his was still not only there but also stuck to the card.

Of course it wasn't. She knew it wouldn't be. It was uncharacteristic for her to make even *one* mistake, much less such a huge one.

Trista fought her frustration and shame. This was no time to make it all about her, but she recognized that this was a huge problem and she couldn't fix it. Anything she did now was just a puppet show, not a solution.

She went ahead and rang the number that had come up on the Google search for the Lowes. It was late, but this felt like an emergency. Surely Burch Jr. wanted his license back too.

The number was disconnected.

"I don't know what to say," she told Brice. "I"—she shook her head—"I really screwed up. Obviously, I'll pay whatever it costs for a replacement and to get it expedited. Anything. And the guy I switched it with goes to school here, so I can call the administrative offices first thing in the morning and try to get a message to him."

Brice, who had been so kind all night, was true to that form now. "Mistakes happen," he said, and he smiled, although she could see the stress creases in his forehead and around his eyes.

"Do you have a passport?" she tried.

He shook his head. "I'm sure I can go to the MVA tomorrow and get it replaced. My flight isn't until the evening."

"If I could go do that for you, I would, I swear it."

He smiled, still tense. "I appreciate that. If you could just keep an eye out for it." He reached into his pocket and pulled out a business card. "You can contact me here at any hour if you find it."

She took the card. "I'll keep looking and I'll find a way to get ahold of the other guy, seriously. With any luck he'll notice he has the wrong license and come back any second."

Brice chuckled. "I don't think that guy would notice a bus in front of him, the way he was drinking. I heard them talking about going to the next place in a planned pub crawl."

Brice was good-natured enough to cringe at the idea. She cringed back weakly.

Of course, they'd gone to a place that would card him. Great. Though when he'd left he was getting damn close to unservable, so the odds of anyone getting so far as to card him seemed unlikely under any circumstances. But then at least the bouncer would probably call him out for the incorrect ID.

This was a nightmare.

He turned to leave. In half an hour it would be closing time and she should leave too, but she couldn't see doing that, just in case Burch Lowe came back.

"Please let me know what the cost is," she said to him as he turned to leave. "And if there's anything in the world I can do to help make this right. Drive you to the MVA? Wait in line for you? Anything, I'm just—"

"Hey, it's okay. I'm sure it will be fine. Mistakes happen."

"I know, but—"

"But nothing. Just let me know if that guy by any chance reappears before tomorrow afternoon."

She doubted that Lowe would even be up before tomorrow afternoon, given the rate at which he'd been drinking and apparently planned to continue drinking. But she nodded. "I'll let you know."

"Thanks." He raised a hand. "I appreciate it."

It was only when she was doing the receipts fifteen minutes later that she realized before any of this had happened, he'd left her a fifty-dollar tip. It made her want to vomit.

CHAPTER FIVE

MARGO

The week began with news from Margo's lawyer that Calvin had offered his one and only settlement: she could keep the house she was currently living in, provided she refinanced and put the debt into her name and took on all the associated costs; a medium-size chunk of cash (could have been better but could have been worse); and a dilapidated farm he'd inherited from his grandparents, located in Lovettsville, Virginia, just across the Potomac, in Loudoun County. It was paid for, unlike the house, but it was also almost uninhabitable, with broken windows and a fair amount of wildlife living inside.

The farm itself had so much potential. The truth was, she'd always loved it, even while Calvin had hated it. Greatly ambitious, she'd gone there one spring to plant vegetables and herbs, intending to use the forty-five-minute drive as a quiet meditation a couple of times a week and to bring the food home for healthful meals.

And that had worked great for a couple of weeks, and she even got to see her seeds germinate and start to grow. But then she and Calvin had taken a trip for a couple of weeks and by the time they got back it was already hellishly hot and muggy. Every day she promised herself she'd go when it cooled down. It had never cooled down.

Weeks had passed before she eventually made it back, and the lettuces she'd planted were too rubbery and the zucchini had grown to the approximate size of a pony. Huge zucchini, it turned out, were tough and flavorless.

So she'd given up on the gardening idea for the time being, thinking a better project might be to fix up the house and make it into a Joanna Gaines extravaganza, but she'd never quite gotten to that either.

Now it was hers.

And on top of that, the lawyer—being thorough, as one would be for his hourly rate—had done some research and discovered that there had been a number of break-ins, mostly teenagers partying, that had been reported to Calvin but hadn't yet been addressed in any meaningful way. In other words, no alarm system, no police patrol, nothing. Plus the place needed some serious cleaning up. Still, the electric seemed to work and the well water ran. It could have been worse.

"I suggest you get a caretaker," the lawyer told her. "Better still, a renter who can do contract work for a reduced rent. Kill two birds with one stone. You have about a year's worth of savings to cover these bills before you start to sink."

"What about alimony?" she asked. "He left, isn't there some sort of law about leaving me high and dry?"

"You signed a prenup when he was in law school. You're lucky he's giving you anything at all, though I suspect he knew he'd have a fight he didn't want to pay for, and that these properties are bound to be money pits."

Margo's heart sank. She remembered that prenup now. He'd been learning contract law and she signed it as a show of faith in his ability as he struggled through school.

When a law professor checks your work, there's little room for error.

"You can turn these lemons into lemonade," the lawyer went on. "With some careful planning."

Margo wasn't so sure about that and she hurried to get him off the phone so as not to have to pay hundreds of dollars an hour for a meaningless pep talk.

For a while after they hung up, she sat there, still, feeling sorry for herself. She allowed that for a limited amount of time each day, usually about five minutes. She couldn't afford to indulge in it, but ignoring the difficulty of what she was going through was impossible.

So here she was, faced with a problem she had to solve. A house she couldn't afford and likely couldn't sell for a profit in this market, thanks to its distance from the nearest highway and all the new developments going up; and a house that was paid for but virtually uninhabitable, as well as being a good half hour of winding two-lane roads from the closest highway, then another hour to get to town.

At least for a now-single woman like herself. Hell, she got nervous being on the property alone at twilight; she couldn't see sleeping in there alone before it was cleaned up and alarmed.

So, like the man had said, her best bet was to put a caretaker in there for a reduced rent in exchange for some work. It solved two problems: generating an income and increasing the value of the farm.

She thought about it for a few minutes, then picked up her phone and scrolled through to find some of the pictures she'd taken back in her brief back-to-nature phase. There were some great pictures, the red barn with a slant of amber sunlight bisecting it, the house shrouded in a morning mist that actually made it look habitable. She posted about six, and then typed:

Local friends: reliable caretaker needed for 20-acre farm, house, and outbuildings. If you know anyone, please DM me. Reduced rent, depending on how much work he or she is willing to do around the place.

Then she hoped for the best, until the phone rang and she was startled out of her reverie. Had someone seen it and was already ready to volunteer?

No. It was Aja, whom she'd met at the cookbook club a few weeks ago. She was calling to find out if Margo had a good strawberry pie recipe she could text her. Aja was having a "hankering," as she said, and thought of Margo first, since they'd talked about her extensive cookbook collection at the meeting.

"I'm sure I do," Margo said, already percolating with the idea. That was a classic southern recipe, not quite shortcake but not quite preserves. It would be in one of those cookbooks. "I'll look and shoot you a picture of whatever I find. Unless . . . do you want to come over and make it here?"

"Oh, I don't want to be any trouble," Aja said, though she sounded relieved. "I'm sure I can figure it out with a recipe. I mean, it's basically just math, right?"

"Sure, but I honestly don't mind. I could use the distraction anyway."

"Are you sure?"

After several minutes of going back and forth reassuring her that Margo meant it, Aja finally agreed, gratefully, and Margo texted her the address with a promise to give her a list of ingredients. Then she went looking for the best recipe she could find.

She couldn't remember which of her hundreds of cookbooks the recipe was in, but it didn't take her long to narrow the search down to the southern section. That's how Margo was, she organized her cookbooks by region first, and cooking type second. Course was third, such as dessert or appetizers. There was also a small section of celebrity cookbooks, but she didn't go much for those, although she had all of Dinah Shore's, a little-known one by the old actor Morey Amsterdam, and both of Chrissy Teigen's.

It had all begun to feel like clutter for a while there, but looking through them now felt like visiting old friends. That she was doing it for an afternoon with a new friend made it feel even more so. Now the books were spread out across the ten-person dining room table she hadn't used in years, and it felt good.

She moved *Eat, Drink, and Be Chinaberry* aside, intending to revisit the buttery-tart Lime Chicken. Sure, it had been one of Calvin's favorites, but it had also been a favorite of Margo's, so she could see past that. She made a mental note to review it tonight and revisit her old favorites.

Patricia Wells's *Trattoria* went right on top of that. She leafed through the book lovingly, remembering the summer she'd gotten it and how those pictures had made her long for a sunny little house in Tuscany.

"There you are." Margo reached for it and pulled out a very old copy of *The Sweet Grass of Home,* a part-cookbook, part-essay book that she'd found at a library sale years ago. It had been a library book, though the stamps showed it hadn't been taken out in years. Too old-fashioned for most, probably. She'd been charmed by the handwritten notes in the margins and the splatters and stains of so many ingredients over the years.

She found the page with the strawberry pie and snapped a pic with her phone, then texted it to Aja.

She was used to entertaining, if not super enthusiastic about it. It didn't make her nervous like it used to, but today felt a little different. Where it was easy to have the book club over because of the clear focus of conversation and the ease of un-imaginative snacks and glasses of wine, she'd really enjoyed meeting Aja and Trista, and she now found herself hoping her screwed-up life and upcoming divorce didn't make her feel like too much drama for them.

Margo wasn't used to being the type of person people avoided. She was used to being the problem solver, the steady, solid friend who had a sensible answer for everything. She didn't want to be the weak link now. Getting married young had made her seem like a grown-up to friends still getting into arguments outside bars with couple-months-in boyfriends. While she did not want to be the burden, she was hoping to maybe shift somewhere into the middle.

She needn't have worried, though. Aja showed up with her arms loaded with grocery bags and a big smile.

"I'm so glad we're doing this!" She beamed, coming in as Margo ushered her, following her into the kitchen. "Your house is gorgeous! The whole drive in was. I think my boyfriend's mom actually lives around here—do you know Lucinda Carter?"

Only by reputation. She was from one of the old Potomac families, and Margo's impression was that she was not one to mess with. But she didn't know her personally, so she was able to answer honestly when she said, "No, I don't know her personally."

"Well, that makes two of us."

"Your boyfriend hasn't introduced you?"

"No, not yet. He can be . . . very private." Aja smiled so charmingly. "I guess he wants to wait and see if we get more serious."

"That makes sense." Margo took one of the bags from her. It was heavy. She glanced in. It had a ten-pound bag of flour in it. "How many pies are you planning on making?"

Aja looked puzzled. "One?"

Margo smiled. "I was just asking because this is a ton of flour."

"Oh, that. I heard that brand is the best, but they only had it in huge quantities. I thought I'd leave some here for you, if you want it. And for the neighbors. And for the soup kitchen. Maybe a local school will need snow for a Christmas play sometime."

"You never know"—Margo hoisted the bag onto the counter—"you may end up becoming an ace baker."

"That doesn't seem likely. But I'd like to at least be good. Competent. I'd settle for competent."

They took everything out of the bags and set the ingredients on the counter island. Margo guessed this one pie had probably cost Aja at least sixty or seventy dollars, maybe even more. Organic butter, organic strawberries, organic flour, cane sugar, she'd even gotten a great bottle of vanilla bean paste.

"I don't know what it is," Aja commented. "I started thinking about strawberry pie and then I just *had* to have it. I don't know what's going on, I've been eating like such a pig these past couple of months."

"What are you, pregnant?" Margo looked at the label of the vanilla. She used to use the same brand to make butter cookies for Christmas as a kid. Just thinking about it conjured the smell and tripped a wire of melancholy she hadn't felt for a long time.

Margo missed cooking for people—*really* cooking. Her family, her friends, even her husband. Her greatest pleasure had come when they rolled their eyes with the ecstasy of a bite of her chicken spiedini, oozing with melted cheese under a crisp crust of buttery fried panko. Or her Cincinnati chili, aromatic with cinnamon and cocoa, which she served on homemade corn spaghetti. Topped with aged cheddar and sharp, fresh-chopped onion, it had been one of Calvin's favorites, and he always had her make it for Redskins games on Sundays. She could smell it now, mingling with the wood fire in the fireplace, and the sound of roaring crowds, on the TV and in the living room.

Those days were gone.

When she looked up, Aja had a strange look on her face.

"What's wrong?" Margo asked.

Aja frowned, then shook her head. "Nothing. Nothing. I was just . . . nothing. Hungry."

"Ah. Okay. So why don't you rinse the strawberries in the sink? I put a colander in there."

"Yes, ma'am."

Margo went to a cabinet and took out the food processor and kitchen scale. Then she took a bowl from a lower cabinet.

She put the flour, salt, and sugar into the food processor and then cut the butter and shortening in, finishing off with enough ice water to make a dough ball. "I've missed butter," she said with a laugh. "My husband wouldn't eat anything that was high in cholesterol." She recalled the cheese fondue and half baguette she had made and consumed over an episode of *Shark Tank* the night before.

"I'm sure I'll die young because I just *cannot* think so much about being so careful."

"I spent almost ten years having to think about it, and I still can't tell you it makes a difference." She rolled the dough out on the counter. It stuck to the roller so she sprinkled some flour on it and resumed.

"Doctors aren't agreed on it either," Aja said. "I brought a pie pan. Should I get it?"

"Yup."

Aja put a ceramic pie plate in front of Margo.

"Oh, this is so cute!"

Was Aja the girl she'd pictured, right before getting so unceremoniously dumped by her husband? Was Aja's kitchen the one filled with specialty pieces from boutiques and trendy stores? Did she have rose-gold coasters and Pinterest prints on the wall at home? Did she have freedom?

Would Margo have it?

Together, they lifted the ends of the dough and placed it in the pan. Aja pinched the edges then put the plate in the oven to parbake.

Then they moved to the berries and started to hull them side by side, tossing the greens into the sink as they went.

"So what brought on the pie craving?" Margo asked. She tossed a green, then popped the strawberry into her mouth. It was good and sweet, the taste of summer in one quick, juicy burst.

"An iced tea commercial."

"Huh?"

Aja smiled. "A bunch of people, summer barbecue scene, strawberry shortcake . . . then I started thinking about pie, and that was it."

"They got you!" She hulled the last strawberry and tossed it in the bowl.

"But not the way they wanted to—no iced tea here." Aja took the bowl and poured a cup of sugar over the berries, then macerated them with a wooden spoon. "This is like making a mojito," she joked.

Margo took the strawberry puree over to a pan on the stove and mixed everything, stirring the vivid red mixture into the gray sugar until it was all one bubbling, candy-scented concoction.

"It would probably be good with tequila."

"What isn't?"

They laughed.

Margo stirred as the mixture reduced and Aja cleaned up. Then Aja's phone rang and she looked at it, paused, then answered. What followed was a quick, tense conversation in low tones.

Margo didn't listen to what was said, but it was very clear that it wasn't entirely pleasant.

Aja hung up, caught Margo's eye, and said, "My boyfriend. Canceling our plans tonight. Again."

"He does that a lot?"

Aja's jaw tensed. "Yup."

"Hmm." Margo considered before saying, "If he disappoints you all the time, maybe he's not the Forever One. Trust me."

"Oh, I don't know that he's the Forever One anyway, but for now he takes care of things, does all the thinking, and after spending my life scrambling to survive, it's kind of a relief."

"So he's domineering."

Aja pursed her lips, then nodded. "Some would say that maybe. I think it's more that he's confident."

"Ah. The other side of the coin."

It was interesting, they'd known each other only a short while and yet it was so easy hanging out together. Was pie the great unifier? Margo smiled at the thought but it wasn't lost on her how important food had become since Calvin had left and her new life had begun.

"It's time," Margo said, and Aja glanced at the recipe.

"The whole lot goes into the crust now, huh?" She took the pan and poured carefully, perfectly. The shining red strawberry mix looked gorgeous against the white marble countertop Margo had chosen so carefully when they first bought the house.

"Now it just needs to chill," Margo said.

"It's not the only one."

Margo laughed. "You are going to feel so good when you have that first meeting with his mother over with. I mean, you're going to have to meet her eventually, right? And when you do I'm sure it'll go fine—you're a great person. She'll have to see that."

Aja shrugged. "You're really nice to think that. I mean, I don't know what's wrong with me; I get nauseated just thinking of meeting her!"

"Nerves can do funny things."

"I guess." Aja didn't look so sure.

"Is something else going on?" Margo asked and immediately regretted it. She didn't want to butt into business that didn't concern her. But it sure seemed like Aja was chewing on something other than pie.

"You asked . . ." Concern crossed her expression again. "I mean, I know you were joking, but you asked if I was pregnant . . ."

Silence pulsed between them. Immediately Margo was certain Aja was pregnant. Not that she was lying or hiding it; she didn't think Aja even realized it. But Margo knew it, sure as can be.

"Is there any possibility?" she asked gently. She liked Aja, but they'd just met. She wasn't sure how to tread this with her. So she waited for Aja's response, trying to arrange her features into a look without conclusion or judgment.

After a moment, Aja nodded. "There is," she said. "I—I honestly don't know how I didn't think of it before, but there is definitely a possibility." Only a beat passed before she started gathering her things. "I'm sorry, I've got to go."

Margo was at a loss. "Wait, can I help? Do you want me to go get a test or something?"

Aja shook her head, a quick jerky movement that showed she was already mentally out of there. "No, I've just got to go. Thanks but—I have to get home."

"Is everything okay?"

"Fine!" But she was already gone. "We'll talk soon!"

The pie and Margo were left behind to chill together.

CHAPTER SIX

MAX

Max Roginski felt sorry for the Beatles.

He hadn't always (most people didn't have the luxury of *feeling sorry* for the Beatles). In fact, he'd been pretty impervious to them once upon a time, but then he'd gotten holed up in a hotel room somewhere in Ohio when his play, *Ironsides,* had become a runaway hit and they'd taken it on the road, and he'd read an eight-hundred-page biography of them over the weekend.

And, not to be vain, but he really started to understand how *hard* it must have been to be them. To never be able to live a normal life, no matter where they went; to be recognized everywhere, despite all efforts at disguise.

Since Max Roginski couldn't take a piss in a urinal in a truck stop on the Pennsylvania Turnpike without being recognized and finding himself shaking the unsanitary hand of the guy next to him, fame had stopped seeming so cool.

Fame was becoming the proverbial bitch.

And suddenly it was all too much. The small, two-bedroom apartment in Gramercy Park that used to be his haven now felt oppressive. Even the deck outside—which had once given him an exhilarating feeling of space to breathe in such a claustrophobic city—now made him feel exposed, with the thousands of windows of neighboring buildings towering over him. Now and then a picture had shown up in the media, clearly taken from one of those windows. The unfunctionally small kitchen, once sufficient with a microwave and refrigerator for a guy who ate out all the time, was now too tiny to cook in if he didn't want to bother with the real world. Which kind of worked out, since the world was too big to shop for food in, but he was hungry.

The delivery people recognized him.

This wasn't what he'd bargained for.

Sure, it's what he'd *hoped* for, or once thought he did. It's what every aspiring actor or singer thinks they hope for. On the rare occasion that he'd prayed, he'd prayed for this.

Now he wondered if he'd made a mistake. It felt awesome to pay his bills, so that had to be considered, but maybe if he'd moved to some bumfuck town in the Midwest and traded his taste for WhistlePig the Boss Hog bourbon to Jim Beam, he'd have been able to pay the bills on his single wide and have a little money left over for some sort of soup gruel at the end of the day.

So, yeah, he rather liked the perks this lifestyle had afforded him. But they never came on his own terms, and *that* was the problem. He was ready for a change of lifestyle. He'd already decided to leave the production—his last show was in two weeks (and he'd still get his 7 percent royalties, which was a considerable amount). But as long as he was here, he was vulnerable. If he could *find* a place to be anonymous, he could probably do that quite happily.

He got up and went to the kitchen, dropped some ice in a glass too big for bourbon, then poured too much bourbon into it. Then he moved out to the deck, where the sun was beaming down on the table he'd had since an ex-girlfriend's mother had had it sent to them a thousand years ago when they'd lived here together. (It hadn't been cheap to get rid of her once he hit it big and she came back wanting remuneration.)

It was a nice table. Sturdier than the crap he'd gotten at some high-end stores, for sure. He sat down on one of the armed chairs and put his feet up. The sun burned behind his closed eyelids, putting patterns of blood vessels before him like an old road map. He'd had an idea for a play about Helen Keller once, inspired by the question of what world she saw and interpreted when she closed her eyes, but too many people told him that it was boring and unknowable.

Not all the ideas were winners.

Right now, though—now he was working on *Clackety Clack* (working title to amuse himself), about the construction of the first continental railroad, but he hadn't told anyone about it, partly because he was so stuck he couldn't move forward on it, and if someone told him it was a good idea, he'd be even more frozen. If they said it was a bad idea, then forget it, he'd never write again. Everyone said artists had egos, but people seldom talked about how easy they were to collapse.

And he was one of the *lucky* ones.

If only there weren't such a daily—sometimes frightening—barrage of recognition.

A window scraped open overhead and someone shouted, "Yo! Maxi! Hows about some tickets? They're goin' for a fortune online!"

Max sighed and tried to ignore it.

"C'mon, neighbor! Don't be a prick!"

That was the other thing. Interactions with the public were seldom polite. People seemed to think they had a right to be abusive. To resent him. Like he'd used up all the success or money *they* were supposed to get and so he *owed* them.

He stood up and walked inside. The last thing he heard was "Fucking prick!"

He wanted to go back out and respond, but he no longer had the luxury of doing that sort of thing without recrimination. Nowadays, it would be caught on camera and splashed all over social media

An hour later, Max was still on the couch, trying to think of a remedy for his increasing life-panic, feeding his hunger with bourbon and wishing someone would leave a large bowl of macaroni and cheese outside his door. He'd prefer that to just about anything else he could think of. Unfortunately, he hadn't a clue how to make it himself, except that it definitely contained both macaroni and cheese, two ingredients he did not have.

His phone pinged. He glanced at it. Someone had tagged him on Instagram. Hopefully it was a friend and not the ticket dude from earlier, but he didn't have enough interest to check.

He put his hands over his face and leaned back. Escape. He needed to escape. Surely he could come up with a disguise good enough to get him on a train and maybe up to Montreal so he could . . . hide in a hotel room there, he supposed.

He picked up his phone and checked Instagram. It was the upcoming star of *Ironsides,* the guy who was about to replace him, standing next to the marquee for the show. No one knew him yet, so he was all smiles, pointing at the marquee, as if to say, *I'm on my way! Nothing's going to stop me now!* And he was right. Unless he totally fucked up, this was going to be a career-changing move.

"Better you than me, buddy," Max said, before idly flipping through the pics. Friends in the business showed up, one after another, and one after another he felt himself getting increasingly sick of looking at their fake, smiling mugs and began to unfollow them.

Jimmy Fallon—unfollow.

Khloé Kardashian—unfollow.

Jen Garner—he hesitated, then clicked. Unfollow.

A "real" housewife he had met when guesting on *Watch What Happens Live* with Andy Cohen—adios, Crazytown.

The weeding went on and on.

Wait, what was this? A tranquil farm on a misty morning. That looked like bliss. It was exactly what he needed.

In fact, where was this? He would buy it right now. That's how strong his feelings were about it. The text under all the pictures said, Local friends: reliable caretaker needed for 20-acre farm, house, and outbuildings. If you know anyone, please DM me. Reduced rent, depending on how much work he or she is willing to do around the place.

Who was this?

Margo Brinker (Everson). Oh yeah. Margo Everson from college. Interesting, he wouldn't have pegged her for a farm girl. He frowned and scrolled through some of the other pictures. A small, rolling-green hill, surrounded by trees, trees, trees. Some big birds—turkeys? peahens?—of unclear origin, and a big red coloring-book barn.

This was absolute Nowheresville, though the tag said Lovettsville, Virginia, which a quick look at Google Maps said was near Leesburg and horse country. Not a cheap spot. But private, as he vaguely recalled it. And right on the Potomac.

He reread the caption. A caretaker. A *caretaker*! He smiled, then chuckled. Then outright laughed. He could be a farm caretaker! How hard could that be?

Something for the memoir, right?

He pictured himself stretching at sunrise on that wide, wraparound porch, the smell of his morning coffee drifting out a screen door into the dewy morning air. No horns honking, only geese. No sirens, just a distant rooster crowing. No thundering footsteps in a too-small hallway outside a too-thin door, just horses galumphing.

No people. He could write. He could *think*.

God, he needed this.

Did he even have her number? He remembered meeting Margo in an improvisation class he'd taken in college. For him, it had been another class in his performing arts curriculum, but for her it had been an elective and an unspoken dream.

He and Margo hadn't been in much touch over the years, but he remembered meeting her for coffee when she was in Manhattan eons ago when he had just started on a soap called *Candlelight Lane*. She'd been a big fan of the show and wanted to know all the scoop on the stars. Since he was just starting out, he felt cool and chatted up a storm, saying a whole lot more than he should have about people who, like he did now, just wanted to maintain some privacy.

To her credit, she must not have told anyone, because he'd never heard the stories repeated.

Margo Everson. Nice girl. He'd liked her. They'd had a lot of laughs in college, before life had gotten real and responsibilities had gotten heavy.

So, sure, he'd like to see her again.

And this was when he pulled out the dichotomy that was his life, and his personality. Now he needed to be Maxwell Roginski, star of Broadway, film, television, sweetheart of the biz.

He called his lawyer.

"Stephen, I'm going to need you to find a phone number and address for me," he said to him.

Stephen Jakes was immediately on alert. "Has something happened?"

"No! No, no, it's for an old friend from college. Her name is Margo Brinker. Maiden name Everson, *E-V-E-R-S-O-N*. I don't know what Margo is short for, if anything, Margaret? I guess I think she's in Potomac, Maryland. Has a farm in Virginia."

"That's it?"

"What do you mean *that's it*? Did you want a scandal?"

"This isn't the mother of some long-hidden child or anything, is it?"

It was pretty amazing how many times Stephen leapt right to that very conclusion when a woman's name came up.

"Still no, Stephen. Just an old friend."

"I have to allow for all possibilities, Max. At all times. I ask the questions, you answer them, I handle appropriately."

The guy was so good that Max didn't want to take any chance on alienating him, so he just let it go. "I appreciate that."

"Any need for an NDA?" Nondisclosure agreements were getting to be the norm for anyone wanting to have so much as a cup of coffee without risk of exposure.

"We were friends only. I just want to talk to her."

"Are you going to see her?"

"I hope so."

There was a hesitation, then Stephen said, "I'll draw one up just in case."

"Just get the number, please." Max hung up and tossed his phone onto the coffee table. How had his life become this? Growing up in the 1990s in Langley, Virginia, even right there next to the CIA headquarters, he'd never dreamed he'd live a life of such paranoia.

He pictured himself on the porch of that old farmhouse Margo had photographed. Surrounded by nothingness. Trees.

Admittedly, he could find a remote inn somewhere, probably. But there were always guests. Proprietors. Advertising and so on. Margo's farm would be private.

He answered the phone and took down the number Stephen gave him, waiting quietly through the obligatory words of caution.

"Be careful," Stephen said in closing. "I realize you think you know her, but it's been a long time and you never know for sure what people will do for a buck."

Even though he knew damn well it was true, Max rolled his eyes to himself. "Thanks for the warning. Buh-bye." He ended the call and then immediately input the number Stephen had given him.

No answer.

He didn't leave a message. In case he changed his mind.

Instead he opened the Insta app and jotted a quick DM.

It was surprising that Margo hadn't answered him.

He recalled his DM.

Margo, hey, it's Max Roginski from college!

Hopefully you remember me? It's been awhile since we've seen each other, I think it was in the old soap days back in the city. Anyway, I saw you are looking for a caretaker for your farm in NoVa, and, believe it or not, I'm looking for a place to escape and get some work done, so maybe we can help each other? I know this probably seems weird and out of the blue, but I'm serious. Please let me know if you are interested and I will come down right away.

Give me a call at your convenience, my number is . . .

Of course, he hadn't meant *at your convenience* in his heart. He'd meant *right away, I am desperate,* but that felt like a bit much to put on the line when they hadn't seen each other in almost ten years.

Still, it had been four days and there had been no response. Why?

Had he done something to offend her when he'd seen her last? Something he couldn't remember? Something he wasn't aware of? Not to be egotistical, but since he'd gotten successful, people didn't tend to take their time in getting back to him anymore.

So four days felt like an eternity.

He was ready to give up and began looking at rural places on his own, but there had been something comforting about segueing in via someone he knew. Not just someone he knew, but Margo in particular. Someone who knew *him*—the *real* him, not the him she needed him to be for her own agenda.

A friend.

Plus, Margo knew the area, the neighbors; he felt she'd be honest with him about all that, instead of just working him to try to get him to buy. Hell, he wasn't even sure if she'd sell, and something about *that* made it better too. He liked it when things fell into place because of fate, rather than because he threw enough money at it.

And he truly felt *fate* was calling him to this place.

The point was brought home to him when he went to the grocery store on a Saturday afternoon to pick up some coffee and creamer. No big deal, but what kind of lazy douchebag would he have to be to pay a premium to have stuff delivered? These were common grocery store items. He should have been in and out in five minutes.

Instead, he ended up in an unexpected altercation by the avocados. He'd never made avocado toast before but he'd certainly eaten enough of it, so he figured it couldn't be that hard to assemble. He picked up a loaf of bread, a red onion (easily identified, he wasn't a complete kitchen idiot), and he was trying to figure out how to tell if an avocado was ripe when someone swatted him on the back of the head. Hard.

He put his hand up to the spot and started to turn, but a voice was already in his ear, a staccato shriek with an unmistakable edge of indignation.

"I *said* I liked your performance in *Iron and Sage,* but you know what? *Fuck you!*"

This time, the hand made contact with his face as he was turning to see who it was—a tall woman, broad in the shoulders and the middle, with long hair in two worm-thin brown braids and a face the color and consistency of seared meat.

"Whoa!" He put his hands up to protect himself. He saw a lot of crazy but it seldom came at him like this. "What the hell are you thinking?"

"You think you're so cool, the big famous actor who doesn't have to pay any attention to the little people who put him on the pedestal he enjoys so much."

He was hard-pressed to figure out how she considered herself a *little person* but he was even more confused as to what she was talking about. "I don't know what you're talking about. I think you have me confused with—"

"To think, I paid *money* to see that play." She sneered. "I think you owe me that money back. *Including* the Ticketmaster fees."

"Even if I was who you think I am, I wouldn't *owe* you any money because I—"

"Entitled prissy boy, that's what you are." He did take exception to that but he didn't have a chance to express it. "Expecting the whole world to fall at your feet like you're so high and mighty."

He could hear people around them talking, speculating on who he was and what the hell was going on.

"I should have known with a dumb title like *Iron and Sage* it would be a dull play, certainly no *Starlight Express,* but I sat through it *out of respect*. And this is the respect you give me?" She lifted her hand.

"That was Bradley Cooper!" he said, dodging another blow. "I was *never* in *Iron and Sage.*"

The woman stopped and wrinkled her bulbous nose, frowning down at the ground. When she looked back at him, it was without any appreciable contrition but, instead, a new expression. Anger that she'd been duped. "Who are you, then?"

By then a small crowd had gathered around and someone said, "That's Max Roginski! Can I have your autograph?"

He didn't even glance in their direction.

"Why did you say you're Bradley Cooper?" the attack dog in front of him demanded.

"I didn't!" He was still holding a too-hard avocado and briefly considered pelting it at her, but instead he put it back in the crate and set his basket on the ground. "You're nuts," he said, walking away. "Take it somewhere else."

"Mr. Roginski." A store employee with a name tag that said CRAIG hurried toward him, his face alight with both excitement and embarrassment. "I'm *so* sorry this has happened to you in our store. Please, take whatever you want. Security will see to it that you're safe."

Safe? That's how this story was going to go down? That he'd been cowering in fear for his safety from this woman? "It's all right," he said, continuing on his way. If he pointed out he wasn't *scared* he was just going to sound defensive. He'd learned this kind of thing many times already. "Thanks, but I'm just going to go."

"Please, Mr. Roginski! I don't want you thinking Lenders is anything but a friendly place to shop." He threw a hostile glance at the woman, who was resisting security's efforts to remove her. She was now talking about Jennifer Lawrence. "I'm sure we can turn this around and make your experience here a pleasant one."

He just wanted out. He felt like a caged animal in the zoo, with all eyes on him. This was just disconcerting. "Thanks, I'm good," he said, striding out the door and onto the bright sunlit sidewalk. It was worse than a spotlight. If it wouldn't have been so obvious, he would have broken into a run, just to get away from the clusterfuck that going out in public had become.

He didn't look back, just kept going, making a mental note to cross Lenders off his list, now that he was on their radar and they were bound to make a big deal of *making his shopping experience pleasant* if he ever stepped foot in there again.

It wasn't until he'd rounded three corners and was within sight of his building that he finally felt like he wasn't being watched or followed.

He had to get out of here.

CHAPTER SEVEN

AJA

How had she not thought of it before?

To be fair, it was probably because she hadn't had anything like a normal period since high school. Taking the pill had made her brain feel whacked, so she'd stopped a couple of months ago with the hopes of feeling a bit less moody and upset. She wasn't. She'd been depressed and upset for months now. Not constantly but often enough to concern her. She would have gone to the doctor, but she figured it was just the blues (or Holly Golightly's *mean reds*) and her deductible was so high that she wasn't likely to go to the doctor unless her head was actually chopped off.

Who could afford $180 for a doctor's visit only to be told she'd had a bad couple of weeks and needed to get out more and meet new people? She didn't need an antidepressant, she needed friends.

That was one of the reasons she'd joined the cookbook

club. She'd had such mood dips, and no one to really talk to. Most of her friends were yoga teachers, like her, and while she loved the practice and the peace of the lifestyle, there were times when she just wanted to hang out with someone who could call bullshit what it was. Someone who understood that maybe not everything was *meant to be,* it wasn't always time to be Zen and *let it be,* and that sometimes life could just plain suck.

How she had pegged Margo Everson as *that person* she didn't know, but she seemed to have been right. The time she'd spent with Margo at her house had been really nice. Relaxing in a way she hadn't felt in . . . she didn't know how long.

Except for the part where Margo had asked if she was pregnant.

Which was what had led her here: standing in her studio apartment bathroom in Rockville, opening a pregnancy test with shaking hands. The packaging was ridiculous: a cardboard box that seemed to have a zillion parts in order to keep the wand exactly in place, an instruction booklet so thick she fully expected there to be plastic gloves included, like with a box of hair coloring—which she'd made a few mistakes with in the distant past.

She had a Solo cup handy, so as not to have to rely on her own aim.

She dipped the wand into it, making sure the fuzzy part was

fully saturated, then set it sink side, and pulled her pants back up to pace for five minutes until the results were official.

A quick glance at the little window showed two very faint lines, including the "pregnant" one, but the instructions had been clear about waiting a full five minutes to see the verdict, so hoping against hope that the line would disappear, she walked from the bathroom into the main room, around the daybed that served as sofa and bed, then into the tiny galley kitchen before returning to the bathroom.

She studied the walls as she went, the things she knew better than the back of her hand since she, herself, had put them there.

Walking the small blueprint of the floor and assessing the things she'd collected over the years that made her feel like herself helped soothe her nerves, which were pulling tighter by the moment.

It felt like forever, but her watch told her that it had only been two minutes and forty-five seconds.

She made another round and sang to herself. "Oops! I Did It Again." Why was early Britney Spears stuck in her head? Why was *any* Britney Spears stuck in her head?

I'm not that innocent.

Her watch said it had been six minutes and two seconds. She went back into the bathroom to check the test.

Two lines.

Two distinct lines.

And the word she'd dreaded: PREGNANT.

As Aja waited for Michael to pick her up for dinner, she was agitated beyond words, but the last thing in the world she wanted was to let him know that. Somehow she had to pull out any acting skills she'd ever had—and to her knowledge she didn't have any—to try to keep things steady and unsuspicious when she saw him.

She *had* thought to call and cancel at least a hundred times, but what then? She couldn't avoid him forever.

He was potentially the father of her child. Or, rather, the father of her potential child.

She was pregnant. She knew it. That was just her damn luck. If it was bad or untimely and the odds should have been against her, somehow they always stacked neatly on her side.

She paced her living room, putting on one shoe at a time then making two rounds to look for the light shawl she took out in summer for air-conditioning. She had to do everything piecemeal because she suddenly wasn't capable of holding tight on to a thought for longer than a second or two.

When she was finally completely ready, she was still alone, waiting to hear from Michael.

He texted her, as usual. *I'm here.* Fair enough. There was no need for him to find a parking space in the crowded lot and come up the four flights of stairs to her door. Just as easy for her to run down, she got that.

And yet she still felt a little "less than" because he didn't make the effort. Ever.

She was on the last flight down when her phone dinged again. *Hello? I'm waiting out front.*

It would have taken longer to answer the text than to run to the car, which she could see at this point, so she opted for the latter, opening the side door of his black Mercedes and climbing into the cool interior, and sitting on the downright icy leather seat.

"Sorry," she said, a little winded, strapping the seat belt on. "I was coming down as fast as I could."

"You gotta get in shape, girl." He chuckled without wit, then raked a hand through the salt-and-pepper hair that reminded her of the old Bob's Big Boy mascot. "You've gotten a little softer in the middle lately." Before she could fully feel the sting of the insult, he added, "In fact, let me feel that middle to be sure." He reached over to her and playfully put his hand under her shirt. "That actually feels pretty nice."

She laughed, though she didn't think it was funny, and pushed him away. "Sir! We are in public!"

That didn't stop him. "Mmmm, even more exciting."

"Gross."

He gave her a devilish smile. "You say that now, but wait until you try it."

It had seemed obvious he was kidding at first, but now she wasn't so sure. "For real? You want to do it in public?"

He met her eyes briefly before putting the car in gear and taking off like a rocket. "Maybe."

Her only option was to take that as a no and make herself believe it for the time being, or to have an uncomfortable conversation. And with the huge uncomfortable conversation that was already swinging over their heads like that big slicing blade in the Indiana Jones movies, she opted to let it slide for now.

"So," she said, trying to establish a new tone. "Where are we going?"

"I've got reservations at Flaps in Potomac for six." He looked at the clock on the dash, as if time precision were of the utmost importance. It was five-thirty.

"We'll be fine," Aja said, leaning back in the passenger seat, feeling her stomach was bloated and obvious. There was no way in the world she believed *anything* would be fine, but what else could she say? If things were as she thought, soon she wouldn't even be able to strap the seat belt around herself. "I hope they have that butternut squash ravioli. Oh, and the brownie sundae! I think they always have that. But I'm not sure."

His hands tightened on the wheel, making his knuckles go white for a noticeable moment.

Aja looked out the window at the passing landscape of old farmhouses, many with new additions, and huge new constructions taking over old plots of land, all along Falls Road. The father of one of her friends used to joke about how they started building "one-acre homes on half-acre lots" back in the day, and the problem of "McMansions" had only gotten worse since then.

Once upon a time, she'd managed to look at those houses as the scourge of the neighborhood, as if she would—but of course!—have much better options in her own future. Now she realized those places cost a flipping fortune and she was living in a studio apartment with no sloping fields or horses or other creature comforts, and she could barely afford that. If she had a baby, how in the world was she going to work less, to care for it, yet afford more, to accommodate it?

What on earth was she going to do?

He drew to a halt at the light in the four corners of Potomac Village. Massive strip mall complexes crossed the road in front of them, but the old Mitch and Bill's Exxon still stood sentry on the left. It had been there forever, right there, a few yards from the road. She smelled the gasoline, even from here, but that had to be her imagination, surely. She also smelled cigarette smoke and saw someone in the passenger seat in the car in front of them smoking, a lazy hand holding the burning butt out the window between two fingers.

Again, she thought it was the power of suggestion, but the

smell made her feel like vomiting. To the point where she actually gagged embarrassingly.

Michael gave her a sidelong glance. "You okay?"

She nodded, swallowing so hard against her gagging throat that she couldn't talk, and gave him a thumbs-up.

The light turned and he pushed the accelerator, jolting the car forward. Aja was both relieved that he stopped looking at her and a little miffed that he wasn't more concerned about her. Admittedly, had she been choking or otherwise in some sort of emergency, she wouldn't have given him the thumbs-up, but still. He should have noticed not everything was all right, since she wasn't able to actually speak.

Would he be like that with a child? What if they were at a birthday party or something and the kid started to choke on cake, or on a balloon or on a Dixie cup of Kool-Aid that he shouldn't have been drinking anyway because that stuff was full of toxins?

She was taking this too far. She needed to get ahold of herself. Michael was no different today than he was yesterday and . . . honestly, even if she was pregnant, she too was no different today than yesterday. She didn't need to put so much weight on everything. She needed to take this one minute at a time at this point. Right now she was in the car with Michael. If she was pregnant, he was the father of her child, so it would do her good to deal with him in a calm and reasonable way, even when the things he did and said might drive her crazy.

"We're near your mom's house, right?" she asked.

He nodded.

"Maybe we should invite her to come along." If she was pregnant, that would be her child's grandmother.

He scoffed, apparently at the very idea. "She's not a last-minute kind of gal." He laughed again, like the idea was even more preposterous than she could comprehend.

"Oh. Okay. It's just, you know, we've been together for a while now and I'd like to get to know your mom a little. Maybe we could even take a weekend trip to Raleigh and Wilmington so you could meet my brothers and their significant others."

"Wilmington!"

"The one in North Carolina," she clarified, as if it would *obviously* be absurd to expect him to go to Delaware. "It's on the beach. It's nice."

"I'm not a big fan of the ocean."

She didn't know what to say to that, so she said nothing. And apparently that was just fine with him because he also said nothing, just turned up the radio when "Bohemian Rhapsody" came on and drove the rest of the way to the restaurant without speaking.

MEETING 2—JULY
The Silver Palate Cookbook

CHICKEN MARBELLA—Better without cilantro,
   good specialty entrée.
GREEN SAUCE—Easy, fast, versatile, but anchovies?
   Ethical to not tell people?
APPLE CAKE—Perfect for fall.
LEMON CHICKEN SOUP—Spring/summer EASY.

Notes: Suspect Aja is pregnant, not drinking, eats a ton, turns green if eggs are mentioned, regardless of context.

Margo asking if I know anyone looking for a place to live cheap; hopefully she's not so hard up for money from the divorce that she needs to take in a roommate. Is it insulting to ask if she needs legal advice?

Must get oven thermometer, think clay oven at restaurant is running cold—chocolate cake was liquid in the middle—must check!!

August

CHAPTER EIGHT

TRISTA

O kay, I'm not going to tell you which one is which. Totally blind tasting." Trista cut three plain cheeseburgers
into quarters and handed one piece to both Susannah, the lead
server, and Ike, the bartender.

"Excellent," Ike declared. "I like the bun. What is this, a
dinner roll?"

"Brioche. But Parker House rolls were an option. This is a
little lighter." She considered. "Though I did give it a quick,
buttery toasting." Butter made everything better, every time.

"It's perfect," he said.

"I agree," Susannah said, closing her eyes and nodding, as if
forming an opinion on a fifty-year-old Bordeaux. "The texture
is good and the bun is great, but the rest of it is kind of ordinary. No offense! I'm sure it would be amazing with toppings
and all."

"Got it," Trista said. "We're going as naked as possible for this test. Now, have a sip of water and try the second one." She handed them over and watched for their reactions.

Susannah's shoulders relaxed and she moaned her approval. "Delicious. Did you grill this or something? The burger is different. Smoky or something."

Trista shook her head. "Everything was done on the griddle. All cooked the same."

"Same cheese?" Ike asked.

"Tillamook sharp cheddar." For eating, she liked Kerrygold Dubliner, but it didn't melt the same way. "There will be other choices on the menu, but the difference here is just the meat."

"It's not something weird, is it?" Susannah asked, setting the uneaten half of her sample down. "Like buffalo or moose? Oh God, it's not oxtail, is it?"

"Are you kidding? I can't afford oxtail. No, it's all beef, no pink slime, no scraps. Just different cuts."

"I think this one is perfect." Ike popped the last bit into his mouth. He could eat like a giant, even though he was slender. He used to model for a local company, but once he hit thirty they didn't want him anymore, and bartending made him more money. Particularly with his dark good looks. The demographic here was weird, there were as many women willing to overtip a hot young male bartender as there were men eager to flatter a female bartender. Trista had one particularly flattering—read *tight*—shirt that got her good tips every single time.

Problem was, it was just so obvious that she couldn't stand to wear it that often, lest her employees think she was playing her assets unreasonably. Not that anyone would actually accuse her of that.

"Next one," she said and handed over her personal favorite. The first had been ordinary ground chuck, good and fatty, seasoned with salt and pepper—the most underrated beef seasoning there was—and smashed on the griddle.

The second was brisket. Toothsome, but leaner than chuck. If she went with that, she'd have to add some oil to the mix, maybe smoky olive oil, to give it some juice. For now, the buttered bun did some of the work for her and kept the playing field even.

But she would probably go with her third option: brisket, chuck, and short rib mixed. It wasn't as expensive as the pure brisket, but she thought it was far better. Then again, the fact that it wasn't as expensive was part of what made it a better option to her, so she wasn't entirely sure she trusted her own taste on this.

"Last one." She handed them the third without further comment. "Then you're free." It was time to set up for the evening. But it was Tuesday, so she wasn't exactly expecting a crazed crowd to run through the door at five.

No sooner had Ike popped the whole thing in his mouth than he said, almost unintelligibly, "This is it."

Susannah was immediately on board. "Incredible. It's almost

like . . . I don't know, sausage? That's not it, but it's just got so much flavor. I don't even *need* toppings."

Trista smiled. Her instincts were on. She'd spend seventy-one cents more per burger, charge a buck more, and beat the competition with a comparatively small difference in margin. The more they sold, the less significant that margin would be. "You're sure?"

Both nodded.

"It's sooo good," Susannah cooed. "Much better than the frozen ones the last owner served."

True, but he still made a ton on them. Until people realized there were better options elsewhere and business fell off enough for him to sell the place at a price Trista could afford.

The door opened, and they all turned to look—no one ever came in the minute it opened—and Trista was surprised to see a semifamiliar face smiling at her.

"Brice Kysela," she said, then added, "See? I know who you are now. No more ID mix-ups."

He gave a nod and said, "And you are . . . Trisha?"

Something in her deflated slightly. "Trista," she corrected, grateful that Susannah and Ike moved away to do their thing as Brice came toward her. "License loser extraordinaire." She almost held out her hand but decided at the last second that would be stupid and clunky. "How was Tennessee?"

"Tulsa."

She knew. "Sorry. The storm. How was it? Did you stay afloat?"

"Well, I went two days late."

Guilt immediately overcame her. "Oh no, the license?"

He nodded. "MVA wasn't open on Saturday. But it wasn't a big deal, at least to me, because I got some work done."

"And your fiancée? Was she okay with that?"

He gave a laugh. "She was not pleased with me." He pulled out a barstool and sat down in front of her. "What's this? Trying something new?"

"Taste test. Want to try?"

He splayed his arms. "I'm game. Add a Sam Adams to the mix?"

"You know we've got a pretty extensive list of craft beers."

"I'm fine to keep it simple."

"You've got it." She went to the cooler and took out a bottle of the lager, popped it open on the side of the bar. "Want a glass?"

"Nah, I prefer to do it the old-fashioned way." He held the bottle up to her then took a swig. "Okay, what are we looking at here?"

"Three meat combos." She gestured. "In whatever order you want."

He started with the middle. Chewed it thoughtfully and nodded. "Brisket?"

She widened her eyes. "Very good."

"Don't get excited; I recognize it because my mother went through a period of taking cooking classes to combat house-wife boredom. Brisket burgers were her specialty."

"Impressive."

Brice smiled, and the light touched his blue eyes. He was really cute, damn it. "Not really, they were dry."

"Oh."

"Not yours, hers. The butter is a nice touch."

"You seem to have a pretty developed palate. Are you in the business?"

He shook his head. "Nope, I'm just a hog. I love to eat. My cooking repertoire consists of about three things, so I should really keep my mouth shut so no one calls me on it." He took another sip of his beer and looked at her long enough to make her face grow warm.

She took out a glass and poured some water in it. Her nerves were getting the better of her, and she was getting dry mouth. "So you're not looking for a job as a cook, huh?"

"No, no, the boss wouldn't take too kindly to me jumping ship for a pretty face."

She turned away before he could see her turn pink and bus-ied herself getting limes. When she turned back to him, he was looking at her curiously.

"By any chance, do you need someone to do chopping or prep work, stuff like that?"

"A line cook? Yeah. Why, do you know someone?"

"My brother needs a job," he said. "He's a little . . . out there." He paused, and she wondered just how bad that meant he was. "But I know he's bored and looking for something to occupy himself. He used to work at the Tastee Diner."

She raised her eyebrow. "Doing what?"

"Flipping pancakes." He shrugged. "Line cook," he added, then smiled. "I'm not really sure, but he was there for a few years until they wanted him to do the overnight shift. Look, he's never been a particularly ambitious guy, but he doesn't really drink anything stronger than root beer and he's reliable." He hesitated. "I can't say he's particularly creative, but he could certainly follow orders."

"Reliable would be great," she said. The lower people were on the kitchen ladder, the more likely they were to seek greener salads, sooner rather than later. "Tell him to come by."

Brice took out his phone and tapped something out. A moment later he looked up and said, "Tomorrow afternoon okay?"

"Sure." What was she getting into? Was it nuts to interview a stranger just because his brother was cute?

And polite. Brice was definitely polite. Even-tempered too— he hadn't blown up when she'd lost his license and been unable to find the guy who had it to get it back. So, actually, he wasn't too bad of an advertisement for a family member.

"Tell him to come in around two," she said, getting him another beer, unasked. "This one's on me. And if he works out,

I'll give you another one, on the house. Maybe even a burger." She winked, then felt like an idiot, because the guy had a fiancée and she had no business flirting with him. "Bring your girl, I'll treat her too," she tagged on, lamely. "What's her name?"

"Whose?"

"Your fiancée?"

"Oh. Of course." He raked a hand through his hair. "Denise."

Denise from Tulsa. She wanted to imagine her as a stereotypical hick, but it seemed more likely she was a gorgeous southern belle, with bouncy blond hair (Trista was six months late on highlights), crystal blue eyes (not denim, like her own), and boobs like large balloons (Trista barely filled out her bralette).

Why had she asked that? Now what was she supposed to say? "Oh, that's a nice name." Stupid. *That's a nice name.* He must think she was an idiot. "What about your brother? What's his name? I mean, since he's coming in. I'm not trying to do a whole . . . inventory here."

Brice laughed. "Louis."

She smiled. "Okay. Louis. I'll look for him around two."

Trista would have bet money she didn't know Brice's brother, but when he came in, he was unmistakable. He looked *exactly* as he had the last time she'd seen him. Fifteen years ago.

In high school.

"Oh my God, Louis Williams," she said, as she thought it. Her voice, she noticed, held the same note of dread she had always felt when he'd huff down into the seat next to her in English and scratch it across the floor toward her just a little too close—okay, a lot too close—so he could yammer at her all the way through class.

There had been three years of that. The only year she'd lucked out of it was her freshman year, so she hadn't even realized how fortunate she was until it was gone. After that they'd been grouped together for English 10, 11, and 12. On top of that, anytime they were lined up in alphabetical order, they were next to each other. Walker, Williams.

He looked puzzled as he continued to amble in, but as soon as he got close to her his round Muppet face broke into a big smile. Actually, he didn't *look* like a Muppet—someone else might have thought he was very good-looking, all gangly tall and dark—but for her his personality had always captured his expression and taken it over. "Trista Walker! I'll be a monkey's uncle. Not actually." He laughed. "You're the boss I'm interviewing with?"

She splayed her arms. "It would seem that way."

"Well, how the hell can this be?"

"I am wondering the very same thing. Brice said his *brother* was coming in."

Louis nodded. "Yup, yup." He didn't offer further explanation or show any awareness that the silence was hanging like a broken branch above them.

"How are you his brother? His name is Kysela and you—you don't even *have* a brother." She'd known him all the way through high school. He had no siblings. Just a single mother who worked in the attendance office. Mrs. Williams.

"Technically he's my stepbrother, but he's been just like a brother to me ever since our parents got married. Well, not *all* our parents, my father died when I was a baby and his parents were divorced, so the way it worked was his dad married my mom and that made us stepbrothers. But we're really more like brothers. So we're not *actually*—"

"I got it," she said, holding up a hand. What the hell was she going to do? "He, ah"—she took a steadying breath—"he said you are interested in being a line cook? That you have experience from working at the Tastee Diner?"

He pressed his lips together and nodded thoughtfully. "Yeah, I worked over at the ol' diner for three years. *Three. Years.*"

He'd aced every test, graduated with a 4.2, so it wasn't stupidity that made him weird. She'd never known quite what it was. His mother was a regular, sweet woman who'd wink and give you a hall pass as long as you didn't try to bullshit her about why you were late.

Maybe it was actually his intelligence that hamstrung him.

He was too smart to have a normal conversation. Or even a normal cadence.

"Okay, as a line cook?"

"That's right."

The conversation went on like that until she finally got a solid grasp on his work experience and, surprisingly, level of confidence in the kitchen. On paper, he was a good candidate for the job, particularly since he didn't mind working for just over minimum wage, which was all she could afford at the moment.

But could she really work with weird Louis Williams every day? All this time had passed since she'd last seen him, but her irritation felt as fresh as it had when she was seventeen. And it had always made her feel bad, because he was a nice guy, he had good intentions, he was just . . . if you let him start talking, it was hard to get him to stop. It had taken three years to scrape him off, and that was only because she'd gone off to college.

". . . and so that's the test that really did it," Louis was saying. "If you put the blueberries *onto the raw side of the cooking pancake,* then you don't get that messy blue swirl." He looked so pleased with himself, she couldn't bear to tell him that she'd heard the same thing on *America's Test Kitchen* years ago. "Now, they weren't happy that I'd made five batches of unusable pancakes to figure it out, but they sure were happy with the results."

Trista nodded. She was going to have to hire him. She already knew it. Perhaps Louis Williams was her lot in life, the lost puppy who always glommed onto her. He annoyed the hell out of her, but she didn't want anyone else kicking him.

"I appreciate your diligence," she said to him. "Not everyone would try to make a better pancake."

"I know!"

"I can't say I'd be wild about wasting all that food here, though. If I give you the job, I'm going to need you to *economize* with ingredients, okay? We're not exactly turning product over like a Chipotle."

He nodded. "Gotcha. Be stingy."

"Well, no, not stingy, just not wasteful."

"Not wasteful. Got it." He was smiling as he looked at her. "My gosh, can you believe it is us, back together again? I always wondered what had happened to you. I heard you were a lawyer."

"Long story."

"Lucky for me. I couldn't work in a law office, but I sure can work in a kitchen." He looked at her hopefully.

Everything in her wanted to say no. But she couldn't.

"Okay, Louis. We'll give this a try. A *try*."

"*Yes!* I *knew* you'd say yes! Brice was worried I'd blow it, but that was when we didn't know it was *you*. All he said was that it was this hot woman I had to make sure not to offend."

Hot? A tickle ran down her spine. Not that it would go

anywhere, Brice was engaged. But. It was flattering still. "All right," she said. "Make sure you don't. Offend me, I mean." She smiled. "We'll see how it goes. But this is a fast-paced kitchen during rush. If you can't keep up, I can't keep you."

"Okay, boss!" He saluted her.

"When can you start?"

He looked around. "Now?"

She gestured. "Okay, kitchen's that way."

CHAPTER NINE

MARGO

She hadn't really expected any great caretaker leads from her contacts on social media because they weren't the sort of people who knew the sort of people who wanted a reduced rent in exchange for working on a house and grounds. Still, it was disappointing after almost four weeks when no one had so much as a distant lead, because the next step seemed to be Craigslist. And Craigslist could be a terrifying place. There were too many stories of people looking for a coffeemaker who ended up dead.

It was several days later, as she was searing some chicken while sifting through her cookbooks, looking for a suggestion for the next cookbook club selection (they were all three supposed to be noodling on it, but she was the only one who was a complete cookbook whore), that she heard from Max Roginski.

As a matter of fact, she was on the meatball soup page of a Dinah Shore cookbook when the phone rang. She remembered because that had been one of the most appealing dishes from the book and she'd made it, following the directions to the letter, despite the rice in the meatballs it called for, which seemed like an odd addition, but it worked, and she was thinking about making it again.

So while the recipe held no current surprises for her, the phone call did.

"It's Max Roginski," the male voice said, sounding confident but not necessarily familiar. Then again, why would it? She hadn't talked to Max Roginski in, what, eight years? Maybe more. "Remember me?"

She'd met him in a drama class she took in college and they'd become friends and actually hung out quite a lot before he moved to New York and got famous.

"Of course! Are you joking?" Who could forget him? Who could have a chance? He was everywhere! Even if she'd never known him, she would know who he was. "I saw you on *Saturday Night Live* not that long ago!"

He groaned. "Not my best work. I can usually remember my lines, but when Hillary Clinton walked on, I went blank."

"That was hilarious! You didn't know she was coming?"

"They thought it would be funny not to warn me."

"Oh my God, that makes it even better." She laughed and then there was an awkward moment of silence where she wondered if he was still there.

"It was funny afterward." He paused. "Kind of."

Now Margo went blank. It had been so long since they'd talked. He was a star. She was caught between wanting to catch up with her old friend, and the fact that all she knew of him lately was his stardom. But she didn't want to embarrass herself by fangirling him. So instead she embarrassed herself by asking, "So what have you been up to?"

"It's gonna sound crazy but I assure you I'm serious." He cleared his throat. "I saw your pictures on Instagram."

She frantically searched her brain, trying to remember what pictures she'd posted that might be of interest to him. Nothing came to mind. She rarely posted. "Which pictures?" The heady smell of chicken rose up from the pan and she turned the heat down.

"Of the farm."

"Ooooh, yes, of course. It's in need of some TLC." Understatement. "I swear I'm not the slob those pictures make me appear to be."

He laughed. "I wasn't thinking that at all. As a matter of fact, I thought it was perfect. I wondered if I could go see it in person."

"Oh. Really? Are you looking for a movie set or something?" If he was doing a horror film, the place could be perfect.

"Not exactly." She could hear him adjust his grip on the phone. "Okay, look, I realize I might not have the qualifications you're looking for, and maybe you've already found someone, but I want to apply for the caretaker position."

"Acting thing didn't work out, huh?" She laughed.

But he didn't. "It's not what I expected."

Rather than sit in awkward silence waiting for the punch line, or making another lame one of her own, she asked, "What do you mean? I don't— What do you mean?" She was nervous. What weird reality had she slipped into?

Was she finally losing her mind, or was this conversation for real?

He laughed. "Look, I know it sounds weird, and I know we haven't seen each other for ages. I'm not looking for favors. I'm willing to pay you the full rent *and* work on the place, it's just that I pretty desperately need to get away and have some privacy."

"Running from the law. Been there, I get it." God, she couldn't stop herself. It was one stupid, awkward thing after another.

"That would be easier. Actually, I just need a break. Quiet and privacy. It's been a long time since I've felt . . ." He paused for a long time, and she suddenly felt like she was intruding on a private moment. "Like myself."

Finally the punch lines left her. She could relate. She sat down. "I think I know what you mean."

"Did you know that the very act of speaking, especially the first thirty seconds, raises your blood pressure?"

It had in *this* conversation. "I've never heard that."

"It's one of a bunch of alarming things I've learned about

why life is so stressful. I think some peace and quiet would be a real lifesaver."

"Wouldn't a fancy spa or something be better for that?"

He chuckled. "Don't make me start spewing statistics about time in nature at you."

She nodded, even though he couldn't see her. "Point taken."

"Besides, no one would ever look for me at a dilapidated farm in Virginia."

"*Dilapidated!*"

"Oh! I'm sorry, I—"

"Kidding," she said. "'Dilapidated' is a kind word for it. But I can pretty much guarantee you that no one would ever look for you there."

He expelled a breath, as if he'd been holding it for a long time. "It's hard to express how great that would be."

"You know, it's funny," she said, thinking of the countless references to his show being sold out for all time. "The rest of the world would think you're in the catbird seat, like you can have anything you want. But you can't have anonymity, can you?"

"*Exactly.*"

"Obviously I'd love to have you come, but I just want to make sure you understand, the place is a wreck." She wished now that she'd posted more honest pictures of the place. "This is the kind of offer that would appeal to someone who has, like, literally no other options. As you know, living is expensive around here, so I was hoping to exchange a low rent for some work fixing the place up. That's not really your situation."

"No other options? Check. I can do that. I can definitely do that."

She poured herself a glass of water. "Remember the end of *Gray Gardens*? You'd be an Edie. Raccoons, coming and going through a hole in the wall. Possibly climbing on you in your sleep."

He hesitated again, then, "I love animals."

She smiled. "Do you like snakes? Because the basement is full of them, and I don't know how adept they are at stairs, so I can't swear they wouldn't join you and the raccoons in bed."

"Sounds like built-in security," he said. "Pest control for mice." He sighed. "And, if all else fails, company."

She laughed. "Okay, and you're going to need that security, because teenagers have been going and hanging out to party there."

"Who doesn't love shit weed and Natty Boh?"

"The feral cats that are wandering all over. They're not sweet and cuddly. They hiss if you so much as look at them." She'd made the mistake of thinking one was cute once.

"Excellent. I've been looking for an excuse to get a dog."

She thought of her old golden retriever, Dizzy, sleeping through doorbells, thunderstorms, just about everything you could think of. She'd be useless with the cats. "Probably better to get a *person* to help you with all the labor that needs to be done inside. Old furniture thrown out, carpets to roll and chuck out. Spackling, painting, lather, rinse, repeat."

"Sounds like exercise to me." He was smiling, she could tell from his voice. "It's very important, with my career, to stay in shape, you know."

She didn't want him to feel like it was a mistake, but it could sure be nice to have him around. "Max, if you do this, I can almost guarantee you're going to be disappointed by the place." She sighed. "I really get the privacy thing, and you'd have it in spades there, but just bear in mind that my husband gave me this with the divorce as sort of a freebie. So he wouldn't have to mess with it himself."

"Nice."

"He's a peach." Then, because she'd done nothing but diss the place, she added, "The driveway is probably a good half mile or so long. Tree lined. Private."

"It sounds perfect," he said, and sounded like he meant it. "Because it sounds *real*. It wouldn't be hard to find a private place that was already the stuff of HGTV. But I've been in situations like that before and word got out pretty quickly that I was there. I don't mean to sound self-congratulatory, it's just how it is right now." A moment of silence. "Come on, Margo. Am I too late? I know it's been a few weeks. Do you already have people lined up for the place?"

"No! Not at all." If this worked out, he'd be a godsend. "In fact, so far there have been no takers at all."

"I don't see how that's possible."

She took another sip. "Right? None of my eight Instagram followers are homeless, as it turns out. In fact, I was just starting to panic over what to do next, since I'd rather eat bees than get involved with Craigslist."

"Sounds like you have just the place to do that. So do we have a deal?"

She smiled. "Obviously there's no way I'm going to say no to this, but I just need to be really sure you understand—"

"Hey, Margo. Seriously. I've got it. So how's tomorrow? Does tomorrow work?"

"Wow, you *are* desperate. But yes! Absolutely, yes. I'd be glad to have you!"

"Thank you. I appreciate this a lot."

This was surreal. "I'll text you the address and meet you there around"—she considered the drive from New York—"two? Would that work?"

His relief was audible. "Perfect."

When Margo arrived at the farm at one-thirty, he was already there. At least a gleaming black BMW Roadster was there. Max was nowhere to be seen. The sound of sparrows and mourning doves in the trees was louder here than at the house in Potomac. There were bullfrogs in the creek at the edge of the property. All in all, it was pretty loud, but a different kind of loud than he'd be used to in the city.

She took the house keys out—they were on a pink John Deere key chain she'd once thought was adorable for a farmhouse—and went to the side door closest to the driveway. There was no garage, which suddenly seemed like a liability in the face of that sports car, but there were plenty of outbuildings that could be converted if he wanted. She wasn't even sure what all of the buildings were for, to be honest. She'd been told the one closest to the house was a "pony barn," but she'd never heard of such a thing. It was the perfect size for a couple of cars, though.

It was hard to quell her nerves as she unlocked the door, knowing that he might show up at any second. It was weird how daunting someone else's fame could be. She never used to be *this* self-conscious around him.

She opened the creaky door and went into the kitchen. It smelled musty, and the first thing she noticed was a gross, dark gray network of cobwebs on the walls, but the surfaces were otherwise smooth. Ready for a coat of paint. It had been a while since she'd been here, and now she saw her bad PR *might* have been a little more extreme than was warranted.

Yes, it was very dusty. Every surface, including the windows, had that gray-brown tinge. The linoleum floor was not only disgustingly dingy, and covered in mouse droppings, but it was also peeling up in so many places that it would be a tripping hazard to cook in here, even if you could get the stove clean enough to keep an appetite.

But the huge butcher block island was something she somehow hadn't taken much note of before. With a little sanding and some oil, it would be a beautiful centerpiece in the kitchen. She could picture it now, with a fresh loaf of bread on it, straight from the oven, ready to slice and butter. She took her phone out and opened the camera, taken by the idea of documenting it as a project. In fact, she could Instagram the whole house renovation. Maybe that would satisfy her need for creativity.

If she put in knotty pine floors, it would be even more beautiful. Knock out the far wall into that small, pointless room to the left and—

"Hello?"

She was startled by his voice, and even more startled when she turned to see The Max Roginski standing in the slant of light coming through the door. "Wow, you look great!" She couldn't help it, he did. Even more polished in person than in pictures, if possible. Some of the awkwardness of his late teens and early twenties had softened into handsomeness.

His eyes lit as they focused on her. "You too." He came over and hugged her, enveloping her in his warmth and in a light scent she hadn't realized she remembered. "As always," he added.

She felt her face grow warm and pulled back, hoping he

didn't notice her embarrassment. "Did you walk around the property some? You're still here, so it's hard to guess."

His fingertips lingered on her arm for a moment, then he looked at them and shoved his hands in his front pockets. "Yeah. Yeah, it's great. I love it. Nothing but nothing as far as the eye can see."

She nodded. "I always kind of liked the idea of being able to walk outside naked and have no one see." Great, now she'd conjured an image for him of her being naked. Hopefully it was flattering. "So"—she cleared her throat—"you want to see the rest of the house?"

"Of course, yes."

"Let's do it. So this is where I'd start to fix it up," she said as they walked through the kitchen. "I can't stand to eat anything that comes out of a gunky refrigerator or sits on a dirty counter, even with a plate in between."

He shrugged. "Doesn't really bother me that much."

She raised her eyebrows but didn't say anything. He had to have been eating in the fanciest places in Manhattan, whereas now the closest restaurant was miles away, and that was a Mc-Donald's. This was no setting to make a gourmet meal at the moment, and a plate of Hamburger Helper in here would have to be repulsive to him, but whatever. "Now, I always thought I'd want to take out the wall between the kitchen and this room," she said as they entered the small square block with a fireplace on the side wall. "Make one huge kitchen, you know?"

"That would be nice," he said, taking it all in. "You've got light from the south and east here. It would be sunny all day."

She nodded, and they rounded the corner to the front entryway. "As you can see, the formal front door isn't really convenient to anything except that random piece of yard."

"But the wraparound porch is pretty great."

She shrugged. "As long as you don't fall through the rotting wood flooring."

"Noted." He examined the bannister appreciatively.

As they started up the stairs she gestured toward the larger room on the main floor to their right. "Good-size family room here. Another fireplace, though I have no idea if it works. I always thought it would be nice to put gas ones in." The stairs creaked ominously under their footsteps. "Be careful," she said, "we might end up in the basement, slapstick trapdoor style."

"These are solid oak," he commented, stomping a foot. "They won't buckle."

"Here's hoping." She reached the landing and stepped into the full bathroom. It had the original black-and-white tile that was popular in the 1940s. "This actually seems pretty tight, but it needs a good cleaning."

He frowned and looked around, tapped at the showerhead, the sink, the faucets. "Nothing too hard to do here."

"This," she said, entering a very long room with stairs back down to the kitchen, "is the master bedroom. I think it has *so* much potential."

"I'll say." He walked around, looked at the windows, then pulled what looked like thin wax paper off the top of one of the sills.

"What's that?" she asked.

"Snakeskin." He dropped it on the floor. "I don't know how it got up there, but apparently it shed while it was there."

Margo felt a lump in her throat and had to struggle to keep herself from gagging. "That's disgusting. I thought I was kidding when I said they'd come up and sleep with you."

He raised an eyebrow. "I didn't."

She was impressed at his utter lack of squeamishness. They'd never had to discuss anything like this before, so it wasn't as if she had any solid reason to assume he'd find it all distasteful beyond the fact that most people would.

She was glad he didn't.

They toured the rest of the rooms, such as they were—and they were all roughly the same—dusty, spiderwebbed, smelly, and empty. But the windows weren't broken, though they were old, and the hardwood floors on the entire floor seemed to be in such good condition they might not even need refinishing.

Eventually they made their way back down to the kitchen, where they'd started. "Well." She threw her hands up in a broad shrug and sighed. "Now you see what I was talking about. I really hope you don't feel like you've wasted—"

"It's perfect."

She wondered if she'd misheard. "Seriously?"

"I love it. If you're willing to make a deal, I am." He walked to the door and looked out at what was an undeniably beautiful landscape. Big red barn that, incredibly, *didn't* seem to need a paint job; split rail fences lining rolling, if overgrown, pastures. "Would you mind if I brought some livestock in? Horses, goats. It would really help trim back the greenery while I work inside the house."

She couldn't think of an objection. "That would be fine."

He cocked his head and looked at her. "Do you ride?"

"I used to. It's been years. I used to take care of a few horses down in Travilla when I was a teenager."

She smiled and felt her face grow pink under his gaze.

He continued to look at her, his blues eyes nothing short of piercing, to use the cliché. His hair was buzzed shorter than she remembered, but with a face like that, why create a distraction with hair? "So if I got a couple of trail horses, you'd be interested in riding with me now and then?"

She laughed outright. Calvin was gone, and with him went his negativity. Now, would she mind riding horses with Max Roginski in the sweet Virginia fields? "I would love it," she said sincerely. "That would be really fun."

"Great!" He put out his hand. "Then we have a deal."

She took it, and shook firmly. "Sure, if you're really up for it."

He smiled and gave a quick, rakish wink. "One hundred

percent. If you can just send me the details about rent, and where to sign for the utilities, I'll send them to my lawyer and have him handle all that."

She cringed inwardly. "I really can't see charging anything."

"Are you kidding? This place is great!" He followed her gaze, and she thought she saw genuine admiration in his eyes. Whatever it was that had appealed to him when this was still just an idea was still working for him, now that he'd seen it. "Send me the deets and I'll have them handled as soon as possible."

She nodded. "You've got it."

"And, Margo?"

She stopped. What would Calvin think if he could see her right now? He'd think he wanted the place back, that's what. He'd see black dollar signs instead of red numbers, and he'd want to dive in and take advantage of it. "Yes?"

"I can't emphasize this enough," Max said. "Please, *please* don't tell anyone I'm here. Not even your closest friends. Please just keep this between the two of us."

A chill of a thrill ran through her, waking a sleeping feeling within her. She hadn't been told a secret in so long, and she certainly hadn't been excited like this when she was told to keep it.

Max and she had a secret. And she wasn't going to tell a soul.

CHAPTER TEN

AJA

She would have liked to believe Michael was finally seeing a future with her and that was why he decided to introduce her to his mother, but, in fact, it turned out that the older woman was trying to set him up with the "horse-faced" (according to him) daughter of a friend of hers and was being relentless about it until he finally said he was seeing someone.

It did very little to reassure Aja. He probably would have asked a cocktail waitress to do him a favor and come along if Aja hadn't been available.

Still, eager to impress, Aja had made what she now considered her specialty—since it was the only dessert she'd mastered—a strawberry pie. It had seemed like a good idea when she'd made it, but now with every mile it felt like a cheaper and cheaper gesture.

She might as well have brought a wrapped Twinkie.

They drove through the posh town he'd grown up in, and she noticed the houses seemed to get bigger on every block.

Finally Michael turned down Alloway Drive, through brick entry posts and past a little guardhouse that must once have contained a security guard of some sort, checking to make sure no riffraff was coming in.

The house was like something out of a vintage *Better Homes and Gardens* cover. Honeysuckle grew on the white picket fence and scented the air. The grass in the front yard was just a little too long, as if waiting for someone to put their iced tea down on the porch and mow it. There was a small barn behind the house, on the other side of where the driveway turned toward a matching freestanding garage.

Michael parked the car, heaved a breath, and looked at Aja to say, "Here we are."

"Is this where you grew up?" she asked, a little breathless.

He threw a cursory glance at the place, then gave the slightest shrug, as if it meant nothing. "Yeah."

But it didn't mean anything. It was a beautiful piece of land, a beautiful piece of nature. The house had been built by people who cared—it *had* to have been, it was so unbelievably perfect. Even the fence that lined the pasture all the way around was perfect, long white rectangles, none of them loose or in need of a paint touch-up. It was a child's play set around a green velvet field with perfect plastic horses, stamped MADE IN GREAT BRITAIN on their bellies, perched about like perfect decorations.

"It's beautiful," she breathed, and found herself imagining the glory of even being a live-in maid here, much less the owner. "Aren't you bowled over every time you come here?"

He looked at her, seeming genuinely puzzled. "Bowled over?" He gave a laugh. "No? Babe, have you been drinking?"

"No." He didn't notice her dry tone, or, in fact, her dry *body*. She hadn't had a drink in weeks. She opened the car door and got out, unwilling to continue the conversation, but as soon as the outside air hit her she smelled the boxwoods and had to wonder how long the house had been here if it had such large, fragrant boxwoods.

She didn't dare ask, though, since she'd obviously already touched a sore spot with Michael, so instead she just walked around the car and joined him to walk up the white stone pathway to the door. For him it was undoubtedly old hat, but for her it was pure beauty.

They got to the front door and, to Aja's surprise, Michael rang the bell.

"It's your house, why don't you just go in?" Aja asked.

"It's not my house, it's my mother's house."

"When you were growing up here, did you always ring the bell to get in?"

"No." He looked at her like she as an idiot. "But I don't live here anymore so walking in would be rude."

Aja opened her mouth to object, but the door squeaked and jerked and then opened. A woman opened the door with a tight smile. She had high, perpendicular hair, and dark, careful eye makeup. She looked like a soap opera matriarch. "Michael. Lovely to see you." She bent forward for fake cheek kisses.

Michael accommodated them. "Mother," he said, all but genuflecting. "This is Aja." He swept an arm in her direction.

"Asia?" his mother repeated quizzically.

"Well, not exactly . . ." Aja started. And really, it wasn't her name. Angela Jennifer Alexander had been going by "Aja"— the nickname she'd inadvertently given herself as a child who could pronounce neither "Angela" nor "Jennifer" fully—for so long that it always surprised her when people thought she was foreign.

She was not. Which would probably be a relief to Michael's mother.

That should have helped her right now to not take someone else's tone to heart. But how was she not supposed to take it to heart that Michael clearly didn't want her to meet his mother and for the obvious reason that his mother wasn't all too pleased to be meeting her?

"I'm Angela," she said, in as strong a voice as she could muster. "My friends call me Aja. *A-J-A*." She smiled and held out her hand.

The older woman looked from her face to her hand but didn't otherwise move a muscle. "I see" was all she said.

Aja wanted to question her on that, but she felt Michael

shuffle his feet beside her, clearly uncomfortable. "Mother, we don't want to keep you long, I just wanted—"

"Come in," the older woman commanded, then looked Aja dead in the eye and trailed her gaze down to her feet. "Wipe your shoes on the matt, please. Then leave them by the door."

Aja eyed her for a moment, wondering what on earth Lucinda Carter thought she might inadvertently bring in.

Then she remembered that she *was* bringing something in; something way more important and consequential than dirt or grass clippings.

She was carrying Lucinda Carter's grandchild.

Having grown up in this area, Aja had seen new money and old money all her life. This was old money. This was gleaming mahogany and equestrian art and the rich smell of saddle leather and fresh cut flowers.

"We'll sit in the drawing room," Lucinda said, with a sweep of the hand, indicating the direction, though Michael would already know it.

He looked uncertainly at Aja, then put a hand on her lower back and guided her to follow his mother.

All Aja could think was that she didn't belong here, carrying this stupid pie that no one had even mentioned. Had Lucinda even *noticed* it? Did she think it was some sort of Security Pie, rather than the gift it obviously was?

Maybe it embarrassed her with its obvious homemade-ness.

Every knickknack on the dark wooden built-ins probably had cost more than everything in her whole apartment. There wasn't a single piece of furniture that cost less than her car. It should be noted that her car was a fifteen-year-old Corolla with almost two hundred thousand miles on it, but still. The thought of being able to pick and choose any beautiful thing in the world to decorate a home seemed like absolute bliss to Aja.

She gathered her nerve and, when Lucinda finally stopped walking, said, "I made you a pie." She thrust it forward into Lucinda's unprepared hands just as the woman was probably trying to shield herself. "Oh, I'm sorry," Aja said.

Lucinda got ahold of the pie dish and gave a tight smile. "Quite all right. You made this? How clever you are."

"It's a strawberry pie," Aja said unnecessarily, as if the pie dish, the pie crust, and the strawberry filling bursting out of the crust like something from *Alien* weren't enough clues.

"Indeed." Lucinda smiled and Aja relaxed fractionally. "It smells delicious. I'll just put it in the kitchen if you'll excuse me a moment?"

"Of course."

Lucinda walked away, holding the pie in front of her like a box of rodents, and Michael said, "That could have been done a bit more gracefully."

Aja nodded. "Right? I'm so nervous I don't know how to talk even." She threaded her hand through his arm and gave a squeeze, but he remained stiff.

"It might have made more sense to leave it in the foyer so she could have the help take care of it."

Aja gave a laugh. "It might have made more sense to bring flowers too, but I can't really put the smoke back in the chimney now." She looked for him to smile but he didn't.

Instead he watched with a tightened jaw until his mother came out of the kitchen. "Sorry about that, Mom. I could have taken that for you."

Lucinda looked at him curiously. "I'm perfectly capable of walking to my own kitchen." She looked at Aja again. "That was really so sweet of you. Now, both of you, please. Take a seat."

She gestured, and Michael and Aja sat on a silk-covered French Provençal settee—Aja couldn't guess as to which Louis it was in the style of—and it creaked briefly under their weight.

"How are you feeling, Mom?" Michael asked, settling in the seat and glancing at his watch before setting his gaze on her.

She waved her hand. "My allergies are absolute madness. Dr. Robbins says I shouldn't go outside at all, lest I should have another spell."

Aja pictured an overly dramatic fainting spell, but Michael said, "Asthma is nothing to mess around with. Do you have Albuterol ready for your nebulizer?"

Aja looked at him in surprise. She'd never seen him in anything that could even remotely be called a caretaking role. He was frowning at his mother, which made Aja want to nudge him to soften his expression, but it wasn't her place and he wouldn't know what her nudge meant anyway. They didn't have that kind of Couple's Shorthand.

"I know it, I just get so *bored* rattling around in here. I barely see another living soul, and when I do it's usually that gardener and he's a son of a bitch."

Aja stifled a laugh. The dichotomy of the language with the carefully powdered and pulled seventy-something face—or was she older than that?—was unexpected. Plus, who hated a gardener? A *landscaper,* maybe, because that implied business, contracts, teams, and noise. But *gardener* conjured a little Englishman with clubfoot, a dead tooth, and the mystical ability to breathe life into nature.

There was nothing more magical than a garden.

"I thought you'd put the idea of a vegetable garden to rest," Michael said, as if she'd suggested she could bury some pennies and grow a money tree.

"It's never a bad idea to have your own organic food, of course," Aja jumped in. "It's just better for you. The strawberries in the pie are organic. Actually, all of it is." God, she really sounded like she was trying to sell the pie.

Michael took what Aja recognized as an impatient intake of breath, when they were interrupted by a tall, wiry blond man with pale blue eyes, skin the color of raw hamburger, and a container of Roundup weed killer in his hand. "Ma'am," he said to Lucinda without an ounce of deference, "I cannot work with the dogs swarming me." He had an indeterminate accent.

Eastern European? Russian, maybe? "I've told you this before. Dogs, children, cats using my beds as litter boxes. I am not a circus act!"

Actually, he was so sarcastically angry that it kind of seemed like he was doing a bit. Ornery millionaire who lost his fortune gambling and now had to work as a gardener for a living.

"Luga, I've told you, I don't know who those animals belong to, and as for the child—"

"Excuse me," Michael interrupted, looking at Luga with interest and not a lot of patience. "Why are you addressing your employer this way?"

Luga swung to face him, and the Roundup sloshed onto the floor. Aja winced. That stuff was toxic. It would probably take the wax right up. It would also probably turn any vegetables Lucinda was trying to grow into poison.

"And who are *you*?" Luga looked him up and down. "I don't know you."

Michael's face reddened almost as much as Luga's.

"This is my son," Lucinda said, her voice tight. "Michael, I can handle this."

Luga snorted. "I should have guessed. Dressed for wine, not for work."

"What business is it of yours how I'm dressed?"

Luga gave a shrug that implied he had Michael, as a type, pegged and thus had nothing more to say to him.

Worse, he was probably right.

Lucinda stepped forward. "Now, please, everyone calm down and be civilized. There's no need to turn this into a— There's no need to argue. Luga, you're simply going to have to work around the distractions."

He looked at her incredulously. "I will not! Everything I do is undone when I return."

"Now, that's not true, you just don't like children or animals and you're exaggerating the perils to your work."

Aja looked out the window, half expecting to see a birthday party going on, with balloons, ponies, puppies, and a bouncy house in the middle of the garden. Some oddly placed cats. There was nothing.

Nothing except the light scent of yarrow lifted in on the breeze that came through the door Luga had left open. Aja could almost imagine the particles of pollen carrying the scent like a great yellow ghost. "The door," she said to Michael quietly, pointing.

"What about it?"

"Pollen." No comprehension. "*Asthma.*"

He nodded and went to close it.

Meanwhile, there was a greater danger sloshing around in the weed killer container Luga was gesticulating with.

"I am not working under these conditions!"

"I'm afraid you'll have to," Lucinda said simply.

"I will not! The tomatoes are rotting, the basil is yellow, and the mint is in a wet pile, all thanks to those animals."

Michael returned, and Aja felt his whole body tighten next to her, his fury was almost as tangible as steam. She hated this. The stress was disproportionate to whatever was going on. Everyone was being a jerk.

"Can you tent the beds with chicken wire?" Aja suggested.

She might have suggested he build a wall out of Play-Doh for the look he gave her. "I do not work with *chicken wire.*"

"But it would keep the animals clear and it would be practically invisible."

"You are now the expert?"

She shrugged and felt her face grow hot. "No, but I've gardened all my life. My grandfather had a green thumb."

Luga looked at her with disgust, clearly not understanding the idiom.

"Like the tomatoes rotting," she went on, knowing she should stop. "That's not animals, that's root rot. You have to throw away the plants that have it and put some lime in the soil to raise the pH. There's still time to have a good crop." She felt Lucinda looking at her but dared not meet her gaze for fear that she thought Aja was being impertinent.

"The plants are very fine," he said with derision. "Heirloom. I saved the seeds myself. This is not *root rot.*"

"It's not about the seeds," she explained quickly. "I'm sure they're very good. It's just the soil. Tomatoes need higher calcium content. If you add some limestone, it should be fine." She looked from him, to Lucinda, to Michael. They all looked blank. All three of them. "It's no one's fault," she finished lamely.

"Well then." Luga gave Aja a cold, hard stare before slowly shifting his focus to Lucinda. "It looks like you have found yourself a new gardener. I quit!" He threw the Roundup down and it splashed across the wood floor again. Aja's first instinct was to run to the kitchen to find something to clean it up with, but she remembered that she was—probably—pregnant. She couldn't risk touching that stuff.

"I'm so sorry," she said to Lucinda. "I didn't mean to make him angrier. I thought he'd be glad to have a solution, since he was so upset about the plants."

Michael put a warning hand on her arm.

But Lucinda's mouth, which moments ago had been a straight, angry line, quirked up at the corner. "What is it you do, girl?"

Girl. "I'm a yoga teacher," Aja answered, knowing that probably disqualified everything she'd said about plants. "Part-time. I mean more full-time, but it's not a normal forty-hour workweek." Why was she overexplaining herself?

"I see," his mother said, though she didn't. "Is that what you've always done?"

"Oh, no, I've had a million jobs." Aja laughed alone. "But actually, I used to work at Potomac Garden Center over on River Road. Before it closed."

"I didn't know that," Michael said.

She gave another laugh. He didn't really know anything about her past, did he? It wasn't as if he asked a lot of questions.

"Well, it's not that interesting. It was just a summer job but . . ." She had no great conclusion. She shrugged. "I learned a few things." She studied his face, trying to determine just how badly he thought this meeting with his mother was going. Of course he had no way of knowing how critical it was to Aja, but she'd have to tell him before too long.

His expression was inscrutable, his handsome face as still as a statue's.

"Excellent!" Lucinda said, with a clap, drawing both their attention. "You're hired!"

Aja looked at Michael, then behind him, wondering if someone else had snuck into the room while she wasn't paying attention, but, no, it was still just the three of them.

She had no idea what was going on.

Clearly Michael didn't either. "What are you talking about, Mom? Who's hired? For what?"

"She is." Lucinda gestured at Aja, as if indicating where to set a vase. "Anya."

"Aja," she corrected automatically.

"That's ridiculous," Michael said, unnecessarily harsh. "What would you be hiring her for?"

"I'm not really looking for a job—"

"To finish the garden! You saw Luga just quit. And your girl certainly seems to know what she's talking about."

His girl. Was that how he'd introduced the idea of her? "No, I'm really no expert, those were just some very basic—"

"She's not qualified for that! Mom, she's a *yoga teacher*. She doesn't do . . ." He lowered his voice just fractionally. "*Real* jobs."

Aja heard it loud and clear, and looked at him incredulously. "I don't do *real* jobs?"

"Don't be ridiculous," Lucinda said to Michael. Aja's chest tightened with gratitude before she added, "This isn't a real job, it's a task that *someone* needs to do, and Aria seems to fit the bill." She leveled that cool blue gaze on Aja. "Don't you?"

"I don't think so," Aja said, suddenly taken over by a cool resentment. She looked from Lucinda to Michael. "I can't believe you two are arguing back and forth about how incompetent and . . . and . . . *desperate* I apparently seem to you. Not that I should have to defend myself to you, but my little job helps a lot of people. Would you have any more respect for me if I was called a physical therapist instead of a yoga instructor? Because that's basically what I am." Her anger rose disproportionate to the offense, and she tried to keep her voice controlled. "The hospital thinks so, anyway, as they have kept me employed there for five years. *They* consider it to be a *real* job when they pay me."

For a moment, Lucinda and Michael both seemed stunned into silence.

"I'll pay you twenty thousand dollars to get the garden set

up," Lucinda said casually. "Is that not enough? Full disclosure, Luga was getting thirty-five, but with his reputation . . ."

Aja's stomach clenched. Twenty thousand dollars? For, what, a *month*? Was there anyone on earth who couldn't seriously, *seriously* use that? Well, okay, there were plenty of people who had enough means to turn their nose up at that, but Aja was not one of them.

Particularly not with the news of the baby.

"She doesn't need your money, Mom," Michael said. "And I find it highly inappropriate for you to try and poach my guest into doing work for you."

"Guest?" Aja echoed, but he didn't answer, he was looking at his mother with heat in his eyes. Maybe *guest* was fair. *Girlfriend* would have felt better, but he probably felt stupid saying that at his age.

He shot her an impatient glance. *Don't interrupt one argument with another,* it obviously said. And he was right, she shouldn't be chiming in on what was a tense conversation with his mother, although it *was* about Aja, so how could she not?

"My schedule during the week is erratic but pretty full," Aja said, thinking it would probably put an end to the question.

Michael shrugged. "There, you see?"

His mother raised an eyebrow. "Works for me. And I can't imagine why you'd have a problem with it."

Aja frowned and tried to read her meaning but she couldn't. Nor could she read his response, which was only to nod and say, "It's up to you, of course, but you're asking her to work a lot."

"Oh, it's not that," Aja said quickly, not wanting Lucinda to think she was a lazy slug who had a few scattered hours of work stretching during the week and couldn't be bothered to help an old lady with her gardening during the weekends. "I don't mind work at all! Actually, I *like* work, but with my schedule, timing can be tricky. And you'd need to know you're looking at autumn crops now at best. But, honestly, I'd love to do it."

And, okay, the money couldn't be ignored either, though the project time would be extended to more than a month unless Lucinda was okay with her working odd hours when she could.

"Excellent news," Lucinda said, and there was no mistaking the checkmate in her voice. "When can you start?"

If Michael had issues with women, and Aja felt pretty sure he did, she was getting a fascinating display of their origins right now. She couldn't tell if this competition between him and his mother was play or not. There was a certain feeling of *to the death* in both of them.

But twenty grand was twenty grand, and no one could blame Aja for wanting to save up as much as she could before the baby came, so she spoke with barely a thought beforehand. "I can start this weekend," she said. "If you can tell me what you want, I'll go take a look at how far Luga got and formulate a plan and calculate planting and harvest times so they're staggered."

"Are you sure you haven't done this before?" Lucinda asked, though this time she didn't sound smug so much as genuinely impressed. "You're certainly saying all the right things."

Aja splayed her arms. "Honestly, it's not that complicated. It's just the earth's rhythms. Everything has different sun and temperature needs, but if you're willing to shell out a little more for some mature plants, and less for things I can sprout on time for their season, there's no reason in the world this shouldn't work out just the way you want. Okay, maybe I'm a little bit of a plant nerd."

"Excellent. May I steal you for a moment to discuss it?" Lucinda looked to Michael. "Can you occupy yourself for twenty minutes or so while I discuss the job with Asia?"

He gave a nod. "By all means."

Relief ran through Aja. He wasn't pissed, thank God. This was just his weird dynamic with his mother. It was nothing to worry about, nothing to do with Aja at all; it was their own weirdness and she was going to stay well out of it.

Lucinda led her to a gorgeous modern kitchen that looked like it never saw any use at all. Given how meticulous the woman's own appearance was, Aja imagined she scrubbed the hell out of it every time she made so much as a pack of Minute Rice.

If she even ate Minute Rice.

On second thought, she probably didn't. No white foods, no carbs. She was as thin as a 1970s rock star and her clothes hung on her like draperies, exactly as she no doubt wanted. To maintain a figure like that, people used to live on cigarettes and clear liquor. The occasional salad. Which was, it seemed, where Aja came in.

They sat at the spotless kitchen table and Lucinda gave a somewhat vague outline of the vegetables that were necessities for her. Tomatoes, squashes, peppers, lettuces of all sorts. She told Aja that more was better but those were her staples, though she wanted vegetables that Aja could "put by" in storage for the winter or the coming terrorist attack, whichever arrived first.

"And what about herbs?" Aja asked.

"I don't know anything in the world about herbs."

"For flavor. They can be used in drinks and food."

"I know what herbs are, dear, I just don't know how all of them are used. You can plant a good variety so that the cook can make those decisions himself, how is that?"

So there was a cook. She should have known. This was not a do-it-yourself house. This was not a do-it-yourself woman. By any stretch. As a matter of fact, in the entire time she'd been with him, Aja had not seen Michael prepare or *eat* homemade food. They always went out. She'd hoped her cooking adventures with the cookbook club might tempt him into a bit more domesticity, but it wasn't looking like it would go that way.

"That's absolutely fine," Aja said. "Whatever you want. I can speak with the cook if he's here on Saturday and see if he has any special requests."

"That would be splendid!" Lucinda clapped her hands together. "I'll see you bright and early on Saturday then!"

Aja smiled, something like hope stirring inside of her. Maybe everything was working out exactly as it needed to. "I'm looking forward to it," she said earnestly. "Thank you for the opportunity."

"You obviously can't really take on this job," Michael said as soon as they were in the car.

Aja felt like she'd been punched in the stomach. "What are you talking about? I thought you were fine with this!"

He jammed the transmission into reverse and backed out of the driveway, guiding himself by watching the rearview mirror. "I think I made it pretty clear to you both that I'm not."

"But why? Why wouldn't you be?"

He pulled into the street, put the car in drive, and accelerated a little harder than was necessary. "She wouldn't even have met you if you hadn't tagged along today."

That made it sound like she was a pesky kid who wouldn't take no for an answer, but she couldn't afford to splinter off into a subargument. "But she *did* meet me and it seems like it was pretty fortuitous timing. Maybe there's a *reason* you invited me today of all days."

The instant, though small, lowering of his brow told her he'd noticed her wording, and probably took issue with it, but instead he just said, "You're not qualified as a landscaper, and you know it. You're going to have to tell her you can't do it after all."

"I didn't pretend I was a landscaper—"

"You're going to embarrass yourself and me. I won't have it." He started to say something else but threw his hand up and expelled a breath almost violently. "This is fucking stupid that we're even having this conversation."

"You won't *have*—" She didn't even know which part to object to first. "You think I'm going to *embarrass* you?" Aja couldn't believe she was actually saying those words to him. She'd *trusted* him. She'd slept with him. For God's sake, she was carrying his baby! Who had she thought he was? And more importantly, who was he really?

Tears sprang to her eyes and her throat closed over a lump of emotion, but she didn't want him to see it. Couldn't let him hear it. Suddenly it felt to her like this man she'd thought she knew would consider it a *triumph* if she cried.

"You worked at a garden center over the summer when you were a kid," he said, softening his voice slightly, if not his words. "That doesn't qualify you to take on a landscape contract."

"And I don't need a *landscape contract* to plant some tomatoes and basil in a suburban backyard!"

He looked at her sharply. "There's no reason to raise your voice at me, Aja."

"I'm sorry," she said automatically. "I'm just hurt that you're talking to me like this. I would have thought you'd have more faith in me. There's no way I would have accepted that position if I didn't think—no, if I didn't *know*—I could do a great job for her. Better than that crazy Luga guy, I'm sure."

"That crazy Luga guy is a professional. That's how he was hired. You're an exercise teacher with a lot of free time."

This was becoming surreal. The whole tone of the conversation had put her in shock. That was the only reason she was able to keep going, because she'd somehow gotten on this ride and part of her wanted to see it through. "I'm a professional," she corrected. "With a complicated schedule."

"A professional," he repeated, as if to himself, and shook his head slightly with a laugh.

"That's funny?"

"Aja, you are, put charitably, a . . . Renaissance woman. With about that much understanding of the way the modern world works. You talk about fate, and things being meant to be. I have no doubt you think you can do this because Mother Earth is one with you and yoga and all the other stuff, but the reality is that you need to . . . stay in your lane."

She did a quick study of his profile. She'd thought he was so handsome once. Even this morning she'd thought that. But now, looking at him, with his words still echoing in her mind, she noticed the thin set of his lips. Like a knife slit cut in a bag of flour. Not a kind or tempting mouth, just a vessel for his judgment and cruelty.

The lines that threaded through his expressions weren't from years of laughter, but years of frowns and condemnations. Thinking about it now, she'd never seen him truly laugh. Definitely not at anything she'd said, but they'd really never even shared a joke. They'd gone to the movies a couple of times, but he always picked heavy dramas that she failed to intellectualize with him afterward.

How had she fooled herself into thinking they had a partnership? In all the time they'd been together, she'd only just met his mother today, and he characterized it as her "tagging along." They had no shared jokes, no secret code, no shorthand. What *did* they have?

Sex.

They had sex. At his convenience. Whenever, wherever he wanted. She accommodated him. She was his . . . receptacle.

"Stop the car," she said.

They were perhaps a quarter mile away from Potomac Village, a cluster of shops and restaurants and a couple of gas stations that were all crowded into maybe one square half mile. It would be easy to get an Uber out of there, even though it would be expensive. But she couldn't even wait the three minutes it would take to get there. She had to get out now or she would lose her mind. "I want to get out." She picked up her purse with her left hand and put her hand on the door handle with her right. "Let me out."

"Don't be stupid."

Her fingers tightened around the leather strap of her purse. She had to fight not to open the door while the car was still moving. "I'm. Not. Stupid."

"Prove it."

"Stop the car."

"Aja—"

Everything inside her felt like it was boiling, bubbling up within and threatening to spill over. "*Please* stop the car." She adjusted her grip on the door release.

"I'm not stopping," he said, but at that moment he pulled up to the line of cars waiting at the traffic light. The simple intersection had worked a million years ago when it wasn't so crowded but now it was an absolute clusterfuck, lucky for Aja. As soon as the car was nearly stopped, she opened the door and stepped out, losing her footing slightly, owing to a miscalculation of what seemed slow inside the vehicle versus what *was* slow getting out.

"Goodbye, Michael," she said, her voice tripping with her uneven footing. She slammed the door.

"What the fuck are you doing?" she heard him yell, but it was behind the glass and mercifully muted, and disappeared behind her as she picked her way through stopped and slowing cars to get to the strip mall where she could regroup and call for a ride.

She watched as he was forced to move with the traffic, looking in her direction, gesticulating, his mouth moving with the force of angry words she could only imagine.

She didn't ever want to hear that voice again.

MEETING 3—AUGUST
Someone's in the Kitchen with Dinah

Forget food—Aja is four months pregnant! Been hiding it—not very well, but you never assume so I guess it was well enough. Explains the yawns, the not drinking, the seemingly bottomless stomach. She dumped her boyfriend and is working for his mother. Bad situation, imho.

September

CHAPTER ELEVEN

TRISTA

She didn't know why, but this random Friday night had been fantastic as far as tips went. Fridays were usually steady, but not slammed like that. She and Ike were pooling the cash, but—thanks to a generous tip for Trista from an out-of-towner who had been thrilled to know how close they were to the *Exorcist* steps and from a woman who looked for all the world to be a drunk, and surprisingly agreeable, Ann Coulter—by 8:00 P.M. they were already pocketing a couple hundred each.

That was gold compared to the state of things when she'd first come back to the bar. Thanks to some nice Yelp reviews noting the renovations to both the structure and the menu, people were slowly starting to come around and give them a chance.

She was making Cathedral Sunsets for a couple who had

recently moved into the neighborhood when Ike came out of the kitchen, visibly irritated.

Louis was right behind him. "Some were as tall as six foot eight, I'm telling you. Most of them. That's the size of LeBron!"

"It's not possible," Ike muttered. "The average human is . . . I don't know, but not that tall. That would be *ridiculous*. We would have heard about this by now if it were true."

Every single day, Louis brought at least one weird fact to work with him. Trista actually got a kick out of them sometimes, although Louis had a problem with reading the room and, specifically, shutting up when a customer was ordering or asking a question.

It had been like that in school too; she'd be trying to take notes and not get in trouble for talking, and Louis would be telling her the manufacturing history of the college-ruled paper she was using and why a different pen would ultimately create less stress on her joints, thereby reducing her chances of having arthritis someday.

"What's in this drink?" the woman in front of her asked. "It's not too strong, is it?"

Trista smiled and shook her head. "It's a fruity rum drink, more juice than booze. Let's see, there's orange juice, light rum, grenadine, and lime." She raised an eyebrow before pouring. "You still want it, or would you prefer something else?"

"No, that sounds wonderful!"

Trista poured as the conversation behind her continued.

"Well, this was thirty-seven million years ago, give or take."

She might have pointed out that people used to be smaller, not bigger, but she didn't want to join the conversation. She knew from experience that it would only lead to frustration.

As Ike was experiencing now. "*Where?* Lilliput?"

"Actually, in Lilliput everything would be smaller," Louis corrected, collecting dirty glasses on a tray. "I think you mean Blefuscu. Though Jonathan Swift invented them both."

Ike rolled his eyes and took two Irish coffee mugs from the sink and added them to Louis's tray. "Dude, they're like a foot tall. You're nuts. I will bet you money."

"Oh, my friend, you do not want to do that." Louis chuckled indulgently.

"Yes, I do. No *penguin* is, or has ever been, six feet eight inches tall. Or weighs two hundred and fifty pounds."

Trista gave an involuntary laugh. "*Penguin?*" She pictured the bow-tied cartoon characters from *Mary Poppins,* towering over Julie Andrews and Dick Van Dyke, outweighing them both by at least a Saint Bernard.

"That's right," Louis said, looking genuinely surprised that yet another person didn't buy his story.

"Actually, you've got the details a little skewed but you're basically right," said the man who was now drinking a fresh Cathedral Sunrise.

"*Kumimanu biceae* was closer to six foot, but still quite an imposing fellow. It was about sixty million years ago." He caught Trista's eye and explained, "I teach zoology at American University."

"Oh." She nodded, impressed and yet wondering where this conversation could possibly go from here.

"You are correct," Louis said. "I'm talking about a species in what would now be New Zealand, thirty-seven million years ago. Go ahead and check it." He gestured toward the man. "It's a new study. Fascinating."

Trista knew she had to change the subject before Ike challenged the customer to some sort of trivia contest. "How on earth did this come up anyway?"

Louis didn't pause for so much as a fraction of a moment before answering. "Ike was saying the rat in the back was the biggest he'd ever seen and he didn't think it was really a rat but I told him a farmer in Ireland found a four-foot one once, and a shoe store in the Bronx found a dead one that weighed at least—"

"*Louis*," Trista said sharply, physically pushing him toward the kitchen. "I've told you, you cannot joke around like this, people will take you seriously." She gave a nervous laugh and hurried him away from the customers. Once safely behind the swinging doors to the kitchen, she rasped, "*What are you doing?* You can't talk about *rats* in the parking lot in front of customers!"

"Oh, he wasn't in the parking lot." Louis frowned and looked down at the shelves beneath the workstation. "He was right in here."

Trista felt sick. No. Please, no. She'd paid an exterminator a fortune to get rid of the rat problem. "Which one was it?" she asked frantically, turning as Ike came in. "Was it Ratricia Clarkson?" Naming them had made them slightly less daunting when she was seeing them daily, but she'd never wanted to have to see them again. This was the kind of thing that could get her shut down. "Please say it wasn't Ratthew McConaughey."

Ike looked grim. "Worse."

"Ratt Damon," she whispered in horror, and Ike nodded. "I thought he was a myth, invented by China Taste so they could take over our space."

"I thought it was a dog," Ike said. "Until I saw the tail. And"—he shuddered—"the hands."

"He was eating a burger bun," Louis explained. "I think it might have been one of ours."

"Okay." She raked her hair back out of her eyes and thought. What to do? "If we close the door and he's outside, then he can't get in. But if we close the door and he's in here, he's trapped. With us."

"Remember when Rattie Lupone ran through the dining room?" Ike shook his head. "Not a good situation."

She took in a long breath and tried to calm herself. "I'll call the exterminator and see if they can somehow get someone over here at this hour on a Friday night. You guys find a way to really secure the doors to the dining room and keep the back door open but *you have to keep an eye on it*. If he leaves, close the door. If he approaches, close the door." This was bad. Just really bad.

And she basically had to count on Louis to get it right.

She thought fleetingly of asking the zoologist at the bar for help, but there was a difference between knowing about a penguin that could be mistaken for Abraham Lincoln and being capable of impromptu extermination of a rat the size of a Great Dane.

She didn't even want to think about the carnage.

She whipped out her phone and googled the exterminator. She called the number and tapped her foot, waiting as it rang and rang. No answer, no machine. She blew through her texts, looking for the confirmation the tech had sent her the last time he was on his way over. She finally found it buried beneath people and bank codes and payment reminders, and shot a quick SOS to him.

Then she put on a smile and went back to the bar to serve what was shaping up to be the biggest crowd they'd had yet.

When Brice came through the door about forty-five minutes after her talk with Ike and Louis, she felt a huge sense of relief.

The feeling was that a grown-up had arrived, and she wasn't sure why she felt that way. Probably because she had been the idiot who had lost his license and he had been the adult who had handled it with aplomb.

But his suit wasn't hurting matters any. Gray, tailored. The kind of classic style and fit that would look right at home on Gregory Peck or George Clooney. She didn't know what he did for a living, but he was obviously pretty successful. There was dressing the part, of course, but some parts couldn't be faked.

"You wouldn't believe what's going on," she said, when he came over to the bar. His smile was disarming and she made a point of picking up a rag and wiping down the already clean bar top.

"I might," he said, with a single nod and a significant look. "Louis called asking my opinion on a really bad idea so I thought I should come right over."

She frowned. "Bad idea?"

"He wanted to do some Good Will Hunting." He lowered his voice and leaned in toward her. "With an improvised kitchen crossbow. If you . . . know what I mean?"

"Ooooh." The horror was too vivid. But it was classic Louis. He'd probably seen it on TV or read it in a book and wanted to try it out in real life. "God, I hope you're not too late."

He gave a quick nod and took off his jacket. "Right. So, if it's okay with you, I'm going to just run back there and see what's going on?"

"Yes, of course! *Thank* you! I really owe you one. Or two."

He held up his jacket. "If you could just do something with this that doesn't involve me taking it into the kitchen, we can call it even."

She took it and had to resist burying her face in the soft fabric. It smelled lightly of . . . clean air? Soap. A bright, ocean-y note. Aftershave aromatherapy. It instantly put her at ease. Or at least a little more at ease. She wasn't going to truly relax until Ratt Damon was gone.

A customer knocked on the bar a couple of feet away, bringing her attention back to the crowd. She glanced at Ike at the other end of the bar. It was even busier down there.

So she took the order and got back to work, hoping, for the first time since buying the place, that the crowd would subside so that she could go to the kitchen and see what was going on.

It was a good half hour before there was enough of a break for her to do that. She took dirty glasses from the two bar sinks and stacked them on a tray that had an old Holiday Inn logo fading in the middle.

She pushed through the door against what turned out to be a fifty-pound bag of sugar, and stumbled so dramatically she nearly dropped all the glasses. In that split second it was easy to imagine the customers' attention being drawn by the noise and then treated to a Jurassic rat scurrying into the dining room.

She righted the tray, sat it down, and caught her breath for a moment before scooting the bag back in front of the doors.

"I don't think a rat is capable of operating swinging doors," Brice commented.

"You don't know Ratt Damon," she said. "And I gather you haven't seen him?"

"Nope," Louis said, flipping a burger on the griddle and pressing down on it with the spatula. She was about to school him in losing the juices when he saw her expression and said, "Smashburger. I'm putting them in the double stack. They seem to be really popular."

It was true, she'd had at least four patrons raving about it. "Great," she said. "Do what you're doing."

Louis lifted the burger to reveal a thin layer of onion. "My secret trick," he said. "It kind of steams until I smash it for the sear."

"That's brilliant," she said. She never would have thought of it. "What a good idea."

He shrugged. "Learned a thing or two in my day."

She smiled at him, genuinely optimistic about his future there for a moment, then turned to Brice and the matter that was still at hand. "If we don't catch him tonight, I'm terrified I'm going to come in tomorrow and find the whole place ransacked. Or, ugh, worse, housing a whole group of rats—"

"Mischief," Louis interjected.

"Okay, creating mischief—"

"No, it's a mischief of rats. Not a group of rats. You know, like a murder of crows? Or a school of fish?"

She paused. "Really? A *mischief* of rats?"

Louis nodded, pleased with himself. An expression she recognized from years ago when he was able to tell Mr. Currey that blood was not blue before it met oxygen, that was just a trick of the light on skin; or when he corrected Mrs. Simon on the exact decimal point effectiveness of birth control, which he knew because he was working at the CVS by the grocery store.

"Sure. You know, like a horde of hamsters, an army of frogs, a rookery of penguins."

She held her hands up. "Okay, let's not get started on the penguins again. What is a single rat called?"

"A rat."

She sighed, and Brice said, with a sly smile, "Come on, even I knew that one."

"Okay, so what are we going to do about our rat?"

Louis shrugged broadly. "I'm really not sure it's not a mischief. They rarely stick around in singles, and you've already named quite a few of them."

"It did sound like you were quite the casting director," Brice said with a laugh. "You'd all but populated a whole Netflix series."

She felt her face grow hot. "To be fair, I'm not sure all the ones I named are different from each other. Maybe they were all Ratt. Maybe he's just gotten really fat as he runs free in the alleyways"—she glanced out the door—"picking up every fried, cheesy, salmonella-saturated bite. He could be out searching for the bubonic plague right now so we can be ground zero for a new outbreak!"

"Technically it's fleas that carry it," Louis began, but Brice shot him a look that shut him up faster than anything Trista had ever been able to think of.

"It's a city," Brice said, taking a slow step toward her. He gave a small shrug. "There are rats. It's inevitable. You can't eradicate them. As long as there's trash—and air—there will be rats." He stopped in front of her and for a moment she thought he was reaching for her arm, but at the last minute he stopped. "You should probably start keeping the door closed, for a start."

"But it's so nice to get fresh air in here!"

"It gets damn hot," Louis agreed.

"Then get a Dutch door so the bottom can stay closed. That will keep out all the rodents." He looked at Louis. "What do you call a group of mice?"

Louis looked at him like he was stupid. "A mischief."

"Of course." He turned back to Trista but Louis continued.

"If you got a pounce of cats that might help." He gave an unmistakably smug smile. And he was right, though the idea was impossible. She couldn't let a pet run free on these streets, and she couldn't build a *pounce* of feral cats that lived outdoors either.

They were interrupted by a shuffling noise out back and the sound of a tin trash can lid clattering to the pavement.

Brice put his finger to his lips and went to look. One glance and he gave them the thumbs-up and grabbed a plastic milk crate and a piece of cheese from the stack Louis had sitting out for burgers.

"That is so cliché," Trista said, but silenced when he shot her a look. The easy smile that followed made her heart trip.

He went outside, and she looked at Louis.

"He's pretty good at this stuff," Louis assured her, for once serious. "My mom is terrified of spiders and when we moved in with him and his dad out in the country, she was constantly finding wolf spiders in unexpected places. I have to admit, I'm not a fan of them myself, so luckily Brice handled them."

She smiled, picturing Mrs. Williams freaking out in a big country house over some spiders. How lucky that she'd met a man and fallen in love and gotten a nice stepbrother for Louis, who, let's face it, needed a comrade who was stuck with him.

Funny, in high school Mrs. Williams had seemed way too old for things like love and romance. Now, of course, Trista realized she had only been in her early forties. Tops. Maybe even younger. Not much older than Trista was now probably. And Trista had never been married, never even been engaged, much less had a child.

Times were sure different now.

She wondered if *Denise* was going to be Brice's first marriage. "So when's the wedding?" she asked Louis.

"Oh gosh, I haven't even thought about that," he said, pushing his brows down thoughtfully. "I don't have a girlfriend."

She pressed her lips together, counted to three, and nodded. "Right. I meant your brother's. Brice's," she clarified quickly, in case somehow it wasn't already clear.

The light came on in Louis's eyes. "Oh, right! I don't think they've set a date yet. Denise keeps trying for the holidays but he's always got a reason not to do it." He lowered his voice conspiratorially. "I'm not sure Brice wants to go through with it."

Details? Yes, please. But it would have been the height of tacky to ask for them. And what if word of her interest got back to Brice? She already thought of Louis as an unreliable narrator, so, with great difficulty, she let his comment slide.

Work continued as usual. Business was steadily creeping up, but *creeping* was the operative word. She still wasn't quite making rent, much less covering salaries and supplies. She'd planned for a bad year to start, just because that was common wisdom, but she'd really hoped her prime location and great enthusiasm would make it all come much faster.

It hadn't.

She also hadn't anticipated a staff shortage. Back in the day, it seemed like everyone was looking for work. It was hard to find someone who *wasn't* desperate enough to wash dishes just to have a little income. Now, though, she'd had an ad for servers and cooks online for weeks with barely any responses and even fewer remotely qualified ones.

That Louis Williams was in her kitchen right now was a testament to that.

Still, if Brice hadn't come, she'd be out there looking for Ratt Damon by herself, and that was *not* a task she relished.

About an hour and a half after he'd gone out into the hot night, Brice returned, this time through the front door. He looked only slightly disheveled, despite having been out in the heat for so long. Trista's immediate thought was that he must not have found the rat, and that Ratt Damon was probably, even now, flattening himself into a pancake and slipping under the closed back door. She didn't know how they managed those maneuvers and she didn't have the stomach to try to look it up on YouTube.

"No luck?" she asked. Then, so she didn't sound ungrateful, she added, "What can I get you to drink? You must need one."

"I think you've misnamed him. *Her* name should be Merlene Ratty."

Trista looked quizzical.

"Female sprinter with more world championships than anyone else," he explained.

She laughed. "You had a bit of time to think of that, huh?"

"I had to google."

"Why not just"—she thought for a second—"Cristiano Rataldo?"

Brice put his hand to his forehead. "Seems obvious now. You just have a gift for this."

"My parents are very proud." She pulled him a pint of the last beer he'd liked. She handed it across the bar to him, and he drank it gratefully.

"I chased that rodent almost all the way to the cathedral," he said.

"That's probably why he kept running," Louis offered.

Brice shot him a look. "And he was really nimble. Left, right, left, right, left, left." He shook his head. "He was a low, gray blur. People must have thought I was nuts."

Trista had to agree, people didn't usually do their evening jog in an Italian suit. "I really appreciate your trying," she said. "Maybe he's at least relocated to a new neighborhood."

"Sorry to say, rodents can easily find their way back two or three miles to a place where they know they will reliably find food." Louis shook his head. "We should probably get a pellet gun."

Trista shuddered. "We're not *shooting vermin* outside the kitchen," she said, and shook her head. Then she looked back at him. "Absolutely not."

"While I appreciate everyone's faith in me," Brice said, "the rat *is* gone for good."

"You killed it?" they both asked, Louis with a hopeful inflection and Trista with a sad one.

"No, I threw the crate over him when he stopped for pizza, then begged a box off the pizza place where it probably came from. So basically I trapped him, came back for my car, and took him for a pretty harrowing ten-minute drive through the back streets to Key Bridge. He's safely in Virginia now."

"Good work," Louis said approvingly, nodding like a bobblehead. "Very good."

"I happened to know about the distance thing"—he shot Louis a look—"for some reason."

"Oh, *thank* you!" Romantic gestures had been made for her before. Sometimes even gallant ones. But no one had ever given her the thrill that removing an exceptionally well-nourished rat gave her.

He tipped an imaginary hat and downed the last of his beer. "And now I have to go," he said. "I was supposed to meet Denise half an hour ago and she hasn't answered my texts. I'll probably have hell to pay for this, but"—he laughed—"no one can take away my pride."

It was hard to imagine being so petty that she wouldn't answer a text saying someone was going to be a little late, but Trista conjured the brightest smile she could. "I really, *really* appreciate your help. Honestly, I don't know what we would have done without you."

For once, Louis wasn't popping up with how he could and would have done something. No one wanted to wrestle a forty-pound rodent.

Her gaze lingered on Brice for a moment, and his on her, before he said, "All in a day's work."

"Where *do* you work, anyway?" Trista asked. She retrieved

his jacket and handed it over to him. "This isn't Humane Society garb, as far as I know."

"He's a lawyer," Louis said.

Brice glanced at him, and then looked slightly . . . embarrassed? "That's right."

"Cromwell and Covington," Louis added, pride shining through in his voice. "One of the best on the East Coast. He just started but he's going to be a partner, you mark my words."

"Thanks, Louis." Brice pulled his keys out of his jacket pocket. "Have a good night, guys. It was fun." He smiled at Trista. "Let me know if you have any more trouble. I'm trying to build my résumé in case the new job doesn't work out."

Her face felt frozen. "Thanks again." She gave a half wave and he was gone.

As soon as he was out the door, she slumped down onto a barstool and sighed.

"Something wrong, Tris?" Louis asked.

"No, no." She waved him off to the kitchen. "Just relieved."

Susannah approached them. "Bud, you better get cooking, this is my third ticket." She handed him an order.

"Aye-aye."

Trista watched them both part ways before whispering, "Oh my God," under her breath.

Brice had taken over her job at Cromwell and Covington.

Brice was the reason she was fired.

CHAPTER TWELVE

MAX

Nothing about living in the country was a *surprise* per se. Country life had not lied about itself: the farm was as quiet and verdant as he'd imagined, the air smelled of earth and greens, and the night sky was far more dark and star filled than it would appear just a few dozen miles away in the city. In a lot of ways, it had been a fantastic few weeks.

Maybe it was Max who had been falsely advertised—to himself. Because he'd pictured himself meditating in the stillness as dusk fell over the fields and filled the rooms inside the house, gaining in sound—crickets, frogs, the bark of a distant dog—what it lost in scenery. This, he'd thought, was a place where he'd put the electronics away and just soak in the peace. It would be a medicine like nothing you could ever find in a pill or potion. It was the antithesis of all the noise and negativity that filled him, day in and day out, in a crowded metropolis where no one had any patience for anyone else, and where public figures were targets for vitriol from strangers who were just looking for something to complain about.

He had been sure that being alone on a farm in the country would be the cure for all that ailed him.

He hadn't planned on being so bored.

He'd been sitting in the musky kitchen on a wooden barstool, nursing a double Casamigos for what seemed like ages. And twilight had come exactly as expected. So had the accompanying quiet. Realistically, it had been quiet all day except for the damn rooster he couldn't locate or block out. Who knew that roosters crowed all day long without regard to the sunrise? *Charlotte's Web* and *Babe* had clearly indicated that there would be one or two cheerful cock-a-doodle-doos at sunrise and that was all until tomorrow.

He hadn't anticipated that the strangled avian screeches would repeat ad nauseam, often sounding like a guttural cat in heat, driving him through all the stages of grief right to his form of acceptance, which was that it was better than the utter silence that surrounded it.

He looked at his phone, having removed it from its sequester within two hours of putting it away, and saw that it was 9:17 P.M. He had felt sure it was closer to midnight. In fact, he'd been sitting there, waiting for the sweet relief of exhaustion to take over after an entire day of fresh air and hard physical work, scrubbing the sinks with Ajax until his hands were red and pruned, and moving the dusty, creaky furniture around to make at least one room feel comfortable and homey.

It wasn't easy.

But he wasn't giving up, he knew that. So he'd gotten his phone out for the singular task of ordering a bed—some things could be cleaned and some things had to be started fresh—and then he'd allowed himself a quick foray into the news head-lines, and the next thing he knew he had familiarized himself with every article on Huffington Post during the last week, and fact-checked each and cross-referenced until he felt sure he knew as much of the depressing truth as he could.

As he went to put the phone back, it slipped out of his hand just as it started to ring. He inadvertently tapped the "answer" button as it fell to the floor. It was Margo. "Hang on," he called. He reached for the phone, gave an embarrassing shriek when he touched something furry (which turned out to be dust on the floor), and finally put it on speaker. "Hey, Margo, what's up?"

"Did you just scream?" She wasn't making fun of him, she sounded concerned.

"No, no." He cleared his throat. "I dropped the phone. And then the chair scraped the floor." Hopefully one of those things would seem capable of making a sound like that.

"O . . . kay." She didn't sound convinced. "Well, I hope I'm not bothering you but I'm wondering how it's going there. It's only occurring to me now that you might not be awake. Sorry if I—"

"Oh, no, I'm up. Up, up, up. Wide awake."

"I was just thinking that it must be really gloomy there at night. Do you need some floor lamps to brighten it up?"

He looked at the single lamp he had turned on—a floor lamp with the kind of shade a tedious party guest might don as a hat—and it was as dim as an evening set on *The Waltons,* but it was on. And it was soothing, in a way. Almost like candlelight.

"I have a light on," he told her. "It probably wouldn't be a bad idea to go around and see how many bulbs to pick up, though." The idea of having something constructive to do for maybe ten minutes or so gave him a lift. "Do you know if anyone delivers pizza out here?"

She drew a breath in through her teeth. "I don't know but I kind of doubt it. Postmates would be hard-pressed to find a way around those dark, winding roads at night. Can you imagine being the person charged with delivering to a stranger in the woods? There's no chance they pay them enough."

"Yes." He laughed. "I can imagine it all too well. That is both the curse and the blessing of being me."

She laughed outright. "Look," she said, "I know you're here for the solitude and all, but I just made way too many biscuits and too much sausage gravy from *Magnolia Table*—it's the source for my cookbook club meeting tomorrow. Do you want me to bring some over?"

He had literally never had a better offer in his life. "I'd love that," he said. "I'm just starving." Like a fool, he hadn't figured out where the nearest grocery store was before he got there.

"It's a deal! It's not much but it's fresh."

"It sounds perfect," he said, and meant it. At that moment, the single lamp began to flicker, then popped off, leaving him alone in the dark, with only the glow of his phone. He hadn't brought extra bulbs, and he had no idea if there were any in the house already. "Oh, and, Margo? One more thing."

"Yeah?"

"Maybe you could bring a lightbulb or two?"

Of course she forgot the lightbulbs from her house, of which she had too many. Fortunately, she remembered in time to stop at CVS and pick up a four-pack, but she was so excited to have something *different* to do that she'd left as soon as she and Max hung up. She did, however, grab a bag of various cleaning solvents and tools from underneath her sink, since the thought of the filth at the farm had been plaguing her all day, even while she didn't want to bother him with offers of help.

Now that he'd asked her over, though, she was glad to give it some muscle.

It was a balmy clear night, and as she drove through the country roads with her windows down, the smell of cut grass was just intoxicating. For months she'd been in bed by this hour—not asleep, that didn't come until about 4:00 A.M., but in bed because there was nothing else to do—and she almost couldn't believe that Max was at the farm.

She really hoped he wasn't put off by the state of disrepair.

The farm, when she pulled up next to the house, was no different. The entire house was dark, except for the slight glow of a light in the kitchen window.

She gave the horn a tap, in case he hadn't seen her pull up, and got out of the car. She collected the food and the bag with the lightbulbs and went to the side door. She gave a knock and walked in.

"Hello?"

"Hello!" She heard creaking floorboards and then Max came into the kitchen, his smile wide and bright in the very dim light.

"Is this it for light?" she asked, gesturing at the desk lamp that was now on the counter by the sink.

He laughed. "Even that one didn't work until I gave it a jiggle. I can't believe it didn't even occur to me to pick up lightbulbs when I was getting cleaning supplies. I really have gotten to be a spoiled city boy. Serves me right."

"I didn't think of it either," she said. "We get used to flipping a switch and witnessing a miracle. Then when the power goes out, we flip the switch a hundred more times, as if something has suddenly changed without our knowing it."

"Exactly." He nodded.

"Well." She set the casserole dish down. It was still warm. Which was a good thing, because she didn't know what the state of the oven was but she had a pretty good idea it was repulsive. Even the smell of the place put her off her appetite, though she didn't want to say anything and show what a picky baby she was. Something about the combination of mold, mildew, and linen-scented cleaner was particularly noxious. "I brought some disposable plates and utensils, since I didn't know what your situation was."

"Oh, it's fine, there are some dishes in the cabinet. And look"—he came over and opened a drawer—"knives, forks, and spoons." And some sort of fuzzball that she hoped had never been alive.

"I—" Her face must have shown her abject horror because he simply laughed.

"It's disgusting." He nodded. "I know. I was joking. I also picked up some paper plates and bamboo cutlery when I was out earlier. I also got a bunch of microwavable stuff but . . . no microwave. Which is probably a good thing, now that I think about it."

"And the oven?" she asked.

"About what you'd think. Well loved, shall we say. There's so much grease you could melt it and power a diesel engine for a thousand miles." He tapped the range. "It's a really nice piece though, did you notice? Viking. Really solid."

She looked now. Six burners and that familiar Viking logo. How on earth had she never noticed that before? It was exactly the sort of thing she cared about. She looked at the fridge and saw the same logo. "I had no idea this stuff was here! It's got to be, what, from the nineties? Eighties?"

"Maybe the nineties," he said. "Maybe newer. I got a better look earlier and there's no structural damage, it's just . . . dirty. I plugged in the fridge and it works—didn't even blow the fuse. How long ago did someone live here?"

Margo thought about it. "Calvin's grandparents died shortly before we got married so"—she shrugged—"at least eleven years or so."

"I'm putting Easy-Off and steel wool on my list for tomorrow. Twice."

"Actually, I brought cleaners," she said, and crinkled her nose in embarrassment. "I don't want to butt in but, gah, the idea of trying to eat or sleep in this place in this condition . . ."

"Oh, I got the bedroom and bathroom in good shape," he said. "I haven't just been sitting on my ass." He laughed. "I just have my priorities, so I've been going out to eat. But not today. I'm starving. Let's dig in!"

"You go right ahead," she said, not wanting to reveal her squeamishness. "I ate not long before I called. I'm going to go out to the car and get the cleaning stuff. I'd love to tackle this range and see what's under it. If you don't mind?"

He was already digging into the casserole dish directly with a plastic spoon. "God, this is good. This is really, really good. I didn't realize I was so hungry. Or that you were such a good cook."

She laughed. "I suspect your hunger is making me seem like a better cook than I am."

He took a huge forkful and shook his head. "I'm not going to turn down help," he said, covering his full mouth with a napkin. "This is *so* good."

"You know," she said, "I think I'll start with the fridge, so if there's anything left we can put it away." But the way he was going at it, there would be little, if anything, left. It was very flattering. Calvin had never relished anything she cooked and he'd certainly never eaten so much as a bite without getting a full nutritional breakdown first.

She took out a roll of paper towels and a spray cleaner with bleach and went to the fridge. She opened it carefully. To her surprise, it wasn't too bad. It was *bad* but not as bad as she'd anticipated. She was braced for live animals at this point. "Huh."

"Yeah," he agreed, mouth full. "I took some Windex to it earlier because that's all I could find, but it's not bad."

"None of the bulbs are even out." She sprayed some cleaner in and started to wipe it down.

"What about the garbage disposal?" She peered over into the sink. "Looks like there's one of those." She looked for a switch.

"There is, but don't flip—"

Too late. She'd flipped the switch and got a shock. She cussed and drew her hand back fast.

"—the switch," he finished. "I figured that one out earlier myself." He laughed. "I can't believe you never even tried to clean this place up . . ."

"Me neither! When I found out about the farm, my first idea was to use it for a massive herb and vegetable garden. Turned out I don't know much about that stuff, so I gave up, but the house seemed like an overwhelming amount of work, and since I was married at the time, I thought we'd just hire contractors when we got around to it."

"And I'm your contractor now," he finished. "For whatever it's worth."

"The world would have a hard time believing that, huh?"

He shot a finger gun at her. "I don't know that the world thinks I can do anything practical at all. I have no idea."

"Even I was a little surprised," Margo confessed. Then she realized she hadn't yet seen if he could. No point in adding that, though.

"You'll see." He smiled. "I wasn't born on a stage in shiny shoes and a top hat."

"You wear a top hat in your show?"

"You haven't even *seen* it. What kind of friend . . ."

She covered her face with her hands. "I'm sorry! I'm a terrible friend! But, to be fair, you know it's impossible to get tickets. Or it *was* when you were in it. People would post their *Ironsides* tickets online like they'd gotten one of Willy Wonka's golden tickets. In fact, a place in Frederick is actually *selling* one of the golden tickets from the movie for three hundred dollars so it's *easier* to get."

"Really?"

"Oh my God, are you kidding? You know that! People have been trying for years to get to your show!"

"I mean about the golden ticket. Is there really one for sale around here?"

"Oh. Yeah. But it was signed in Sharpie by the guy who played Mike Teavee." She shrugged.

"Ah."

"No one's favorite." She turned back to the refrigerator and sprayed the second shelf area. "Now, if it was Violet Beauregarde, we might have something." She wiped. "*I want an Oompa Loompa now, Daddy!*"

"Was she the one who turned into a blueberry?"

"Yup."

"What about the German kid? What was his name?"

"Augustus Gloop." She gave a laugh. "I'm kind of an expert on Willy Wonka. I had a crush on Gene Wilder when I was little and watched it so many times the VHS tape ripped. Don't judge me."

"Huh. Wish I'd written it."

"You're doing okay." She wadded the paper towels she'd just used and tossed them. She moved to the next level, sprayed and wiped. "If there's one thing we learned from the Wonka Chocolate Factory tour, it's don't get too greedy."

"Salient point." He milled through the cleaning solutions on the counter. "Which one of these is best for the oven?"

She paused. "Is it self-cleaning?"

"I don't know."

"Look at it. Does it have a self-clean cycle?"

He went and frowned in front of the collection of dials on the front of the range. "There's a warming drawer."

"Nice."

"I never knew what that was for."

"Warming food." She laughed. "Well, *keeping* it warm. Honestly, I haven't used mine since the great hockey puck roll saga of Thanksgiving 2018. It was a little too warm. Dried them out completely." She shook her head, remembering.

"I prefer mashed potatoes, for what it's worth."

"Me too! But it was still a pretty major failure. Now I just keep my broiling dish in the warmer, like the rest of the world." She pulled the crisper drawers out and took them to soak in the sink, then returned to finish the back and walls.

"Self-clean!" Max clapped his hands. "Should we give it a go?"

"Absolutely. Set it and lock it with that handle and push 'start.'"

"That's it?"

She nodded. "It doesn't clean it like magical elves or anything, but it will burn off anything gross and make it easier to scrape and clean." She stepped back and looked at the inside of the fridge. It gleamed like new. "This is really satisfying, I have to say."

He came up behind her, his proximity making her shoulder blades tingle. She actually shivered and, embarrassed, said, "Man, it is hot in here."

He didn't move away. "It's not so bad."

"Glad you think that, because there's no central air."

"When I get the ceiling fans cleaned up, they'll do fine. I turned that one on earlier"—he pointed to the far end of the kitchen, where the table should go—"and a plume of dust kicked up off of it."

"Nice. Who needs Parmesan cheese when you have the dust of ages?"

He made a face. "I probably should have left it running and vacuumed."

"Let's do it." Margo took the casserole and put it in the now-clean fridge and closed the door while Max went to the switch for the fan.

Sure enough, a cloud of dust shook down underneath it.

In fact, the whole place suddenly seemed dusty. There was a mist filling the entire room.

"What's burning?" Max asked, alarmed.

"Oh no." She looked at the oven. Smoke was rising from the back and there was no vent overhead to clear it. "All that crud is burning off in there."

"Is it okay?"

"Yeah, but maybe not the best place for us to hang out. Good thing it's nice out. Want to go breathe?"

He laughed outright. "Stellar idea. I even have some warm beer on the porch."

"You went out and got beer but not food?"

He shrugged. "Priorities."

They opened all the windows and propped the door open. As they stepped onto the creaky porch, Max reached down and grabbed a six-pack of Flying Dog Numero Uno. It was one of her favorites, a Mexican-style lager, but with a little kick and lime zest.

He brought beer. He wasn't a complainer. He was hot. He had become the damn-near perfect man.

"I'll grab the chairs." She picked up the two light plastic chairs that had been there forever, and hoped they wouldn't break when challenged with weight.

Then she hoped if one broke it wasn't hers.

They walked far enough into the yard that they could no longer smell the burning oven and propped the chairs up. A field spread out in front of them, with the large empty barn to the left, and a hill in the distance on the right, dotted with the silhouettes of horses quietly grazing in the night.

A creek ran the perimeter of the property, and the frogs were as loud as if they were three feet away. Crickets too, though they probably were. The moon was almost full, suspended in the sky like a distant balloon, slowly moving across, under stars and through tree branches, never speeding and never stopping on its course.

"You seem to have it all," Margo said after they'd been there awhile, talking and dipping into silence, then talking again. The warm beer was lubricating her nerve. "Do you regret that?"

"No," Max said quickly. "Not regret. Never regret. I've been poor. I don't ever want to be poor again. The feeling of not being able to buy so much as ramen noodles at the grocery store is . . . unforgettable. No, I never want to go back to that. But I wish I'd set myself up for a private life more realistically."

"How?"

He considered, tipping his face up toward the sky. She watched his profile in silence, thinking of the boy she'd known and the hugely successful—frankly iconic—man he'd become. "I guess all it would have taken was to grab a piece of land like this under another name. It's easily done. Not the loan, of course, but the title." He chuckled. "But who the hell has that kind of confidence when they're just starting out? For a long time, I was glad to be able to buy a block of good cheese without checking the price, but I sure didn't have the money or confidence to buy anything substantial. Honestly, Margo, I wasn't even trying to be famous."

She looked at him for a moment and said, "God, then you're a real failure."

He gave a laugh and looked back at the moon. "In a way, yes, I am. And I feel like an ungrateful jerk for not enjoying the success more fully, but it's just that . . ." He paused for a long time. "It always felt like a mistake. Like it was someone else's success and it was being piled on me. I mean, hell, this was just an idea I came up with while I was working and bored. It never occurred to me that I, of all people, could come up with something that resonated with others. It just . . . happened."

"Luckily."

"Oh yes, very luckily," he said quickly. "Which is why I feel like such a jerk for not just lapping it up and enjoying the notoriety." He looked in her direction. "Sometimes I feel like I can't breathe. Like I can't get away. In fact, I honestly thought I couldn't until now." He leaned back and sighed heavily. "Not one siren. Not one horn. It's been so long since I experienced this kind of quiet that I don't even know if it's real."

Margo nodded and returned her gaze to the sky. "It's real. I've never needed it in the way you do, but I spent a lot of lonely nights with the blinds open, looking out at the stars as I fell asleep, hoping that every old love song about fate was right."

"'Stardust.'"

"Yes. And 'Deep Purple.' I don't know what, exactly, 'sleepy garden walls' are, but I know I want that garden."

"'And the stars begin to flicker in the sky,'" he said. "My grandfather used to play that on the piano."

"I had a CD of World War Two songs and it was on there."

Max nodded and reached out his hand. Margo looked, uncertainly, for a moment, then put her hand in his.

He squeezed, and they spent the rest of the evening in silence, while the moon crossed the sky, making way for the sun.

CHAPTER THIRTEEN

AJA

For a moment, she thought it was the heat getting to her. Aja had moved ten bags of topsoil from her car to the garden in heat so muggy it felt like she was slapped in the face with a hot wet washcloth when she got out of her car's air-conditioning. She was trying to stay hydrated and thought she was doing fine until she found the ring.

It was buried in the dirt right next to the small stone wall that partitioned off a section of flowers from the vegetable garden.

The area had been in shadows until that moment, when the sun had moved just enough to touch the stone with its light. The sparkle caught Aja's eye and she dug carefully, worried that there was broken glass in the soil.

But it wasn't broken glass, it was a gold ring with what appeared to be a large emerald-cut diamond flanked by smaller diamonds and, now, dirt. She pulled off her gloves and tried to examine the ring more carefully, pouring her bottled water over it until the dirt loosened and ran onto the ground.

It was still dirty, of course, and Aja was no jeweler, but it sure looked like the real thing. And it had the heft that rhinestone baubles just never had. A certain, telling weight in her hand.

She sat there for a moment, completely unsure of what to do. If this was some old piece of junk that she was mistaking for precious gems and she took it in to Lucinda like she'd found pirate's gold, she was going to look like an idiot. And, really, how could it be anything else? Michael had grown up here, which means it had been Lucinda's property for a long time. Why would she have real jewelry buried in the garden?

She was still contemplating her next move when she sensed someone watching her and looked up to see a child dodge behind a tree about five yards away.

"Hello!" she called, but the child remained hidden.

Again, she questioned whether the heat was making her imagine things. Why would a kid be roaming this property? She stood up, tucked the ring into her pocket, and headed for the tree.

When she got to it, she was half sure she was going to look and there would be no one there, but, sure enough, a narrow, tanned girl with a wild tangle of dark hair and bright blue eyes looked up at her. She appeared to be about ten or eleven, though Aja wasn't very good at the age-guessing game with kids.

"Hi," she said to the girl. "Who are you?"

The girl straightened her back and crossed her arms in front of her. "I'm allowed to be here."

Aja laughed. "Good. Me too. But that doesn't answer my question. Who are you?"

"I don't have to tell you that."

"No, you don't," Aja agreed, and put her hand out. "My name is Aja."

The girl ignored her outstretched hand. "Like the country?"

"It's a continent, but no. It's *A-J-A*. It just sounds the same."

"That's a weird name."

"I suppose you have a better one?"

"Yes, I do."

"What is it?"

She lifted her sharp little chin. "I don't have to tell you anything. You're just a worker."

Aja swallowed a laugh. "I can think of much worse things to be called than that."

"*I* can't. It means you're just a hired hand and you don't really belong here."

"Oh, wow. Do you?"

The girl pressed her lips into a hard, thin line. "Well, *I* don't think so but *they* do, so they make me come here."

"Who are *they*?" Aja wondered if this was a runaway or if she should be alerting the authorities.

"My parents. They leave me here because they think it's good for me or something, but it's just stupid. I hate it here."

That didn't answer any of the more pressing questions Aja had. "Where are your parents now?"

The girl shrugged, her bony shoulders rising up then flopping down in pretty classic nonchalance.

"Are you lost?"

"No!" Indignation colored the girl's cheeks. "I'm not *stupid*. It's kind of hard to get *lost* here."

"Well, you just said you don't know where your parents are," Aja pointed out, trying not to insult her by showing her humor. "That sounds like you're lost."

"I *meant* they're at *work* or something."

"Ah, I see."

"And it's none of your business anyway."

"True."

"What are you even doing here?"

"Working, as you pointed out."

The girl rolled her eyes outright. "On what? Why are you *digging*?"

"I'm making a garden for the lady who lives here."

She looked over the yard. "There are already like a million gardens here."

"I'm making a garden filled with things you can eat."

"Eat?"

Aja nodded.

"I don't eat stuff from the dirt."

"Of course you do! Where do you think"—she was going

to say *carrots* and changed her mind—"french fries come from? You do like french fries, don't you?" What kid didn't?

The girl nodded reluctantly. "But they don't come from the dirt."

"The potatoes do."

"They come from the store."

Maybe this kid was younger than Aja had initially thought. "That's true," she said, "but before that they are grown in the ground. And then the farmers pull them up, package them, and sell them to the store. Or the restaurant."

"Whatever."

She could have—and probably should have—told the kid to scram and gotten back to work, but she'd always had a soft spot for snarky preteens, given that she was so able to remember the hell of being that age herself. It made her want to dig in a little, maybe see where the girl was coming from and give her some much-needed understanding.

"Do you like to dig?"

The girl's eyes darted away. "Why?"

"I thought you might want to help make the garden." She'd finished with the larger plants and was now working on a border of herbs along the stone wall.

Apparently it was exactly the wrong thing to say, because she squared her shoulders and said, "I don't have to help you do your work. You're just being lazy. I'm going now." And with that, she turned and walked away, across the wide-open lawn toward the overgrown and now-obsolete bridle trails that ran behind the property.

Aja watched her go, wondering where she'd come from, which house had a nanny or sitter who was supposed to be watching her but wasn't. It wasn't worrisome, it was a very secure area, but it seemed clear that the child was lonely and maybe shouldn't have been quite so alone.

She went back to work, methodically pulling the dirt from the plastic bags and smoothing it over the plots she'd laid out, but she couldn't get her mind fully off the interaction. Something about it was really sticking with her, and she couldn't figure out why.

It was probably her hormones free-falling with pregnancy that made her feel so sad and so driven to help the child, when the fact was she didn't know anything about her. For all she knew, the girl had gone back to a wonderful home filled with brothers and sisters and was playing a rousing game of Monopoly right now, sneaking extra cash out of the bank and putting it under her side of the board the way Aja could remember doing years back.

She worked for a while in silent thought and it wasn't until she stood up to stretch her legs that the ring in her pocket dug into her abdomen and reminded her it was there.

She took it out and examined it again. It sure looked real to her. Whether she'd look foolish or not, she had to take it in to Lucinda and let her decide what to do with it.

She stopped at the hose bib at the back of the house and rinsed herself and then the ring again, before going in the door to the kitchen. Under the overhead light, the stone looked even more brilliant, despite the bits of dirt and grime that mere rinsing hadn't been able to remove.

"Hello?" she called. "Mrs. Carter?"

No answer.

She crossed through the large room where she and Michael had sat with her and went to the bottom of the staircase. "Mrs. Carter?" she called again. Then, a little louder, "Mrs. Carter!"

Finally there was an answer and the sound of heeled shoes walking on the hardwood floor overhead. Lucinda Carter appeared at the top of the stairs, silhouetted by the sunlight that poured into the hall behind her. "You don't need to scream, I'm here."

Aja took a moment to remind herself this wasn't about her, this was the way Lucinda probably was with everyone she regarded as "beneath her." Which, yeah, would be easy to take umbrage at, but it would be wrong nonetheless.

"I'm sorry to bother you, but while I was working I found something I think you should see."

Lucinda started down the steps. "Dear lord, please tell me it's not another bone."

"What? No. It's— No, it's a ring."

"A ring?"

"Yes, and it looks to me like it might be real." She braced herself for a sarcastic rejoinder about an imaginary ring, but fortunately that didn't come.

"Buried treasure, you say." Lucinda had her glasses on a chain around her neck and she raised them to her eyes. "That's a first. Let's see what you have."

Aja produced the ring, and the woman took it as gingerly as if Aja were handing her a tarantula.

"Hmm." She crinkled her nose and turned the bauble over in her hand. "This looks like . . ." She closed her fingers over it and looked up the stairs behind her. "But that's impossible."

It seemed rude to question her, so Aja waited in silence to be addressed or, preferably, excused.

"This is my mother's engagement ring," Lucinda said, leveling a steely gaze on Aja. Her eyes had darkened from the vivid blue she'd passed on to her son to a battleship gray. "How did you get it?"

It was only then that Aja realized she really hadn't offered much detail about where she'd found it, so it was reasonable for Lucinda to be concerned. "I was digging by the stone wall, just using the trowel, so it had to be within, I'd say, five or six inches of the surface, and it came up with a scoop of dirt."

"You're saying this was underground in the *garden*?"

"Weird, right?" She was getting the distinct feeling that this was weirder than she knew.

The woman's frown showed just how deeply her age was etched into her features. "Was there anything else?"

"I . . ." Why hadn't she looked? "I don't think so. I got distracted and then moved on to putting the sage into the ground because it was starting to look unhappy, so I didn't specifically look." She knew she wasn't guilty of anything and yet her words sounded like a feeble explanation even to her own ears.

"Mm-hmm."

Anything further she could say would sound like a scramble for exoneration. And it did. "Honestly, I lost track and it didn't occur to me to investigate further. See, I thought it *had* to be a fake."

"You thought my mother's heirloom Tiffany diamond was . . . a fake." She sniffed. "Interesting."

"To be fair, I found it in the dirt. It was hard to imagine it could be real, though the more I looked at it, the more I thought it was. Which is why I brought it in to you."

"Was it an attack of conscience, girl?"

Aja was taken aback. "Conscience?" It wasn't like she'd planned on keeping it. Fencing it, or whatever that process was called. She wouldn't even know where to begin with something like that.

"I know that without a husband or any obvious support, you might be feeling desperate, but—"

"Wait, are you saying you think I *stole* this from you?"

"I'm saying it's from my dressing room and you've just brought it in covered in dirt. This is well over the standards of grand larceny."

"Grand *larceny*?" She felt ill. She should have known after the other day that working anywhere near Michael's domain would be bad luck for her. "Let me get this straight, are you saying you think I snuck into your house and somehow ferreted out wherever you keep your valuables and somehow bypassed what *must* be some sort of security, and took this so I could rub it in the dirt and bring it back *pretending to have found it*?"

"I'm not saying that makes good sense." Lucinda raised an eyebrow. "Yet you might have guessed there would be a reward in it for you."

Aja couldn't help it, she laughed. "With all due respect, if I went that far with that plan, it's reasonable to guess that there *could* have been a lot more in it for me than a *reward*. Particularly one that, I have to say, seems unlikely to have been forthcoming."

It didn't seem possible, but was Lucinda stifling a smile? She gave a single nod. "It does seem crazy."

"I'll say! If I were, I'd probably be smart enough to come up with a hustle where I didn't actually work so hard? Like, I wouldn't be toiling away in a garden in this heat while struggling through the exhaustion of pregnancy—" She stopped. What had she done? How could she have said that? How foolish could she be?

Lucinda was the last person in the world she wanted to know about this. Or, rather, the second-to-last person.

"Exhaustion," Aja corrected, too loud. "And the heat." She tried to think of something that rhymed with *pregnancy* to pretend that was what she'd said but came up short.

Now Lucinda did smile. It was small and tight but a smile nevertheless. "You're a real spitfire."

Aja didn't know what to say to that. She couldn't lurch from insults to compliments—if that *was* a compliment—so fast. "Say what you will, but I'm not a thief."

"Perhaps not."

"Definitely not." The former gardener, Luga, came to mind, but she had no idea who had done this and she didn't want to cast blame on anyone who might be innocent. "So I guess you, and perhaps the police, will have to figure out this mystery. That's not my job."

"Correct," the older woman mused, pressing her lips together and frowning, as if in thought.

Aja gathered her nerve. "Now, if you'll excuse me, I want to finish working before the sun goes down. That is . . . if I still *have* a job?"

Lucinda looked at her as if she'd just been roused from a deep sleep. "Hmm? Oh. Yes, yes, you're not— Yes, you can go finish what you were doing."

Aja took a short breath and started out of the hallway as quickly as she could, but when she heard the footsteps coming

behind her, she knew it hadn't been fast enough and she definitely hadn't covered her slip of the tongue. Wealthy people
worried about being sued all the time, probably because they
were sued all the time. Though there were laws to protect pregnant women from discrimination, there were a million ways to
get around them.

"I'll do some careful digging to see if there's anything else
out there," Aja said, hoping to keep the woman's mind on
the near loss of her gem and not on firing her so she wouldn't
have any perceived potential liability for having a pregnant
woman doing physical labor for her.

"Aja."

Aja stopped. She could have kept going, but this was going to catch up with her no matter what. She didn't have the
luxury of magical thinking to get her out of this. She was going to lose the best-paying job she'd ever had, right when she
needed the money the most.

"Aja," Lucinda said again, this time softening her voice.
"Please."

Aja turned to her and decided to go fast and hard with her
lie. "Okay, yes, I probably should have told you that before you
hired me, but legally you can't discriminate against a pregnant
woman, *especially* since I'll finish the job well before I'm even
halfway along. My doctor says I can do everything I've always
done physically as long as I'm mindful of any unusual symptoms."

Lucinda looked at her quietly and when just a single uncomfortable moment passed without anyone speaking, Aja filled it.

"I'll sign a waiver, indemnifying you or whatever the word is. I'm sure Michael could write it up for you. Except"—now she'd really stepped in it—"I'd rather he didn't know my private business. Particularly after the way things ended between us."

"I see." Lucinda nodded.

"It's just . . . delicate."

"Indeed."

"It's not his," she blurted. "It's— I'm seeing someone else."

Lucinda inhaled through her nose, making it even more narrow and pinched for a moment, which gave the impression of a sharp-eyed eagle, about to swoop down and grab her with sharp talons. "Aja."

"Yes?" It took all she had to resist adding *ma'am*.

"I am not a fool."

That makes exactly one of us. "All right."

"I'm also not cruel."

Aja straightened her back and gave a nod. "That's good to hear."

"I'm not going to deprive an expectant mother of an income I have agreed to provide. I appreciate how important that can be to your personal calculations."

"Thank you." Aja waited a moment, then gestured toward the door. "May I . . . ?"

"Of course."

She started to leave but she heard Lucinda behind her.

"There's just one thing."

Aja stopped and turned around. "Yes?"

"I will not allow my grandchild to be raised without family. Not under any circumstances. If that child is a Carter, he will be treated as such."

"It's not," Aja lied firmly. She bunched her fists by her sides, trying to pull some convincing force into her words. "Like I said."

"I see."

"Good. Now if you'll excuse me." She didn't wait for permission, she just left.

But she could tell Lucinda didn't believe her.

MEETING 4–SEPTEMBER
Delish

REUBEN EGG ROLLS–Nothing short of genius.
   Can make with beets instead of pastrami.
CHICKEN FRIED CAULIFLOWER–Vegetarian option, fried
   so everyone will love.
HAMBURGER SOUP–Du jour/1 week/month.

Margo is distinctly lighter than air–something is up.
I'd think she was in love but how? And who?

Aja, on the other hand, is tired all the time. Pregnancy seems exhausting.

October

CHAPTER FOURTEEN

MARGO

H i, guys, so . . . okay, today we're going to make braised garlic pasta. I know some of you have dietary restrictions as far as gluten or carbs go, but I trust you have already figured out what your pasta needs are. This one's about the sauce primarily—you can put it on anything. Even spaghetti squash, which is pretty diet-friendly, no matter what the diet." Margo smiled at the camera. "And, Mom, I know you're going to want real spaghetti, so, since you make the sauce by itself, go ahead and make that for yourself but give Dad the lentil pasta. You're going to make up for it in garlic, believe me. This one has a *ton* of flavor, especially if you layer the garlic by putting it in in thirds, at the beginning, the middle, and the end."

There was a knock at the back door. She glanced over and was surprised to see Max standing there. He gave a small wave, and, flustered, she hurried over and unbolted the door. "Come in! I'm surprised to see you here!" She hoped that didn't sound rude. "Delighted too, though. Really." Now she sounded desperate. "Just surprised. Can I get you something? A drink?"

He ambled in, looking as relaxed as she felt nervous. "Sure. Got a beer?"

"Absolutely." She reflexively checked the clock—4:45 P.M. Calvin would never have approved of this for her, despite the fact that his blood alcohol level would likely have been elevated from lunch. She took two cold Coronas out of the fridge—Calvin also didn't like "overpriced piss," no matter how craft—and asked, "Lime?"

A quick shake of the head. "Nah, give it to me straight, baby."

She laughed and popped the top off one and handed it to him, careful not to lose her grip on the glass as the condensation made it slick.

To get a slice of lime for herself would seem fussy at this point, so she opened hers and went over to join him next to where he was leaning on the counter.

"Given up on the farm finally?" she asked, only half-joking. She wouldn't blame him if he had.

"Not at all! Which you'd know if you'd been by in the last couple of weeks."

"I didn't want to bother you."

"That's ridiculous."

"Well, I've also been taking a refresher real estate course. Not interesting, but important. I'm looking for a brokerage to join without a huge commitment. It's not that easy."

"Everyone wants commitment. That way *they* can decide if they want to keep you, not the other way around."

"That's definitely the impression I'm getting." She didn't elaborate on how much she hated it. She'd gotten so used to having her own schedule over the past few years that she'd forgotten what it was like to get a real job and work within someone else's time frame.

When she thought about it, she had to wonder if that was part of why she'd stayed in an unsatisfying marriage for so long. It wasn't *bad* and it allowed her to do her own thing on her own time. Maybe she hadn't realized just how important that was to her.

"So what brings you out this way?" she asked.

"Actually, I was on my way to a specialty lumber place near Great Falls and I wanted to ask for your input but realized I didn't have my phone."

She frowned. "No Google? No Waze? I'd be lost. How did you find me?"

He produced a piece of paper from his pocket. "Wrote down your info from your text when I hit the road outta New York. It was still in the car." He slipped the sheet back into his pocket. "I don't trust technology that much."

"Good thing."

"Yeah, except I didn't write down the address of the place I'm going."

"So you needed to borrow my technology?"

He flashed a pirate smile. "That *and* your input on up-grades." He glanced at the camera, then did a double take. "Is that on?"

"Oh my gosh, it is." Mortified, she hurried over and grabbed it from the stand. "I'm so sorry, that's probably just the kind of thing you worry about, being filmed without your knowledge. I'll erase it, honest. Right now, you can watch."

He touched her forearm. His fingertips created three spots of heat on her skin. "Whoa, Margo, I was only worried about your battery, since I interrupted you and the camera kept running." He gave her a squeeze then released. "What were you filming?"

"Oh, you know, just a little striptease." She shimmied, then felt stupid. "I make a little extra cash by doing some live streaming."

He furrowed his brow in mock consideration. "Do you need a manager? For twenty percent I'll make you a star."

"Ten."

"Fifteen."

She held out her hand. "Deal."

He took it and they had a moment of looking at each other in silence before she hastily drew back and said, "No, actually I have a little cooking channel on YouTube for the fine folks at Sullivan's Island Shady Palm Retirement Village. In other words, my parents and their friends."

"Cool!" He took a sip of beer and shook his head. "That's

really nice of you. I don't know a lot of people who would bother. Though that might say a lot about the kind of people I know these days."

Margo was sure he knew a lot of very interesting people. Far more interesting than she was. "I'm just trying to keep my dad alive. He's already had one heart attack, and my mom just kept on making him his rib eyes and buttered potatoes, so I had to figure out some dishes that, you know, wouldn't actually kill him."

"So you live-stream?"

"Actually, no." She raised an eyebrow. "I edit and produce *very* professional videos. And by professional I mean that they don't see me sneezing into the salad or tripping over the dog or any of the other things I've had to"—she made a scissors motion with her fingers—"hide. I protect my viewers from the rough stuff."

He laughed outright. "How many are there?"

"Thirty-six. Unless I've lost any today."

He looked surprised. "Oh, does that happen . . . often?"

"So much." She realized what he was thinking and said quickly, "Oh! No, no. They don't *die off*. I think sometimes they accidentally click 'unsubscribe' when they mean to shut the video off. I've actually seen my mom do that more than once." She shook her head. "They could get a bird's nest of wires to make a Nintendo work on a TV that still had rabbit ears, but when it's right in front of them, they can't click for shit."

"It's true. I remember my parents setting up an adaptor on another adaptor to get RCA cables to work on an old Zenith they got from my grandparents." He chuckled. "My dad is not one to waste anything that he deems *still usable*. He was forty-two when I was born, so he's basically on the heels of the Victory Garden age. Computers are never going to come naturally to him."

Margo nodded. "My mom was thirty-eight, which was still pretty old back in the day. I've heard a lot about the accommodations she had to make for her *high-risk pregnancy*." She sighed. "Anyway, they're with people who get them now, so it's all good. But, seriously, don't worry about the video." She added, "I promise I'll edit you out so it doesn't seem like I'm capitalizing on your fame to get a thirty-seventh subscriber."

He took a moment, then put his hand out. "Give me your phone. Turn it on and hand it over."

She clutched it to her chest. "Sir?"

"Come on, lady, we don't have all day."

"Fine." She turned on her phone and the video app and handed it over. "Have at it."

He took the camera, held it in selfie position, and tapped the "record" button. "Hello—" He hit "pause" and asked Margo, "What are their names?"

"My parents? Charlie and Elise."

He cleared his throat and started again. "Hello, Charlie and Elise, and all the subscribers to Margo's YouTube channel—"

"June's Cleaver."

He stopped again. "What?"

"The channel. It's called June's Cleaver. From an old TV show. It's a pun."

He quirked his mouth into half a smile. "I know what it's from. *Leave It to Beaver*. Very clever. Clever Cleaver work there."

She felt her face grow warm at the compliment. "I— Yeah, yep."

He held the phone up again. "Hello to Charlie and Elise Everson and all the June's Cleaver viewers out there. Margo is cooking up something that smells absolutely delicious here." As an aside he said to her, "It really does. Am I going to get some?"

"I thought you had to go to the wood store."

"Aren't you coming?"

"To the *wood* store?"

He rolled his eyes. "Specialty lumber store."

She smiled. "Oh, well, if it's boujie . . ."

He looked back at the camera. "So, as I was saying, we're going to give this soup—"

"Pasta."

"—this *pasta* a try, then we're going to the boujie lumber boutique to make a bitchin' kitchen counter and shelves at Margo's farm."

That sounded good. "Really?"

He kept his eyes on the camera. "Really. The last piece of

the job is the floor, so we're doing all the stuff that's higher up first."

She was impressed. "Excellent."

"So where are we in this process, Margo? Have you finished the lesson or . . . ?"

"No, not quite."

He took the camera off himself and trained it on her. "We're going to do this *Blair Witch Project* style now, I'm going to film the rest of the process. I want camera *and* producer credit."

"Oh." The idea of Max watching her every move was far more daunting than having the camera on her. "Okay, well. I've chopped ten cloves of garlic sort of roughly and I'm putting just a teaspoon of olive oil into a nonstick pan over medium-high heat." She turned on the burner and went back to the chopped garlic. She knew her hands smelled of it and hoped she didn't reek entirely.

"Go on," Max said. "I'll follow you. You can edit me and my prattling out later."

"Yeah, people just hate when you perform." She made a face, then looked back at the camera. "Start by putting about a third of the garlic into the pan." Since she'd done a number of these videos already, she was pretty used to the process, and it took over her self-consciousness fairly fast. "Honestly, I'd normally use more. A lot more. But I realize not everyone likes vampire-level pungency. Or buzzard breath."

Max chuckled.

Margo felt a flush come over her. "So if you aren't a fan of sharp garlic flavor, you can put it all in right now and it will mellow over the heat." She stirred with a bamboo spoon, waited a few awkward moments, then said, "Now I'm going to add a little more garlic"—she did so—"and about a cup and a half of chicken broth." She poured it from the measuring cup and it sizzled onto the pan and shivered the garlic scent into the air.

"Can't wait to try this," Max commented, like a golf voice-over admiring a fine drive.

But there was something much more sensual to it. The steam, the scent, the low lilt to his voice. She'd call it the practiced masculinity of an actor, but for one thing there was a rasp to it, and for another she'd known this voice since well before he was an actor.

She cleared her throat and returned to the job at hand. "It's time to start the water boiling because we're almost ready to eat." She got her favorite four-quart All-Clad pan down from the pot rack and took it to the sink to fill with water. "As usual, you're going to want to cover the pot so the water boils faster." She did.

"Care to explain the science behind that?" Max asked.

"Nope." She returned to the stove, smiling as she felt his amused gaze tickle down her back. "Now I'm going to add some white wine to the sauce, about a half a cup. Don't worry, this won't make you drunk, the alcohol will cook off." She could already hear the fretful old voices picking and plucking about the amount of alcohol. "If you don't want to add it, you can just let the chicken broth carry it, that's fine too."

"I like a nice glass of chicken broth at five P.M. every night," Max said casually. "I find it just helps me relax, let the day go."

"Hey, no one's judging."

"My doctor says it's fine, all right?"

"All right, all right." Margo laughed. "And there you have it. Max Roginski's secret to health and relaxation. A nice hot mug—"

"Flute."

"I beg your pardon?"

"I drink it from a flute." He pantomimed drinking a glass of champagne, pinkie out. "It's more festive."

"Ah. A nice flute of chicken broth every evening. Very civilized. *Meanwhile*"—she turned the stove off—"our broth has boiled down nicely and the pasta water has come to a boil. I'm using fresh pasta, so I'm only cooking it for three minutes but follow the directions to al dente on the package you use."

"I used to work with Al Dente," Max commented. "Terrible actor. Just terrible."

Her laugh was completely spontaneous. It was an old dad joke, but so unexpected it got her. "He was on *General Hospital,* right?"

"*Passions.*"

"Oh yes. With the, ah"—she tried to remember the show—"the doll that came to life, right?"

Max shot a finger gun at her. "Bingo. You can edit all of this out, right?"

"Definitely." But she knew she wouldn't. She dropped the pasta in and watched the water bubble up and cover it as she stirred the noodles. Once again she could feel his eyes on her, and even though he was three feet away, it felt like he was touching the back of her neck. "All we do to finish the sauce is add a tablespoon or so of brown sugar and a splash of balsamic vinegar and it's ready." Trying to concentrate on cooking and not Max, she stirred the brown sugar in. It dissolved into the hot liquid immediately, and the pour of vinegar turned the sauce to a warm amber color. The smell rose again, and she realized she was being perfumed with it, her skin, her hair, everything. She was going to be like a skunk in the car with him.

She frowned and returned to her task with perhaps a touch too much efficiency. "So. The pasta is done, so I'm just going to quick drain it, reserving a little of the cooking liquid, and"— she poured it into a strainer over the sink and flipped it back before the starchy water was all drained—"then pop it into the saucepan." She worked too fast and it sloshed up and over onto the stove. Instead of commenting on it, she just went ahead and touched it a little bit with some tongs and said, "Now I'm going to let it sit while I get plates out and . . . there you go." She set two plates on the counter next to the stove. "It's done. Top it with some pecorino Romano or Parmesan and enjoy!"

She smiled for the camera and then at Max. "Mom and Dad are going to be thrilled to see you."

"Don't forget the other thirty-four."

She held a flattened hand out and tipped it from side to side. "Usually my videos get like eight views so . . . maybe *some* of the other thirty-four will see it, assuming it's not just my parents playing the videos over when they want to pretend the whole family is there." She took the phone and turned it off, excited to edit later on so she could see how it came out.

Max gave a laugh. "Now that I know about your channel, I'll be making up at least a hundred views of each. You are a star. I couldn't take my eyes off you."

Her face felt hot, and she knew she looked like a goofy tomato. If only there was a way to control the unflattering splotches of pink that crept into her cheeks like splashes of paint every time he said something sweet or sexy or flirtatious. "You couldn't or you'd have spent the whole time filming the floor or the refrigerator."

He smiled. "I got you, don't worry." He came over to the stove, moving in close to her. "Got a fork?"

"I don't like to brag but I've got a whole bunch of them."

"May I borrow one?"

She smiled and opened the drawer between them. "Take your pick."

He took one and scooped some pasta out and into his mouth.

He wasn't even finished chewing before he said, "This is *incredible*."

She shrugged. "It's pretty simple."

He took another bite. "You say that, but it's perfect." He wound more around the fork and held it out to her.

She had no choice but to open her mouth and let him feed her.

It was a big mouthful. She chewed, just hoping she didn't choke and die right there in front of him.

"Right?" he asked.

She nodded and gave a thumbs-up. "And it's light," she managed. She swallowed and added, "There's almost no oil or fat in it."

He looked at her like he was appraising an antique ring. He touched her cheek with his knuckle and said softly, "I don't know how that idiot JB let you go."

She blinked, then expelled a breath, brought back to the moment. "You mean Calvin?" JB had been her college boyfriend for a bit when she and Max had been friends. He'd comforted her through that embarrassing breakup, and here he was for another one.

This time it was Max whose face went red. He stepped back, the moment broken, his touch gone. "Calvin. Of course. I was thinking . . ." He shrugged and looked down. "I don't know what I was thinking."

"I do. You were just confusing names on the ever-expanding list of guys who have dumped me," she said. "JB was in college. You met him a few times."

"Yes, I—" He shook his head. "I remember him. He was a moron, and so was Calvin. They're both fools."

She shrugged. "It's hard not to notice there is one common denominator." She pointed at herself. "Hard to say who the biggest fool is. It feels possible that they both found something *really annoying* about me. Go figure."

"Impossible."

"*Anyway.*" She was terrible at transitions but she didn't want to talk about the myriad reasons someone might have to break up with her. "How about we eat and hit the road? I need to get some garlic in you so that you can't smell how much I reek of it when we're in the car."

When he smiled she noticed, for the first time, the faint lines that were forming around his eyes and how he looked even better with a little bit of age on him. "How can I say no to an offer like that?"

"You can't." She started to pile pasta onto his plate. "You really can't. Trust me. It's for your own good." She made him a plate, and then one for herself (smaller), and they sat down at the table together.

"You're a hell of a cook, you know that?"

"If only there were money in it."

"There could be. Isn't your YouTube channel monetized?"

She gave a laugh. "Again, thirty-six subscribers . . . and always dropping and shooting up, lingering around a measly number."

He nodded. "Noted." He finished up the last of his pasta and stood up to take the plate to the sink. Something she'd rarely seen a man do. "Are you finished?" he asked, nodding toward the single noodle left under her fork.

"Um . . . yeah, hold on." She took the last bite, and then handed it to him.

He smiled and took the dishes to the sink. She stopped him when he turned it on.

"I'll take care of those later," she said. "Let's go."

He looked uncertain. "Are you sure?"

"Yeah, the dishwasher is full, and I don't want to mess with it right now. Besides, I don't know how late this wood boutique is open, but I imagine they don't keep Lowe's hours."

"Probably not." He set the dishes down. "Got your phone? We're going to need directions. Or at least an address."

"Got it." She held it up then slipped it into her purse.

"Good thing one of us is on the ball."

"Oh, I'm on it." She smiled. "I'm all about the ball." She shut up quick, horrified. What could that even *mean*? What a stupid thing to say! What was she supposed to say now?

Nothing, it turned out. Max just grinned and said, "I'll keep it in mind."

They left without saying anything further.

CHAPTER FIFTEEN

MAX

He should have kissed her. Damn fool. The moment had been perfect and he could *feel* her wanting it the same way he did.

Instead he'd decided to comment on the guys who'd dumped her. Because what could be a better aphrodisiac than that?

He would have thought, with more than a decade of experience under his belt since they'd met, that maybe he'd finally have at least an *iota* of cool when it came to being with her, but no, he was as nervous and romantically inept around her as he'd ever been.

What *was* it about her? It's not like she was some ice queen with a withering gaze. She was a nice woman, and she always had been. She had the softest, sweetest blue eyes, the kind you'd expect to see on the first angel you meet in heaven.

He'd always thought so. From the very first moment he saw her, she looked familiar.

Which was why he'd put that line in *Ironsides*. She'd never guess it was about her. No one would. He'd buried his boyish unrequited love all over that play and covered it so thoroughly that no one would guess that he'd been, at heart, an insecure kid carrying a flame that was a little too heavy and wobbly for him to hold gracefully in front of her.

So now he was a man with enough success under his belt to proceed with confidence in almost any endeavor, but what did he do when he had the opportunity to kiss her?

Made her feel like he was calling her a loser, of course.

He pulled his car up in front of the back porch at the farm and looked at himself in the rearview mirror. "You're an idiot," he said, then shook his head and opened the door. "Absolutely stultifying," he told the fireflies that hovered in the evening air.

"It's not that hard," he said to the uneven ground on the way to the back door, nearly turning his ankle in a few holes. He made a mental note to get some ground fill. *That* he could do.

He caught his reflection in the glass of the door and said, "The worst that could happen is that she'd say no, we're just friends. And you've been *there* before, God knows, so it wouldn't be new. Maybe this time she'd be into it. You just don't know until you try."

He went in, flipped on the light switch, and the new lights he'd installed in the kitchen bloomed to life. Nothing special, just dimmable LED bulbs in the recessed housings, but it made a difference in the mood of the room, even though the rest of it was still in dire need of a face-lift.

That was why they'd gone to the lumber store. The pieces he'd ordered were going to be cut and delivered in three days. In the meantime, he was going to paint the walls a lighter color than the current Years of Cobwebs and Dirt that was there. Brightening up the room with a good paint job would not only make a world of difference visually, but he hoped it would also freshen up the smell a little. There was the distinct smell of rotting wood and antiques in the air. But fresh paint combined with fresh air would get rid of that.

No wonder her shit ex-husband had left it to her. He knew the guy's type from Margo's descriptions—the kind who wouldn't see the potential in a house like this. He'd left it to more or less rot, and now he unloaded what he thought was a dump on his soon-to-be ex-wife.

But he saw the potential, and he knew Margo did too. He could imagine her, getting the idea and industriously putting on some sort of "gardening costume" and going to the hardware store for spades and rakes and plants and seeds.

But it was an overwhelming task for one person. And if she never got help, she could never have tackled this alone. And despite his own capability, thanks to his early years working for his dad's contracting company, there were moments when he looked around and felt like he'd bitten off more than he could chew.

But that was his loneliness talking, not his laziness. It was a lot easier to do manual labor with someone else to help out, or even to have a glass of iced tea with on the porch at the end of the day.

Truth was, it was that mental picture—making the place beautiful so Margo would want to hang out here more—that kept him going forward into what could well be a huge mistake.

Well, not huge. Maybe not even a mistake necessarily. What he had wanted and needed most was to get out of the city and have some quiet to think and create. He definitely had that now. In spades, no pun intended. Sometimes the quiet felt like someone had put earmuffs on his head and was holding them tight against his ears so the loudest thing in his head was his own heartbeat. It was silence like he'd never known, even as a kid growing up on a sleepy suburban street. There, at least, there was the occasional car, the laughter of neighbors cooking out in summer or shoveling snow on asphalt in the winter. Here there was none of that. If a plane landed on the nearest two-lane road, he might not even hear it.

This was what he'd signed up for. And this was what he wanted, for the most part. It was.

But it sure wouldn't suck to be looking over at Margo's face in the whisper of amber light that nudged through the age-encrusted sconces that flanked the porch door and illuminated the wrought iron patio furniture that had probably been there for decades.

He needed a power washer.

Among so many other things.

He took a glass out of the cabinet and filled it from the tap. No ice. Oddly enough, the water didn't smell funny until it was frozen, which probably spoke more to the state of the appliance than to that of the well. He took an Oreo from the package on the counter, blew an ant off it, and went out to the front porch to contemplate his next day or two.

That was the luxury of country life, or at least he was allowing it to be. Frenzy was a bad habit, one that everyone in the city was trapped in. He'd had it for years, but he was going to kick it now if it was the last thing he did. There was no schedule to adhere to, no rush hour to take into account, no employees to accommodate. If he wanted to sit here on this thin old cushion, feeling the iron poke into his back, and listen to the crickets and birds for the next twenty-four hours, he could. If he didn't answer his phone, no one was going to come running with the police; hell, most people didn't even know where he was.

He didn't even have an emergency contact. That was the definition of being single, wasn't it? No emergency contact. He could die, unknown, in a hospital in some strange town by himself. Completely alone until his face was splashed all over the internet.

He kicked back. Yup, anonymity had its value but so

did companionship. He checked his watch. It was just after 9:00 P.M. Borderline, but *probably* not too late to call Margo.

But what would he say if he did? They'd just spent hours together. He couldn't say he'd forgotten something in her car, they'd taken his. He couldn't say he missed her, that would sound psycho, even though if he examined his feelings realistically enough, that would probably be an accurate assessment.

He definitely couldn't come right out and tell her he wanted another chance to do what he'd been meaning to for fifteen years and kiss her. She'd never made a first move either, and this was an equal opportunity world. Maybe the fact that she hadn't meant that she wasn't interested.

Except she'd always been shy, especially about that kind of thing. He remembered one of their first conversations. It was before she'd started dating that unworthy twit JB. He had written it out in a word document, to relieve his brain of it (which didn't work), and hopefully for a scene to be used someday in the future. He opened the document on his computer from the folder marked TAX STUFF. It was where he hid everything vulnerable that he couldn't imagine sharing with the world.

"So there's a guy I like," she'd said as they sat outside the library in the autumn shade during a fifty-minute free period they both had. "And I just can't tell if he likes me too."

Max had scoffed. "You sound like you're in seventh grade!"

Her cheeks went instantly pink, the way they always were when she felt self-conscious. He'd already seen it happen countless times in class, as she was forever thinking she'd been called on and started to talk before realizing someone else had been indicated. "Thanks," she'd said, clearly trying to attempt anger through a scorching embarrassment. Her gaze flitted to his, then she blinked and looked away, the pink of her skin blooming into red.

He felt like an asshole right away. He was an asshole. Why had he said that? Apart from being pissed off that she—really obviously—liked JB DeWitt, the douchebag who was always asking her to take notes for him while he skipped class. All JB had to do was make a few elementary celestial references and she was putty in his hands.

Guy like that wouldn't be hard to get. At least not for a night or two, depending on how much she gave up. Then she would invariably be hurt, and no matter how much Max loathed the idea of her hooking up with that guy, he definitely didn't want her hurt for any reason.

By anyone.

"Hey, I'm sorry, I didn't mean it that way."

She lifted her chin. "What way?"

He was flummoxed. "Well, any way that hurts your feelings."

"Cool. You didn't mean whatever you meant. That definitely makes it okay."

"I didn't mean to belittle you. What I meant was you're great, you should just tell him how you feel." He'd shrugged and probably did a little involuntary eyeroll. "If he's too wimpy to make a first move, then maybe he's hoping you will."

She'd considered him for a moment, then sighed. "Whatever. You're right, he's obviously not interested."

"I didn't say that." But he was careful not to say otherwise either.

What could he say? Granted, he'd probably implied JB was disinterested by pointing out he hadn't made a move, but given that he, himself, had never let on to her that he had feelings, he did know it was possible that JB didn't have the confidence to say something to her even if he wanted to.

But it wasn't Max's job to play matchmaker or figure out every other guy's psychology. He liked to think he was a good friend in general, but there was such a thing as going above and beyond, and in this case he just wasn't going to do it. Why should he?

He didn't know if the guy was into her or not, so what was the point in going out of his way to encourage her? He didn't know.

He just didn't know.

She met his eyes for a long moment, searching. "At least I always have you as a friend, right?"

It was a crushing conclusion but true nevertheless. It was where he'd expected her to land anyway.

"Right," he'd said, then, since it sounded so lame, he'd re-affirmed it as strongly as he could. "We are absolutely friends for life."

"Great," she said, without a spark.

Seeing her deflated like that was almost enough to make him do a reversal on everything he'd just said, just to make her feel better. He could say he'd seen the way the jerk looked at her and he was definitely crushing on her. He could say the most intense interest was often characterized by a paralyzed inaction—it was certainly true in his case. Hell, he could even say he'd heard something through the grapevine that would make her heart and ego soar.

As dumb luck would have it, before he had to make any con-cessionary decisions, JB and his little group of minions walked by in front of them—not going to the library, of course, but passing the building. So, in what Max had considered a greatly unselfish act, he'd gestured toward them and said, as cool as he could possibly muster, "There's DeWitt now. Go for it. I'm sure he'll be open to you."

"Gee, thanks for the huge vote of confidence. Maybe I can beg him for a little attention."

"I'm sure you won't have to beg."

She widened her eyes at him. "Wow."

Everything he was saying was wrong, but he couldn't fig-ure out why. He was just trying to be encouraging. He was terrible at this. Terrible at love, and apparently even terrible at friendship. "Sorry!" That came out a little too harsh. He softened his voice and tried again. "Look, I'm not good at this stuff, okay? Just . . . do what you want."

That had effectively ended the conversation, save for a few small comments that accompanied them gathering their things and going to their different classes.

They hadn't spoken again for about three weeks and by then she was dating JB DeWitt, so Max figured he'd probably done her a favor, even if it hadn't seemed like it at the time.

Part of him was pissed that she'd trampled all over his feelings like that, in her scramble to get to the guy she really wanted, but he knew her well enough to know she didn't realize what she was doing. She'd just had no idea that Max was in love with her.

In love?

Had he really just thought that?

He turned the idea over in his mind and examined it. The feelings he'd had today, the feelings he'd had when she came to visit in New York, the feelings he'd had when he was looking at her Instagram—far from the first time he'd done it, by the way—and seen that she was looking for a person and that, for once, maybe he could be the one.

Sure, yes, it was fair to call it love. It had always been there.

There had been so many times along the way that his feelings had swelled for her over the smallest, least consequential, hardest-to-define things. The way the waves of dark blond hair framed her face when she took it out of a ponytail. The melody of her laugh when she was taken by surprise. The unconscious swing of her hips when she walked slowly, lost in thought. To say nothing of the more obvious appreciable qualities, like her kindness to strangers, her patience with children and adults who needed help, the way she was always ready to give up her own time to be there when someone else needed her.

She didn't usually ask for help herself. It had been remarkable to find her post, looking for a caretaker. It was surprising, and a bit disappointing, even while it left the opportunity open to him, to learn that no one had stepped up to offer assistance before Max had. Sure, it could be argued that it was *meant to be* and that any other volunteers would have muddied the waters, but at the same time he felt sad that she wasn't surrounded by people who cared about her as much as she always cared about everyone else.

It didn't matter now, he supposed. That fact was, he *had* seen the post, he *had* gotten back in touch with Margo, and he was here now, repeating all the same mistakes he got so good at fifteen years ago.

If cycles needed to be broken, he was the one who needed to break them. Particularly if he was the only one who saw them.

He picked up his phone and went to "recents." Hers was the

first number there, and he tapped it, then ended the call immediately. He didn't have a plan. He was a man without a plan. He wasn't going to make a bumbling ass of himself again.

The phone vibrated in his hand, and he looked at it.

Margo.

Had she picked up on his thoughts? Was it possible that she was thinking about him at the same time he was thinking about her? Would that even *mean* anything, or was his romantic teenage self getting too wound up in the mix?

"Hey, Margo, what's up?" He congratulated himself on pulling off sounding casual.

"You just called me."

"No, I didn't."

"Hmm. It showed up on my phone just now. It says nine forty-two P.M."

Damn these stupid phones. They registered everything immediately these days. You couldn't rethink your actions halfway through dialing, couldn't have the satisfaction of slamming a phone down in anger, couldn't even hang up before the first ring without it trumpeting to the other party that you were sitting here aching for them.

"Oh. Huh. You know, I just picked the phone up. Out of my pocket"—he leaped on that—"yeah, I just got the phone out of my pocket so maybe I hit the button. Sorry about that."

"No problem. I just thought— I was hoping nothing was wrong out there."

"Well, it's hot as hell, but that's to be expected this time of year." He gave a laugh. For an actor, he sure did suck at improvising in real life. "So, nope, nothing's wrong."

"This is quite a heat wave we're having."

He nodded, then said, "For October."

"They say it's the record."

"I can believe it."

"Max." She stopped, and a silent pause stretched between them. "I have this big house to myself and if you're uncomfortable or anything, you're welcome to come stay here. In the guest room. I have two guest rooms, actually. You could take your pick."

He would like nothing more than to get in his car and drive back to her house and generate some heat, but not from the guest room. Or one of the two guest rooms. She was making it pretty clear she meant this platonically, so he decided it would be best for him to simply suck it up and stay where he was. He was here to man up for her, and cowering in the heat and making her prepare a room for him in her air-conditioning was no way to do that. If anything, it would just solidify their outpost here in the Friend Zone.

"Nah, I'm fine here. It takes more than a little humidity to knock this man down." He made a point of yawning extravagantly. "In fact, I'm about to hit the hay." What a stupid bunch of things to say! If he'd come up with one more dumb cliché about manning up, he would have hit the trifecta. "I'm beat," he finished lamely.

There was a hesitation before she said, "Okay. Let me know if it gets unbearable. My door is open twenty-four hours."

He almost—*almost*—said something about being careful and locking that door, but he managed to stop himself. Maybe he really *was* tired. At any rate, he needed to stop himself before he said anything irretrievably stupid.

"Thanks, Margo." He shook his head to himself. "Everything's fine here, don't worry about it."

"Okay," she said again. Her voice sounded small. "I'll talk to you later then."

He hesitated.

"Later," he said, then hung up before the conversation became ridiculous.

For everything he'd realized about his feelings for Margo before he came here and everything he hadn't, one thing was becoming crystal clear to him now: he had it bad for her.

CHAPTER SIXTEEN

AJA

I heard from Michael the other day," Aja told Margo when they met in front of Trista's restaurant for the *Magnolia Table* cookbook club meeting. Margo had a casserole dish of biscuits and sausage gravy, which smelled like heaven in a nine-by-thirteen to Aja, and Aja had brought the vanilla cake dough-nuts with maple glaze because they were easy. Unfortunately, they were also delicious, and she'd had to make a second batch before the meeting because she'd eaten three-quarters of the first batch before Monday had arrived.

"You did? I wondered how long it would take him. What did he say?"

Aja drew her shawl tighter around her as the wind lifted. "I guess he noticed my work at his mom's was taking longer than expected and he was uncomfortable with me still being around." She stepped over a crack in the sidewalk. It was amazing how often she found herself doing that still. Didn't want to break her mother's back. "Or maybe she told him . . ." Even as she spoke she wasn't sure whether to mention the incident with the ring. "I don't know what she might have told him."

Margo looked concerned. "Hopefully you aren't worried about it. Right?"

Aja flattened her hand and tipped it side to side. "I'm going to have to tell him sometime, it's only right. But I'm dreading it. So as far as that goes, yeah, I'm a little worried about it."

"Well, you've got us. He's not going to hurt you."

"I know. I appreciate it." She sounded so much more casual about it than she felt.

Margo stopped. "I mean it."

"Thank you. That means more to me than you know. Even pregnant, I'm so much happier without him." It was only when she said it that she knew just how true it was. It was a weight off, a real relief to not be spending so much of every day actively hoping she hadn't said too much, pushed too hard, or otherwise offended Michael's standoffish ways.

They got to the restaurant door then, and Aja took the moment to change the subject. "Anyway, I am so up for this," she said to Margo as she opened the door. "I ate a huge lunch, but this is going to be really, really good."

Margo nodded, still eyeing her but far too polite to push a subject she obviously realized was being avoided. "I had to make a second batch myself."

"You too?"

"Yes. *You* too?"

Aja felt her face grow warm. "I couldn't stop picking at them. They're so stinking good. And I went to Costco for my neighbor, who has a hard time getting out so I run errands now and then, and they had the most *amazing* array of baking stuff. Oh my God, have you *been* there?"

"To Costco? Sure, of course."

"Well, the maple syrup is fantastic." Breakfast. She was glad Margo had brought the biscuits and gravy, she was definitely in the mood for that. "And the sous vide eggs that you put in the microwave for a minute and then top with hot sauce and . . ." She rolled her eyes. "Bliss. Pancake mix, a hundred pounds of Dubliner cultured butter, fresh orange juice, I mean, the place is just amazing. And my kitchen is way too small to accommodate everything I got, so I had to consume a bunch."

Margo laughed. "Jeez, you sound like you've been on *Survivor* or something. Pregnancy is everything they say, huh?"

"And then some."

Margo nodded but her gaze was intense. "Just remember." A pause. "I just want you to know if you *did* need to talk about anything, or if you need to get away, I'm here."

Aja's emotions were a quick trigger lately. She felt like she could cry just because of the kindness of the gesture. "Thank you."

"I mean it."

They stepped in and it took Aja's eyes a moment to adjust to the dimmer lighting, but when she did, she couldn't believe how perfect the place was. Antique clocks and clock pieces adorned the wall over a tall and wide lit bar housing every liquor Aja had ever heard of. The taps for beer were carved wood, rather than the brightly colored ones the breweries sent for free advertising. The bar was a rustic bloodwood, which probably only Aja would recognize and know how expensive it was. She admired Trista for that touch.

"God, I love these old wood floors," Margo commented. "I wonder if they were here or if she installed them. What a job!"

"You thinking about putting them in at your farm?"

Margo smiled and her face went a little pink. "I'm getting it done. Or my . . . my handyman is." She made herself laugh, describing one of the world's favorite celebrities as not only a handyman, but as *hers*.

"Handyman, huh?" Aja raised an eyebrow. "Is that as interesting as it sounds?"

Margo made a face. "Suffice it to say, it's been a weird couple of months."

"Agreed." Aja was about to ask Margo to elaborate when Trista swooped up, followed by a tall guy with a bad haircut and a baby face. His bright blue eyes added to the childlike effect of his visage.

"Hey there." Trista gave them each a hug. "Glad to see you

both! Was this cookbook fattening or what? I couldn't decide what to make, so I did almost everything. The fact that I landed on the arugula salad is a direct statement about my waistline."

They laughed and agreed.

"Um." The guy behind Margo gave a small wave of his hand. "I helped with the salad."

Irritation flashed across Trista's face and she said, "Right."

"And I set up on the pool table."

There it was again, that annoyed look. Trista gave a smile that looked forced. "Louis—Margo, Aja, this is Louis; he's just started here, though we went to school together a long time ago. Anyway, Louis, the thing about a pool table is that you *really* can't spill anything on it or it will be ruined because the felt will be off."

"I'm not putting stuff *on* the table."

Aja watched with interest to see how this would play out.

Trista looked confused. "But you just said you set up on the pool table."

"When you told me you were doing this tonight, I used some old wood pallets I found out back to retrofit a table cover. I thought you could use the space. Don't worry, it was *after* I cleaned the grill."

"Let's just set everything on the bar," Trista said, but her expression softened at the disappointment on Louis's face. "I really appreciate your doing that, Louis, but in this particular case I think the bar is a good way to set up. Your table topper sounds great for"—she frowned slightly—"trivia night? It will give them a place to set up the equipment."

That did it. "Good point." Louis nodded. "Ladies, would you like me to carry your dishes to the bar?"

"Sure, thanks." Aja handed it over. The poor guy just wanted to be needed. He was an odd bird, for sure, but as birds went, that was her favorite kind. "I really appreciate it."

He beamed and took Margo's dish and took a few steps toward the pool room before stopping and turning back to the bar.

"Wow, that guy does everything," Margo commented, apparently not noticing the undertone of aggravation coming from Trista. "Lucky find. I only got one response when I was looking for a caretaker for the farm and *that* included a place to live."

"Ah, yes," Aja said. "Good help is so hard to find. And I know it because I'm good help. The last guy"—she shook her head—"it would *seem* he stole a ring from the homeowner and buried it in the garden."

Trista looked interested. "And you found it?"

Aja nodded. "Dug it up."

"Whoa. And it was valuable?"

Aja had looked up the value of comparable diamonds as soon as she'd had the chance. "Very. And I was nearly fired and/or arrested for letting Lucinda, the owner, know. No good deed goes unpunished, huh?"

"That is outrageous," Margo began. "You should tell that woman—"

"Oh my God, Margo Everson, I saw your video!" A woman with a pale blond pixie cut and the slight figure to match came running up. "Can you introduce me to Max Roginski?"

Max Roginski? Aja looked from the woman's eager face to Margo's, expecting her to look as puzzled as Aja felt. Instead Margo's face was so red, it was visible even in this dim light.

"I— How did you see that, Tula?"

"Well, you posted it, didn't you? Isn't June's Cleaver your channel? Everyone's talking about it. There were a bunch of videos of you there."

"Well, yes, but—"

"Doing what? What in the world is this about?" It had never even occurred to Aja to look Margo up online.

"They were cooking in her kitchen," Tula said knowledgeably. "I'm completely serious. At least I think it was her kitchen."

"And you think it was Max Roginski," Aja added, hoping to be helpful but it fell on deaf ears.

"But how did you even find my channel?" Margo asked in a thin voice. She didn't exactly look thrilled. "It's not very popular."

"It is now. Girl, you've gone viral."

"What's the channel called?" Aja asked Margo, taking her phone out of her pocket.

"June's Cleaver," Tula supplied. "But it's all over Facebook too."

"*What?*" Margo looked stunned.

Aja was lost. "You're not saying there was anything . . . *indecent* or anything, right?"

"No, but it looked pretty hot to me."

"How long has *this* been going on?" Aja asked, half fascinated and half pissed that she hadn't already known about it.

Margo's face was nothing short of scarlet. "He's an old friend. We went to school together. Just like Trista and that guy. There's no more to it than that."

Aja waited for YouTube to load on her phone, then went to the search bar and typed in: June's Cleaver.

There it was.

A little over twenty thousand subscribers and twenty-two videos. She scrolled down to "Latest from June's Cleaver" and saw a still picture of Margo and, yup, Max Roginski. The title was simply *Braised Garlic Pasta*. It made no sense.

"Can you cast it to the TVs?" Aja asked Trista, absolutely awash with excitement.

Trista looked at Margo uncertainly. "Do you want me to?"

If possible, Margo began to look even more mortified. "Ugh, no! That was just a thing I did for my parents! I've been sending my mom videos on how to cook healthful stuff for my dad, and Max came in while I was filming one." She looked lost and looked back at Tula. "And now it's all over Facebook?"

Now another woman joined them. She wasn't even remotely familiar, just a customer who knew Margo even though Margo didn't know her. "The Roginski cooking video? Someone posted it on my page because it looked delicious and your tag was local."

"Would your parents have shared the video?" Trista asked.

"They barely know how to click on it!" Margo shook her head. "But maybe one of their friends did. Or something. Obviously someone did. It's not like the channel is set to private or anything, I just can't sit here while everyone watches me bumble my way through something I thought no one else would ever see."

Aja felt bad for how embarrassed Margo obviously was, but Trista patted her back and said, "You can't really post something publicly with a huge star in it and expect it to stay private."

"I could change the settings," Margo said.

Though the sound was off, Aja could see the video was of Margo talking to the camera in her kitchen and then getting interrupted by Max Roginski.

What was it about star quality that made certain people's light shine so differently, even in a candid context?

"Margo," Aja said. "This looks really cute. And you've got tens of thousands of followers!"

"But that channel was just for my parents, really. I didn't mean for it to become . . . something."

Aja shrugged. "Well, it looks like it has and you can monetize that, so why not?"

"I don't want to take advantage of a friend."

"You could do a video right now and get this restaurant in front of all those viewers," the second woman added, apparently ready for her close-up.

Margo looked at Trista. "It *is* a lot of people," she said. "Maybe some of them are local."

Trista's eyes lit. "I would love it."

"I'll film it," Louis said, appearing out of the blue. "I majored in film."

Aja was not surprised.

"You have your meeting and I'll edit it into the best advertisement ever," he said. "I've been waiting for just this kind of chance!"

Aja was exhausted when she went to Lucinda's the next day. The night at Trista's had turned out to be really fun but really taxing, with Louis catching spontaneous moments and then asking for repeat performances when he didn't have the lighting *quite* right. It was annoying at times, but when she saw some of the clips he got, it appeared it might be worth it. They'd know soon enough, since he'd left happily talking about how he was going to be up all night, editing.

For her part, Aja was fine with being part of it, since she was well aware that soon she would look very different. Last night was kind of a time capsule, capturing the last period of her alone-ness and prebirth figure.

She picked up a trowel and started digging, ignoring her fatigue as best she could. It was an illusion, she reminded herself. She'd gotten enough sleep, her body was just doing a lot inside to create a self-sufficient home for the baby. As long as she took breaks and didn't overdo it now, she could work through it.

She had to.

Then a sparkle in the dirt, very similar to what she'd seen a few weeks ago. She dug gently with her fingers and pulled out a thick gold rope necklace. It was heavy, and if it was real— there was little reason to doubt it was now—it was worth thousands. She knew that because not long ago she'd sold a gold bracelet she had, to help cover her bills after going to the emergency room with a sprained ankle. The bracelet had gotten her over a thousand dollars from one of those emergency stores that took a huge commission. This easily weighed four times what that had.

Was this a joke? A test? Did Lucinda come out and put it here to see if she was honest, or brave, enough to return it again?

She set the piece aside and dug around some more, working gently so as not to damage anything that might be there.

Twenty minutes later, she had the hole she'd needed to dig anyway, as well as three more rings, a tennis bracelet, an elaborate diamond (or stone anyway) earring, and what appeared to be an emerald choker.

The earring threw her, and she dug for another ten minutes, certain a second one must be there, but the search produced nothing. She sat back on her heels and wiped her brow with her forearm. It was hellishly hot in the sun, today was the first day of a heat wave that promised to get worse throughout the week. She'd thought 10:00 A.M. would still be early enough to avoid the worst of it, and maybe it was, but tomorrow she was going to aim for seven. Either A.M. or P.M., just anything but midday.

She took a swig of ice water from one of the double-insulated steel bottles she'd brought and felt it snake down the center of her body, cooling her from the inside.

When she saw movement out of the corner of her eye, at first she thought it might be a mirage, but a moment later she realized it was the child again, watching her from that same place behind the wide oak tree. Today she was dressed in black pants with a neon pink top. She stood out against the bleak landscape like a flower in the sand.

"You!" she called. "Little girl!" It was classic grown-up speak, awkward and bossy, but she didn't know what else to call her. She softened her voice so as not to spook her. "Hello? Come on out!"

It worked. The girl peeked at her.

"Yes, you," Aja said. "Please come over here. Just for a moment or two?"

The girl obediently started toward her, and Aja put a towel over the pile of jewelry so it wouldn't catch the light. "That's my stuff," the girl said defiantly, as soon as she got close enough. "I saw you pull it up." She frowned, and her small nose crinkled in a way that looked more angry than charming. "It's mine. You can't have it."

Ah, this added a new twist. "What is?" she asked, almost sure she already knew the answer. "I can't have what?"

"You know what." The girl shifted her weight and stamped her foot in the process. There was a reason these clichés existed.

"Your . . ." She picked up the trowel. "Garden tool?"

The girl glared at her.

"Your rock?" She held up a gray pebble.

"No! My *gems*!"

"Ohhhh. I see." Aja sighed. "I think you know that's a problem then, because Mrs. Carter said they're hers."

The girl paled.

"I'm *Miss Carter*."

"You're . . ."

"Michelle. Michelle Carter. You're Aja. *A-J-A*. So not like the country."

How was she a Carter? Michael had no siblings. He definitely—had said—he didn't have any children. Perhaps she was a tertiary relative?

Although, this was Michael in question. Anything was possible.

"Where do you live, Michelle?"

"Nowhere. My parents live in different places, so I come here after school. It's my grandmother's house."

Aja nodded and asked the million-dollar question. "Is your dad Michael?"

The girl looked amazed. "Do you know him?"

"Not very well." She said it more to herself than to the girl, her gut plunging. "Okay, listen, we need to find all the jewelry you took and give it back to your grandmother."

"I can't do that!" She looked stricken, and Aja could understand why. "She'll be *so* mad."

"I know it's hard to admit when you've done something you know is wrong." Aja looked at her with compassion. This was her child's half sibling. "But it's a lot harder when you get caught and confronted and you *have* to tell the truth. I'm sure she'll be glad you did the right thing."

The girl shook her head rapidly. "I can't! I'll tell her *you* did it."

Aja's first reaction was to laugh, but this was no joke. "I don't think you want to add lying to stealing, do you?"

Michelle's brown eyes brimmed with tears and her lower lip started to tremble. "They'll all be mad."

Aja patted the ground next to her. "Have a seat, let's talk this through." When she sat, Aja handed her the water bottle. "Cold water. It will make you feel better."

The child drank, then wiped her mouth with the back of her hand. "You can't make me tell them anything."

"I don't intend to. I can just take the jewelry inside and tell her I found it in the garden where I found the ring before, but how long do you think it will take her to figure out who did it?"

"She doesn't know."

"She'll know." Aja had some water. "Why did you do it? What did you want to bury her jewelry for?"

The girl shrugged her narrow shoulders and looked down, pulling up grass blade by blade.

"You know it's very expensive, right?"

Another shrug. "She hasn't even noticed. Besides, maybe if she didn't have so many fancy things she'd have a smaller house."

"Oh. You don't like this big house?"

"It's always empty."

Aja recalled the coldness of the house, even in summer, and how cavernous the place had seemed. A child could feel frightfully alone there. As a matter of fact, without supervision, she could even get hurt and no one would know it.

There was no combatting the logic, so Aja just said, "Maybe it's so big that when things go missing, no one notices at first, but that won't make her move to another place. This is her home. She loves it, and you will too someday."

"I hate it. And I hate all the stuff in it."

"Michelle, at least one of the rings belonged to her mother. Maybe all of it did. Think about it, that's your great-grandmother. You don't want all her pretty things ruined, do you?"

"She's dead."

"Well, yes, but that makes things like this even more special. Because she was your great-grandmother and someday you might want to, I don't know, wear her earrings when you graduate or wear her necklace when you get married or . . . there could be all kinds of reasons you'll want them safe and sound and not buried in the mud for years."

Michelle appeared to consider that.

"Trust me on this. I just have one question—I found this earring and not the other one." She showed her. "Do you know where it is?"

Michelle pressed her lips together, hesitated, then reached into her front pocket and pulled it out. "It was my good luck charm."

"See, they do mean something to you." She looked at this child, the vulnerability in her eyes. This was going to be *her* child's sister.

This was real.

And it was bigger than her, more important than her own insecurities, or fears, or selfishness. This girl was going to have a sibling. Her child was going to have a sister. Lucinda was going to have another grandchild.

And, okay, yes, Michael was going to have another child.

Of course she was going to tell him. It had always been the case. She'd known it all along. She just wanted to stretch out her solitude in this a little more.

Keep it her own just a little bit longer.

"We'll look for a four-leaf clover instead. That's luckier anyway. Come on," Aja said gently, picking up the priceless pieces. "Let's take them inside and explain to Mrs. Carter what's going on. I'm sure she'll be understanding." She wasn't sure of that at all, but she *was* sure that someday the kid would be glad she'd learned this lesson.

And, although the thought was almost beyond comprehension, she would likely remember it was Aja who had helped her with it.

In fact, Lucinda *was* understanding. Shockingly so. When Michelle had dredged up the nerve to speak, standing before her like a little whippet who might be blown over by one angry word, she told her everything she'd said to Aja, and even added that she was scared of the house and didn't like to be inside it.

Lucinda had remained quiet for a long moment before saying, "Have you seen my reading room upstairs? It's very small, with room for only two chairs. It's my favorite place in the house. I can't stand all these echo chambers either."

Aja and Michelle must have both had the same look of surprise because Lucinda actually laughed. "Goodness, look at the two of you! You aren't the only ones allowed a bit of human sentiment, you know." She smiled at Michelle. "Do you like to read?"

She nodded.

"Why don't you join me in my reading room, then, until your mother comes to get you? I think there are some Nancy Drew and Trixie Belden mysteries that will be right up your alley. Plenty of hidden jewels." She winked at Aja and reached her hand out for her granddaughter.

MEETING 5—OCTOBER
Magnolia Table

BISCUITS AND GRAVY—Breakfast all day? Maybe just on Sunday. Will gain four hundred pounds if on the menu full-time.

HAVARTI AND TOMATO SANDWICHES—Summer app.

BEEF ENCHILADAS—Permanent entrée on menu—delicious!

Margo talking about farm a lot. My bet: she moves there and sells her house. Worried it will be lonely out there alone though. Maybe Aja can rent room? She seems unhappy. Wish I could say something, but don't want to be rude.

November

CHAPTER SEVENTEEN

TRISTA

"Got any rats?"

Trista looked up from the bar and her chest tightened when she saw Brice walking in.

He wasn't a typical head-turner. There were women who wouldn't have given him any notice at all. Nice-looking, with medium brown hair and dark blue eyes. Clear skin and the kind of five-o'clock shadow that was perennially *in*, but which looked, on him, like an accident. Solid, straight nose, not remarkable. He had a good, albeit *medium*, build.

Really, the first impression a lot of people would have had was that he was ordinary. But for some reason, Trista found everything about his looks to be just . . . correct. Right. He radiated reassurance. Kindness. Confidence. Competence.

She smiled at him. "Not a one."

"No?" He rubbed his chin. "But I've been putting a trail of

cheese out back every night in the hopes that you'd call me for help."

"Oh, was that you? It was delicious. Gruyère is my favorite."

"Cave aged for more than sixteen months."

"What woman or rat could resist?"

He laughed. "I ask myself that every single day. About everything." There was a split-second pause and he met her eyes. "You'd think my engagement would have worked out."

She damn near squealed but maintained her composure. "Your engagement didn't work out?" She picked up a clean glass and went through the motions of drying it with a bar rag, and just hoped she didn't drop it.

His engagement didn't work out. This was coming directly from him. He was cute, he was nice, he was chivalrous in the face of rats, and he was *available*.

That didn't mean he was interested in her, of course.

Boy, it had been too long since she'd dated. All the time she'd devoted to work, and then to being fired, and then to starting over . . . she'd forgotten the basics of guy-girl dynamics.

"Nope." He pulled out one of the barstools and sat with a sigh. "It did not."

She wanted to ask why, obviously she was practically desperate to know what had happened, but there was no tactful way to do it. In fact, she couldn't think of *any* follow-up that wouldn't reveal her adolescent glee at the idea of him being free. "I'm sorry," she said without an iota of sincerity. Hopefully he couldn't tell. "I'm sure that's rough." She looked at him but reflexively looked down when his gaze met hers. Much as she wanted to read his expression, she didn't want him to read hers.

"Ah." He shrugged. "Things just weren't right between us. She . . . she didn't appreciate cheese enough."

"Oh dear." She gave a sly smile. "Literally or figuratively?"

"Both. But to be fair, I wasn't that into the things she loved either. Outlet shopping."

"Ugh. They're really not even discounted anymore."

"Correct. It's just an outdoor mall that smells like Chick-fil-A, pizza, and Yankee Candles."

She laughed. "It's true."

"I wasn't a fan of whatshisname either. The singer with the cowboy hat and bare feet?"

"Kenny Chesney?"

He snapped his fingers. "That's it. Make up your mind, dude. Who are you?"

"It's true, he's a conundrum. Not quite country, not quite beachy. It's like jean skirts. It makes no sense to me."

He nodded. "I hear you. I could have gone Tim McGraw or Jimmy Buffett, but those are two completely different moods." He tightened his mouth. "And if I never see another three-hour musical onstage it will be fine by me."

"There you go, it all comes back to *Cats*," Trista said. Then, thinking he didn't get it, added, embarrassed, "You know, rats and cheese and musicals? Cats and . . . well . . . *Cats*?"

"I got it." He nodded with a chuckle. "Very clever girl. Always rounding up the rodents. How did you get rid of them anyway? Did they all go off in search of Ratt Damon?"

"Actually, they don't like my cooking." She smiled. "I'll explain, but first, do you mind if I belabor the rodent pun for one more second and ask you to be my guinea pig?"

He gave a rakish smile, which made her heart trip. "I don't even know what that means, but I am one hundred percent willing."

"Give me a second." She went into the kitchen and rounded up her most recent experiments. "First, cheese. I wasn't kidding about that. I'm trying to pick one to multipurpose beer cheese as a pretzel dip, burger cheese, and appetizer."

"I'm all yours."

"Careful what you promise." She bit her lip and bent down to the minifridge below to retrieve two bowls she'd set in there earlier. "Here you go"—she set them down in front of him—"sample number one and sample number two."

He looked at the bowls and then at his hands.

"Oh! Shoot, sorry. I'll get a pretzel, hang on." She hurried back to the kitchen and got a soft pretzel. "This should help." She put it on a small plate and slid it in front of him.

"Okay." He ripped the pretzel into pieces, and salt tapped onto the bar top. She moved in front of him and gave it a quick swipe with a rag. He met her eyes and dipped the pretzel into the creamy golden dip, which was uncooked and therefore sharper. He put the morsel in his mouth and closed his eyes while he chewed. "Very good. *Very* good. Nice garlicky bite. Good . . . cheese flavor."

She nodded. "It's cheese. So."

"But it's also got a note of . . . Hot." He widened his eyes and swallowed. "Pretty hot!"

"Sorry!" She grabbed a mug and pulled some Sam Adams lager into it, then handed it to him. "I forgot to warn you. Some people are more sensitive to that than others."

He took a sip and shook his head. "Don't get me wrong, it's great. It just sneaks up on you." His eyes shone as he looked at her, probably a reaction to the hot peppers, but it made her heart trip nevertheless. "I like it." He drank more of the lager. It was the same one she'd used in the dip, so she felt like it was probably a nice symmetry of flavors.

"It does the trick too," she pointed out. "The point of traditional Kentucky beer cheese is it's supposed to make patrons thirsty so they drink more."

"Devious."

She laughed and absently wiped the rag across the gleaming bar top. "Got to stay in business."

He leveled his gaze on her and gave a slow nod. "I'd been wondering what sorcery you were using to make me want to keep coming back."

She blinked, suddenly blank. No clever quips came to her. He was flirting with her. She was sure of it.

Well, *almost* sure of it.

She'd been out of the dating game for so long she wasn't sure what to do. What to say. Then again, she'd taken the rat joke way too far and he was still here, so maybe she was doing all right just by being herself. Isn't that what she wanted in a man? Hell, in a *friend*? Someone who liked her for herself?

"If I knew any sorcery to bring people around whether they wanted to come or not, I'd be very, very rich." She tapped the darker bowl. "Now try the other one. Don't worry, it's not as hot."

"Did I say I didn't like it hot?" He mocked offense. "I absolutely like it hot."

She raised an eyebrow. "Do you now?"

"The hotter, the better."

"But you looked a little alarmed at the first taste."

"First tastes are always unpredictable." His expression was very still, though that dimple was showing very slightly on his left cheek. "That's part of what makes them exciting."

"I mean, I agree."

He nodded. "I've learned if it's not exciting right up front, it's probably never going to be."

"But, as you said, sometimes it's more subtle." She swallowed and tried to keep her voice smooth and confident, even though she felt anything but. "It sneaks up on you."

"That's true. But then you realize you suspected there was spice in it all along."

She'd thought his eyes were blue but she was noticing now that they were more gray, darker than she'd thought at first. Like storm clouds.

She loved a good summer storm. "Uh-huh."

"Goes for more than just food. You know?"

He was definitely flirting with her. Definitely. And he seemed just about as nervous as she was.

Something about that was really endearing to her.

"Well then. You like hot and spicy. What do you think about saucy?" She took out three plastic bottles she'd filled with her hot sauce experiments earlier.

He gave a surprised laugh. "You're good at this. Saucy is good." He met her eyes. "Bring it on."

She hated to be so cliché in her visceral reactions to him, but she couldn't help it, her chest went tight and a tremor ran straight down her core. "All right then." She took the pretzel and tore off three small pieces, aware of the light overhead and how it happened to be shining down directly onto her cleavage. Her shirt wasn't overly skimpy, but it was flattering. Thank God she hadn't just gone with a plain T-shirt.

"This one is medium-spicy." She picked up one of the pretzel pieces and squeezed some deep orange-ish red sauce onto it. The smell of onion hit her first, then the peppers and the mellowing of roasted garlic, sea salt, and finely milled black pepper.

His hand touched hers when he took it from her. "You make hot sauce yourself? I never thought about doing that from scratch."

"I'm not sure I would have if it weren't for the rats," she said, then smiled. "Let me explain."

"Please."

"I didn't want to put poison all over my kitchen or restaurant so I googled it. Turns out they hate hot stuff, so there was a suggestion to puree a bunch of peppers and, you know, sort of *splat* it around. On the trash, in the alley, wherever they are."

"Makes sense."

She nodded. "But I got a ton of peppers, so I decided I'd splat some and make the rest into sauce. Go ahead, try it."

He did. "Mmm." He nodded while he chewed. "Man. That's good. A little smoky."

"Alderwood smoked salt and a tiny bit of chipotle."

"I like it. I'd buy it."

"Not too much heat?"

"Maybe not quite enough." He picked up another piece. "The next one is hotter?"

She shrugged. "Hotter or sweeter, it's up to you. There are two of them."

"Surprise me."

If there was a strategy to be played here, she didn't know what it was, so she just went with logic and started with the savory one. "Here you go." She handed it over to him.

He tried it. Again he closed his eyes and chewed thoughtfully. "Nice. Really dances on the tongue." He didn't smile, but that dimple dented in his cheek.

She suppressed her laughter. "It is a tango for the tongue for sure. It seduces one into taking another bite, and then another, before they even realize what they're doing." She dipped a pretzel piece into the other cheese and topped it with the hot sauce. This time when she held it out to him, he leaned in so she could feed it to him.

"I see what you mean about the cheese," he said. "It's mild, perhaps understated, but the sauce adds some zip."

"The sauce is cooked so there's no sharp edges on the flavors, everything melds together."

He tore off more pretzel and dipped into more of the cheese. "It's like really, really good macaroni-and-cheese cheese." He paused and looked puzzled. "If you know what I mean."

"That's a good idea." She made a mental note to put macaroni and beer cheese on the menu. It was something that always caught her eye when she saw it. She couldn't believe she hadn't thought of it herself. "Now the last one." She picked up the last of the pretzel and put the sweet hot sauce on it.

"That's it!" he said, two seconds after tasting it. "*That* is *incredible*." He stopped and thought for a moment, then nodded.

"The first impression is sweet, then it heats up until you think it's going to be too much, then *poof* it's gone."

She couldn't help smiling. She'd actually been really proud of that one herself, but she wasn't sure if anyone else would like it. "You really like it?"

"I *love* it." He put some directly on his finger and tasted it again, then nodded enthusiastically. "You need to bottle this and sell it."

"Come on." She rolled her eyes. "Everyone thinks their spaghetti sauce or elderberry wine or whatever is the best and they should bottle and sell it."

"But yours *is*. I've never had anything like it." He took another bite. "What's *in* it?"

"Grasshoppers."

He cocked his head.

"And wolf spiders," she added.

He smiled, his relief clear. "You almost had me."

"It's been done. But not by me, I promise."

"Grasshoppers are the new protein," he said. "Or is that crickets?"

She screwed her face up. "Both. Grasshoppers in tacos. Crickets . . . somewhere, I'm not sure." It was hard not to gag at the thought. "I saw it on *Shark Tank*. I'm proud to say this is a cricket-free restaurant."

"The people who came up with it probably made a fortune."

He laughed and had still more sauce. "So this is sweet. Some sort of fruit, right? Not just sugar."

She nodded. "Mango and peach."

He looked surprised. "No kidding." He tasted it again. "Got it. Now that you tell me, I can taste them. What kind of chilies?"

"Mostly fresno. A cherry pepper here, a poblano there. A little habanero." She hadn't gotten enough fresnos, so the truth was she just used everything she had. Fortunately she'd written it down. "Some honey too. Seasonings."

"But there's something I can't quite put my finger on." He tasted more then looked at his finger and said, "No pun intended."

She smiled. "Curry."

"*Curry*."

"Yup." She nodded. "I needed something to segue between the sweet and the savory and I thought of curry."

"It's incredible."

"Wow, you're actually selling me on my own sauce." She upended the bottle and put a few drops on her own finger. It was just as good as she'd remembered, exactly as he'd said, with the heat that snuck up and away. Suddenly her mind reeled with the possibilities. She could use it as the base for a barbecue sauce and start serving pulled pork on the menu. That, with the beer cheese, Aja's cheese soup, and the biscuits Margo had made, she had a theme developing suddenly.

"I never knew anyone who made their own hot sauce," Brice commented. "Though I honestly haven't known many people who could boil water. Cooking isn't a big activity in law school."

"Then you're lucky to have me." She hadn't meant to say that. Her face went scarlet immediately, she knew it. She could feel it. "I mean, the restaurant. Where you can come eat anytime."

"What about if I took you someplace else so you didn't have to do the cooking?"

"You mean . . . what do you mean?" She didn't want to make any assumptions. There were too many ways for that to go badly.

"Look, I'm out of puns. But you *are* hot, and spicy, and saucy, and all of those things, and I would really like to take you out and talk without you having to bring me food and pour my drinks."

"I would like that. A lot."

CHAPTER EIGHTEEN

MARGO

Margo had felt unreasonably excited after the night Max accidentally called her. There was a spark between them, she knew it. Or at least she was *almost* sure.

Just not sure enough to make a fool of herself.

If he wanted to, he could have asked her to dinner, suggested a movie, or even just taken her up on her offer to have him over when they'd talked about how dark it was getting in the farmhouse at night. Though it had only taken moments for him to decline, it had been enough time for her to imagine preparing a gingerbread cobbler and pouring some of the Irish cream she'd made into aperitif glasses to enjoy in front of some candlelight. It would have been so romantic.

But Max wasn't interested in a romantic *anything* with her. Maybe she'd waited too long to really feel this way, always taking him for granted as a friend. In college, when she'd felt the first stirrings of what she was feeling now, he'd steered her toward the huge mistake that had been JB.

Perhaps that was a lesson she needed to learn, or perhaps life was as random as some said it was. There was no real telling if there was fate or not. She was inclined to think not these days.

So there it was. She had feelings for her friend. He didn't appear to reciprocate.

And now he was famous, a big star, though it was hard to connect with that part of reality, even though the proof was right there in the number of followers she'd gotten since their video had gone viral. It was close to fifty thousand now. And probably every one of those people would have thought she was a foolish rube to even hope he'd want to come over.

Still, her heart persisted.

She tracked the shipment of wood they'd ordered for the kitchen floor, trying to think of a reasonable way she could help with the work. She was useless with tools, but she could use stain and a rag, and she could wrangle a paintbrush without too much mess.

It had been more than a week since she'd seen him, and though they'd texted some about the house, he seemed to be getting along quite well without her. He'd come here hoping for privacy, so it wasn't surprising, and she definitely didn't want to intrude on him. It was just disappointing.

Meanwhile, Calvin's lawyer had been in contact with hers no fewer than six times with an ever-increasing list of things that Calvin wanted from the house that he had not been allowed to take while she was present. Things outside the settlement.

Most of them were his belongings, not assets of any real value. She had no problem with him taking the remainder of his clothes, and the overpriced office furniture he'd purchased to impress the clients he never met at home, but when he demanded the Baz Allende painting they'd gotten as a wedding present from her godfather—who was once Calvin's boss—she drew the line. Sure, he'd been fond enough of Calvin, he was happy for the couple, but the gift had been because of his relationship with her, not with him.

Unfortunately, every minute his lawyer spent talking with her lawyer was a billable minute, and though it was reaching a point where it would have been cheaper and easier to just let him have it, she shuddered to think what he would claim next if she did.

So she spent the morning and the better part of the afternoon collecting everything portable that she was willing to give up to him then took a picture of it all and emailed it to him, cc'ing her lawyer, and told him to hire someone to get it at a time they could agree upon, maybe when he came back to the home office. She had no idea how often that was, but it seemed like a reasonable offer for her to make.

If they'd had kids—and thank God they didn't—there would have been a necessity for him to keep her apprised of his plans, but since they didn't, their parting was disconcertingly fast and complete. Years of marriage were severed as easily as a high school romance.

But then again, she didn't want it to be otherwise. There was nothing left to say to him, definitely nothing she wanted to hear from him, and the call to start over was clear. But sometimes, when circumstances and mood collided in just the right way, she missed the security she used to feel. The hope for simpler things, like love and family. She'd thought she'd had that. There had been days where just the sunshine, or a seventy-two-degree temperature, or brunch at Normandie Farms in Potomac, was enough to look forward and be happy with.

Now there were days, like today, where she worried she was doomed to spend the rest of her life alone. The eternal third or fifth wheel at events, the party guest everyone feels sorry for, the lone traveler on a tour bus through Paris.

Okay, yes, she was still pretty young, but given how fast the last five years or so had flown by, it wasn't hard to see herself slamming hard into forty, then fifty, then sixty, and so on.

So she decided to bake bread. She could use it for stuffing if she couldn't finish it.

Baking was always therapeutic. She couldn't anticipate the next fifty years of life, but if she started proofing yeast, she knew in three hours or so she'd have a piping hot loaf of delicate cheese bread.

Twenty minutes later, she was kneading the bread on a flour-dusted granite countertop and trying to work her agitation and uncertainty out. She could have used the KitchenAid, and, in fact, usually did these days on the rare occasion she baked bread, but there was something therapeutic about doing it all by hand, and she put herself into the task wholeheartedly.

She had just plopped the dough into a greased bowl to rise when Calvin walked in and scared the hell out of her.

"What are you doing here?" she asked sharply, her heart pounding. She'd never felt fear at his arrival before but it was so unexpected, and so inappropriate, that he might as well have been a seven-foot buffalo in a ski mask. "I thought you were in California!"

"I had a meeting here, and need to talk to you," he said, pulling one of the barstools out and sitting down. "What are you making?"

"You can't just come in here like this."

"The house is still half in my name. Until you sign the paperwork."

She tried to take a deep breath to calm herself but it wavered, as if she'd been crying. She'd *agreed* to the settlement, how long did she have to wait for bureaucracy? "We have a separation agreement that says you're signing a quit claim over to me."

He gave a relaxed shrug. "Look, I don't see why we can't just talk like civilized people without paying lawyers to interfere."

"Mediate," Margo corrected. "They mediate. Sadly, that

seems necessary so things like"—she gestured at him—"this don't happen."

"This?"

"You barging in." She put plastic wrap over the bowl and set it by the stove. "You can't be here, Calvin. Please go."

"We need to talk about the painting."

"We don't, though. I told you I'm keeping it. It was from *my* godfather, for me. If he were still around, I'm sure he would tell you himself." She edged over by the refrigerator, where her phone was on its charger, and pocketed it.

"You're not being reasonable. I'm giving you the house *and* the farm."

She gave a sharp spike of laughter. "The house still has ten years of mortgage on it, which you're also giving me, and the farm, as you know, is a wreck." She hoped he hadn't heard it was being renovated. "It's probably worth less than the taxes owed."

"Bullshit." He rolled his eyes, but in a way that told her he felt he'd been caught. "It's fifteen acres in Loudon County."

The last thing she wanted now was for him to take it back. "Twenty all-but-undeveloped acres," she corrected. "It's primarily land, and wooded land at that. The house needs hundreds of thousands of dollars' worth of work, which is why you didn't keep it."

He gave a semi-concessionary nod. "You always liked it."

She had so many responses, but none of them were appropriate, given that he was trespassing. "Calvin, leave. Now. I mean it. If you don't, I'm going to call the police."

He chuckled. "Like I said, my name is on the house."

"Like *I* said, we have an agreement, and you're not allowed to be here."

He pushed back and got off the stool. "All right, I'm just going to go upstairs and pick up a few things."

"No."

He looked at her with pity. "I am."

She took the phone out of her pocket. Her heart was pounding and felt like it was squeezing up into her throat. "Please don't make me do this." She made a mental note to call a locksmith. Or, really, just to lock the doors from now on.

He shook his head and went into the hall, and while she hoped he'd go out the front door, he turned and headed up the stairs.

So she did it. She called 911.

"Nine-one-one, this line is being recorded, what's your emergency?"

Margo swallowed her hesitation. "I have . . . an intruder." She should have followed through on that restraining order she'd threatened him with. "My ex-husband is here and he's not allowed to be."

"What's the address?"

She gave it to the dispatcher, growing more anxious with every second. "Can you just send someone?"

"Can you give me a description of the suspect, ma'am?"

"He's not a *suspect*, he's my ex-husband and I've asked him to leave but he won't."

"Description, please?"

Margo took a quick, steadying breath. If she killed him, which she'd like to do, they'd magically be here within seconds. "Six feet tall, a hundred and ninety pounds, dark brown hair, wearing a dark blue three-piece suit with a red and blue tie. And dark leather Johnston and Murphy shoes I gave him, size eleven. Now can you send someone?"

There was a skip in the connection and the dispatcher said, "How did he arrive?"

"*Please* send someone!" She hoped he couldn't hear her, but he probably could, so he knew he had time to take what he wanted and get out. Then possession would be on his side.

"Ma'am, a car has been dispatched. Now can you tell me how he arrived?"

Frustration threatened to consume her. "I don't know, probably in his car, a mahogany Lincoln Navigator."

"Year?"

"I'm not sure." She was close to tears. "What if there was a murderous stranger in the house, would you still be playing twenty questions with me?"

"A car is on the way," the dispatcher said again, without apparent regard to Margo's panic. They must get this kind of response all the time.

Margo hung up angrily and went to the foot of the stairs. "The police are on the way," she announced to Calvin. She almost added that a locksmith was too, but decided it was probably best not to warn him she was going to change the locks, lest he find a way to leave an opening for himself to return, whether it was by unlocking a window or doing something else that would be harder to find or think of.

He came down the stairs carrying a large Louis Vuitton suitcase. She noted, with relief, that it wasn't large enough to contain the Allende painting, even if he'd taken it out of the frame and wedged it in there. "You're really nuts, you know that?"

She wasn't nuts. She knew that. He had created this entire situation, this entire atmosphere of mistrust. "There's a reason we have lawyers, Calvin," she said. "And there's a reason you have to go through yours and not take matters into your own hands."

There was a strong knock at the door then and she hurried to get it. Two uniformed police officers stood on the step. No backup, she noticed, only one car in the driveway, but at least they had come.

She ushered them in and stood back so Calvin was the only thing in their sights. "This is my ex-husband," she said. "He's not allowed to be here, per a separation agreement we have. And he's not allowed to help himself to whatever he has in that suitcase."

"It's my stuff!" Calvin objected.

The police exchanged a look and moved forward. "Sorry, sir, we're going to have to escort you out."

"Leave the suitcase," Margo said.

Calvin looked at the police in question.

"Does the agreement involve him being allowed to take his possessions out?" one of the cops asked her.

"There's a list, yes. But I wanted him to send someone to get them."

"What if he showed you what he has right now while we're here? Would that be all right with you?"

She thought about it. "Why not? Go ahead." She gave Calvin a look of disgust. "You always have to make things harder, don't you?"

"Fuck it," he said, dropping the suitcase and pushing out of the house. "You'll hear from my lawyer," he threw over his shoulder.

She watched him go, gradually becoming aware that she was shaking. The adrenaline had been going so strong that she hadn't even realized it.

"Do you need anything else, ma'am?"

She shook her head. "Thank you."

They exchanged a look and followed Calvin out the door. Fortunately he was gone in an instant, so she didn't have to watch another confrontation in the driveway.

As soon as all was clear, she went to the kitchen and poured a glass of wine. Her hands trembled so much she sloshed some onto the counter, but she didn't care. Most of it went in the glass and she downed it in one long gulp. All those days of beer bongs had come in handy. She poured another glass and took it with her to the table and took out her phone.

She googled locksmiths and clicked on the first one, AAA Locks. She got an answering machine, so she tried the second one, A-Plus. This time there was an answer but they weren't available to come out until the next day. This was the case with everyone straight through to Mike's Locksmith and Security. He sounded nice, and the picture next to his business on Yelp was of him holding a puppy, so she went ahead and made an appointment with him for the next morning.

Just as she hung up, she got a text from Trista. It was a link to the video that Louis had finished editing. She sent the link to Max. She hoped for a response so as to open up conversation and maybe invite him over, or vice versa. This time it wasn't just because she wanted to see him but also because until the locks were changed, she was going to be ill at ease in the house.

But there was no quick response. It was Trista she heard from first.

Well? Isn't it awesome?

Fantastic! Louis is really talented!

The text bubble appeared and then Trista said, *He's not the world's greatest barback or busboy . . . or cook . . . but I agree, he did a damn good job with this! His stepbrother told me he was really excited to do it. You must thank Max for me, again and again.*

I sent it to him, Margo typed, resisting the urge to whine that she hadn't gotten a response. *I'm sure he'll be impressed.*

Then Louis will probably quit and pursue his filmmaker dreams. I'm not sure that would be a bad thing. :/

Why'd you hire him if he's terrible?

Long story.

I've got time. Want to meet for a drink? Margo hesitated, then went ahead and added, *My ex came by and I had to call the police. The locksmith can't come change the locks until tomorrow so I wouldn't mind getting out.*

Trista's response was immediate. *Girl, pack a bag and get over here! Slumber party! You pick up some wine and I'll make some snacks and we can watch a terrible movie. Deal?*

Margo had never been so grateful for an invitation in her life. *Deal!*

MEETING 6—NOVEMBER
Deep Run Roots

SPOONBREAD WITH SAUSAGE RAGOUT—Seasonal for fall.

**SAGE HONEY-GLAZED PORK TENDERLOIN WITH BACON-
ROASTED RUTABAGAS**—Insane, October/November
special.

BEET SALAD—Buttermilk! Honey! Blue cheese! Winner!

Time to advertise for more group members? Will
announce December meeting at the restaurant and
let people sample the wares. Hopefully there will be
a good crowd.

December

CHAPTER NINETEEN

AJA

The nausea hit hard.

One minute Aja was making a pan of buttery slow-scrambled eggs that she'd just read about in the food section of the newspaper, and the next minute the whole kitchen smelled like a wet dog and she barely made it to the sink in time.

It had been months since she'd had morning sickness. In fact, she'd been feeling pretty good. Despite being almost eight months pregnant, she could get away with looking a little chunky with a flowy top. Everything was going so well.

She did *not* want to start puking again.

She stood there, bracing her hands on the counter, breathless and shocked by the suddenness of the attack, and suddenly it was gone. The eggs smelled good, her stomach growled, and it was as if she hadn't gotten sick at all.

She looked around, as if to commiserate with someone, but she was alone. Dreadfully, painfully alone. She opened the

cupboard and took out a glass and filled it with tepid tap water, then drank half of it in one gulp to get the taste out of her
mouth and her airway.

Then she went to the pan and halfheartedly pushed the
eggs with the silicone spatula that was still there. They looked
good, but she was afraid to try them for fear it would hit her
again. Then again, she hated to waste them.

This was what she got for giving eggs another try. She wasn't
ready.

She contemplated the pan for a few minutes then decided
that if she was going to puke, she was going to puke, and it
was better to have something come up than nothing, so she
scooped them onto a plate and sat down at the tiny bistro table
she'd fit into the corner of her non-eat-in kitchen. The Christmas lights she'd strung over the window in an attempt at holiday cheer winked at her sarcastically.

It took a while for her to try a bite. At first she just sat there
with the plate in front of her, unable to move, the blinking
lights throwing colors onto the plate. She was hungry and full
all at the same time. Bored and agitated.

And more than anything, she was lonely.

She took a forkful of eggs and made an effort to chew before
deciding there was no point and swallowing with a gulp of
water. It wasn't just nausea that had come over her suddenly, it
was sadness. Fear. Confusion.

What was she doing? She looked around at her small studio

apartment, the string lights and the little rosemary tree she'd put a few tiny ornaments on, and wondered where she was going to put the baby. At first it would be fine to share the space, but they couldn't do that forever. What was she thinking? How was she going to pull this off?

She thought about Lucinda Carter's words: *I will not allow my grandchild to be raised without family. Not under any circumstances. If that child is a Carter, he will be treated as such.*

She thought about texting Michael, just letting him know the whole truth right now. Assuming Lucinda hadn't already. But she knew she hadn't. She knew Michael well enough to know he couldn't have ignored that information, if only because he'd be afraid of her showing up with a lawyer and a bunch of demands. He thought they'd had a normal relationship and a normal breakup, nothing more than that. She hadn't heard from him so much as once since they'd ended it.

And she'd been glad of that. Until now, when it was plain that everything was going to be a lot more awkward.

She was going to tell him in person this week. Trista was drawing up a custody agreement for her so she could get him to sign it before he had time to think.

She quieted and listened to her heartbeat in the stillness. The clock said it was 8:00 P.M. though it felt later. She tried to breathe deep into her abdomen to quell the panic that was rising in her, but she'd feel a moment of half-relief and then the heartbeat seemed to come back stronger than ever.

SOS, SOS, SOS, SOS, SOS.

She stood up and paced the floor. Everything in her felt like it was reaching a crisis apex, but there wasn't one single thing she could point to as an addressable emergency. If she went to the ER, what would she tell them? That she felt like she was going to freak out? What was the medical definition of that? It wasn't just a panic attack, it was justified fear about the future.

She needed someone to talk to.

If she'd given it just a little more thought, she might have stopped herself, but she picked up her phone and called. "It's Aja," she said, as soon as it was answered. "Can I come over and talk?"

Evening Lucinda was different from Daytime Lucinda, at least visually. Whereas during the day, she was immaculately dressed, head to toe—coiffed hair and makeup in place—when Aja arrived just past 8:30 P.M., she was wearing a matching nightgown and robe, slippers, and no makeup. Only the sheen of night cream.

"You'll forgive my appearance, I hope," Lucinda said. "This is most unexpected."

"Of course." Aja moved in uncertainly, wondering with every step if she'd made a mistake. Actually, every third step she was sure she *had* and yet the reality was that this truth would come out eventually, things like this always did, and it was better to confront it now than let the fear hang over her head.

"Drink?" Lucinda asked, stopping at the kind of credenza bar that always seemed to be in soap opera living room sets, complete with filled ice bucket. She picked up a distinctive brandy bottle and poured some of the amber liquid into a snifter.

Aja felt her face grow warm. "No, I . . ." She gestured vaguely toward her middle.

Lucinda gave a nod. "Ginger ale? Mineral water?" She picked up a blue bottle of Tŷ Nant.

"Oh." It was Aja who had made the wrong assumption, not Lucinda. "Sure. Yes, that would be nice."

"Or perhaps tonic with some lavender bitters? Perfectly safe, but more relaxing than plain water."

She hadn't realized how badly she wanted something with a bite until she said it. "Yes. That. Please."

"Have a seat, dear."

Aja sat on the unexpectedly comfortable antique sofa, and tried to figure out what to do with her hands. The house had been professionally decorated for the season—or so she guessed, since it looked like a very high-end department store. There weren't any colored lights at all, instead there were lots of white lights, red poinsettias, and plush creamy white ribbons. The air held a strong scent of spruce.

For a moment the only sounds in the room were the ticking clock over the mantel and the ice plinking into the glass.

Then Lucinda swept over to her and handed her the bottle and the glass. With a quick extra glance Aja's way, she then took a coaster out of the holder and set it rather obviously on the table in front of her.

Aja wanted to point out that she wasn't just going to set a sweaty glass on the antique wood, but she didn't need to get into such a petty discussion. Instead she simply said, "Thank you."

Lucinda sat down in one of the wingback chairs opposite her and said, "Tell me why we're here."

"I think you know," Aja began.

"I think I do too," Lucinda interjected, and Aja wished she could just get up and leave. "But let's be sure, shall we?"

"Well." Aja cleared her throat. "As I indicated before, I am . . ." *Pregnant* suddenly seemed like a crude word for this 1940s movie she found herself sitting in. "In a somewhat delicate position—"

"Let's call a spade a spade, all right? Otherwise we're never going to get anywhere with this discussion. I don't have time for nonsense."

Maybe it was the hormones, maybe it was her own natural sense of pride, Aja wasn't sure *what* it was, but her anger suddenly rolled up inside of her like a special effect from one of the Harry Potter movies and spilled out.

"Please stop the superior act," she said, with a sharper edge than she'd intended. "Don't mistake my politeness for weakness. Despite your wealth, you are not more important than I am, and you don't have more rights to decent treatment than I do. You know what I'm here to tell you and you must be able to figure out that it's not easy. But you are this baby's blood family, which entitles *me* to invite you into his life or not. It doesn't entitle you to bully me."

Lucinda shrank back as if she'd been slapped. "It's . . . it's a boy?"

Aja reeled in confusion for a moment, then said, "I have no idea. We'll know in a little over a month." She paused. "Does your welcome depend on that?"

"No." She regained her composure. "No, it doesn't. But you said *his* life, so I thought perhaps you'd found out the gender."

Aja gave a brief, humorless laugh. "I told the doctor I wanted to be surprised. That's how it began, that's how it should end."

"So this was . . . unexpected."

"That's an understatement."

"Mm." Lucinda nodded, and then, after a considered pause, added, "I understand."

"Ma'am." A soft voice came from the dining room entrance. It was an older woman, quite wrinkled, with hair so pale it could have been blond or gray, pulled back into a neat bun. "Is there anything you need before I retire for the night?"

"Liv! Yes, thank you, could you bring some of those lovely thumbprint cookies? And gingersnaps?" She looked at Aja. "Are you hungry for something more savory?"

She'd burned calories being upset and had been too nauseated to even think of eating. Now she was starving. The tonic water was fizzing in her hollow stomach like Pop Rocks. "Maybe a little cheese or something?" She would have settled for a Slim Jim.

Lucinda looked her over for just a moment then frowned and said to Liv, "Perhaps a cheese plate with some fruit and that wonderful pasta you made at lunch?" Liv nodded and disappeared into the kitchen. Lucinda turned to Aja. "She makes the most wonderful Italian food, of all things, makes the noodles from scratch. Odd, she's from Stockholm."

Aja's stomach clenched in hungry anticipation. She wouldn't have said she was in the mood for pasta, but the mention of homemade noodles was pinging all her appetite receptors. "Thank you."

Lucinda swirled her brandy. "You are sure it's Michael's, aren't you?"

"I'm sure." She couldn't even be offended. It was a reasonable question.

"I'm not surprised. He has a habit of getting beautiful women pregnant. May I ask if you're intending to keep the baby?"

Aja hesitated. "It hadn't occurred to me to do anything else . . . actually. That's a little odd. I always thought I'd be unsure, but . . ."

"I understand. As for his involvement, if you don't desire

any, I'm sure he'll have no problem with that. His ex-wife, Marnie—"

"Wow! He was *married*, huh? Wow."

"So briefly that it's hard to acknowledge. I insist on having Michelle come after school, but what I know, and what Michelle does not, is that she and Marnie will be moving to Seattle in the new year."

"Seattle. That's pretty far."

Lucinda fluffed her hair and straightened her posture a bit. "Yes. It is. I expect I won't see much of them again. Not until they need money for college."

Aja didn't expect it, but Lucinda laughed.

"Is Marnie . . ."

"She's a nice woman. Was always too smart and good for Michael." She shrugged a pointy shoulder. "She has a good job. Plenty of pride. Doesn't need much from anyone. I had to convince her to let me see Michelle, but not because we don't get along well. Just because she is perfectly happy having just the two of them. Which I understand. I'll try to be part of Michelle's life, but"—she lowered her voice—"I'll respect Marnie as well."

"You're awfully understanding."

"Yes, well. I, myself, was there some decades back."

"*You?*" Aja couldn't believe this admission was coming from her.

Lucinda gave a nod. "It's not something I talk about often, though I think about it quite a bit."

Aja wasn't sure what to say. "I'm sorry."

"As I am. For you. For me." She gave a sad shake of her head. "It was before Michael came along. Before his father came along."

Aja relaxed against the back padding, listening to Lucinda's story.

Around nine, and without allowing for second-guessing, Lucinda had insisted that Aja change into something more comfortable. She had swept her upstairs to a gorgeous room straight out of a castle in the most romantic of novels Aja had ever read.

"I didn't go a day of pregnancy in everyday clothes. Pregnancy is permission to wear anything from kaftans to muumuus. Anything tight is out. Pants are an absolute no. It's the only way to keep yourself sane. Here, take this one, I've never worn it."

With that, she'd handed Aja a silky-but-solid kaftan printed with paisley swirls. She would have tried to object, because ordinarily you don't go over to your ex-boyfriend/baby daddy's mother's house and accept formless clothing. But as soon as she saw it, she was drawn to it. The idea of being in something shapeless and flowy seemed like just the thing.

Then the two of them had sat down in the grand parlor-like room, drinking tea and eating too many cookies, talking. Thankfully, Lucinda did most of the talking.

She told the story of her one true love. It conjured golden-sun-soaked images of dusty roads and speeding Cadillacs. The man, Nico, had been Italian. Tall, dark, and handsome. High cheekbones, firm brows, a broken nose that looked just perfect, and pillowy—but masculine—lips. He had met her when she worked at a flower shop. He'd been buying flowers for a girl. Lucinda had told him not to buy a girl flowers, because all it did was give her something she would watch die.

"And judging by the looks of him, I told him, she would already have their love affair to grieve soon enough."

Aja had laughed and listened as she went on to describe the way she'd run away with him, away from her family with no notice. She had been nineteen, but it wasn't *the way* to just go off on one's own. Apparently. She had left, and with him, she had traveled around from horrid motel to horrid motel and stopped in every state worth visiting. She had called home only to scream, "This is Lucinda, I'm alive, and I'm fine!" at one of the family's housekeepers.

"No matter how kidnapped they thought I was, they still never answered the phone themselves." Lucinda rolled her eyes. "A dynasty of brats."

Eventually Lucinda's story darkened. Nico and she had to return home. The money had run out, and she had none of her own, since she'd left her family behind. He dropped her at the end of her driveway, and she never heard from him again.

"If I hadn't opened the newspaper that particular Wednesday, I might never have known what had happened to him."

He'd been shot after an underground poker game, in which he'd won the pot. The shooter was caught, so she got to know some of the details. Otherwise she might not have known about the game—or known how unfair it was. He hadn't deserved what happened to him. She hadn't deserved it either. It was all just senseless.

The shadow cast over Lucinda's face made Aja's heart ache in a way she'd truly never experienced.

It wasn't until after Lucinda found out he was dead that she also found out she was pregnant.

Numb enough to agree to anything that would keep her slice of Nico healthy and taken care of, Lucinda agreed to a shotgun marriage with the son of another wealthy family—they'd always wanted them together anyway.

"We'd only been married a week when I lost the baby," she said.

Aja had melted with empathy. "No."

"I entered a strange state of delusion after that. I desperately wanted to be pregnant again, as if it would mean getting back that same baby. Of course that wasn't how it worked, and so I married a bad man. I had a son who loved that bad man more than he loved me. I spent his childhood trying to make him into a good man. But I was bitter. Tired, always, those days. Angry and resentful. And it bled through. I don't think I failed to raise a good man. Not exactly. Though you might disagree." Lucinda laughed. "But I didn't raise a man I admired. And that was worse than anything."

Aja had felt like a lifetime of pain had been exorcised by listening to Lucinda's story. She knew it was certainly the hormones, in part, but it was also the dark realization that she had been shutting off emotion for years. The emotion of being left by her father. The emotion of worrying, irrationally, as a child that it was her fault. The emotion of not getting enough from her working mother, and the emotion of feeling guilty for asking.

No wonder she hadn't noticed the way Michael could hurt her, until her hormones wouldn't let her deny her fragility any longer. She was in the habit of taking small scraps and not only not asking for more, but also feeling guilty for wanting to.

What she was learning now was that she was enough. And she was going to make sure she was *more* than enough for this baby.

When she told Lucinda this theory, she had smiled and said, "Then you can rest assured that your baby is already looking out for you, just by bringing you this strength."

CHAPTER TWENTY

TRISTA

Trista was arranging crackers around wedges of Morbier and Brie on a plate when Margo rang the bell to her apartment.

"Come in!" she called. "I'm in the kitchen!"

"I could be anyone," Margo said, coming in and setting two bottles of Charles & Charles chardonnay on the counter. "You need to lock your doors, lady."

"Oh, come on, everyone knows how safe this town is."

"Exactly." Margo twisted the top off one of the bottles. "Where are the glasses? I need this badly."

Trista opened one of the frosted glass cabinets and took two stemless wineglasses out. "Hard to believe you were married to him, huh?"

Margo poured the wine and handed it over to Trista. "I thought I was going to spend my whole life with him. I *promised* to spend my whole life with him. Now I'm afraid to be in the house we shared—the house we were so excited to buy together just a few years ago!—because he might come over unexpectedly." She took a sip of wine and shook her head. "I used to look forward to him coming home. I used to *watch the clock* waiting for him to get home."

Trista watched her as she spoke, saw the sadness in her eyes. There was nothing small about this, despite the fact that Margo seldom mentioned him. "People can change so unexpectedly. Even after years, after *decades,* you think you know someone and suddenly they turn on you."

Margo set her wineglass down. "Kind of makes marriage seem like an insane idea, doesn't it?"

"I didn't practice family law, but everyone I know who does has horror stories. The fights can get so ugly. Particularly when there's infidelity involved."

"If only I'd been that lucky. My husband just"—she shrugged—"changed his mind. Got a better offer. Whatever. Basically I'm nothing more than an ex-girlfriend to him now, and he's a San Francisco resident now."

"San Francisco?" Trista took the basil to the sink and rinsed it off, squeezing the water off before dropping it on the counter between them. She picked up a stem and began pulling the leaves off and dropping them into the mortar she had by the sink.

Margo nodded and reached for some basil to help stem. "His firm has an office out there and he's transferring. Getting about as far away from this life as he can without living on an island or in another country." She glanced at Trista. "And I don't really blame him for wanting a change. For the split second that I thought we were going together, I was into the idea myself."

Trista chose her words carefully. "Well . . . it kind of seems like Max might be a good travel companion."

Margo's face turned pink. "We're just friends."

"Look. Margo. Would it make it easier for you to move on if you knew something bad about your ex?"

Margo stared at her. "Where could *this* be going? And yes, anything makes it easier. Even the harshest truth." She sort of laughed, sort of swallowed a sword.

"I hope you trust me. If I had known this sooner, I would have told you, or at the very least would have done what I could to find out if you'd really want to know. And if I wasn't absolutely sure, I wouldn't be telling you. Okay?"

She could barely speak. "Okay."

"And just for the record," said Trista, looking nervous, "he's clearly a total tool and you're going to win—you win this divorce, dignity-wise. Because this is all about to come out."

"Trista."

"No, I know. Okay. So I used to work for Cromwell and Covington. I think I told you I was a lawyer, but, yeah, anyway it was there. And Calvin—"

"Has worked there forever, yes."

"So when I worked there, he was sort of . . . sort of a joke. I'd been a bartender, so to me he was just par for the course. He would hit on everyone, but always in a way that felt like— less sexual and so therefore more unsettling? He would invite people into his office, asking them for advice or their opinion, or just to get to know them—"

"Tell me he's not really another Harvey Weinstein."

"Um. Well, no."

Margo thought of herself, how she would look to be married to someone who *was* a Weinstein type.

"I can't say if it's worse or better, at least for your emotions."

"Great. Hold on one sec." She took a knife to the Brie Trista had set out and took a massive bite before topping off her wine. Through cheese, "Go on."

"So he talked to me a lot. And the meaner I was, the more he liked me."

Margo's gut lurched. Please, no . . . She took a gulp of wine. "Mm-hmm."

"And I couldn't shake him. One time I told him he was a desperate sycophant and he sort of . . ." Trista looked embarrassed and disgusted. She took a sip of wine too. Then another. "Then he sort of, like, bit . . . his . . . lip?"

"I'm—I'm sorry, like, how?"

Trista sighed. "Like it *was* a sexual thing. I immediately freaked and asked him what was wrong with him, and I said

I thought he was disgusting, and that he should be put away.
I'm not pretending my insults were on point, but I was in full
gross-out mode."

Margo felt seriously ill.

"I finally just escaped the situation, and only later, when I
was over the initial shock, did I start to put it together. Everyone
who had complained about him had never quite known how
to complain. And these are *smart* people. People who know the
law inside and out. And couldn't quite figure out what was so
weird. But so many of the people who complained had said
something along the lines of being shocked they didn't get fired
because they were so short with him, or they snapped at him."

"And . . . so, you . . ."

"I guess the reason it escalated with me was that I was done
with that fucking place as it was, he was just the last straw. So
I said whatever I wanted, no holds barred. They couldn't scare
me. And I guess it sort of, like, got him off."

"So, hang on."

"Hanging. Sorry. I hate this. I'm sorry." Trista had more
wine.

Margo had more wine. "So you're saying he's been, like, hitting on people via having them insult him? And by the way, I
noticed you didn't just say girls or women, so . . ."

"I . . . did not."

"So."

"So, anyone. The part that pissed me off the most was that

he made interviews weird. I saw it on Glassdoor, but again, no one could quite say what was so weird."

Margo made a quick mental note to find a way to talk herself out of looking that up.

"I'm so sorry," said Trista. "I only put it together because I met someone who I liked, I realized he had filled my old job, and wondered why Calvin hadn't. And so, then . . . Margo, he hasn't worked there in almost a year."

Margo almost spat out her wine. "O . . . kay, what now?"

Trista shrugged. "We have— They *have* a location in San Francisco, but he's definitely not working there. He got fired."

"I can't believe I don't know that."

"I mean, when you're married you sort of take certain things as the truth and never even think to look into them. I imagine."

Margo's gaping mouth would not close. "Huh."

"Huh. Yeah. Hell. I hate to tell you."

Margo made a sound even she could not identify, and then let her wineglass make harsh contact with the counter before she put her arms and head down on the counter. Her body started to convulse, almost, and when she sat back up to take a breath, barely conscious of Trista's hand on her shoulder, she realized she was laughing.

Cracking up.

Losing it.

Dying laughing.

"Margo, are you . . ."

She could barely catch her breath. "Oh my God. Oh my God. Holy. I cannot."

Her misery had shattered into a million pieces and had attached to her hysterical giggles. The parasites cascaded out of her at machine-gun speed.

When she finally got it together, she lay a hand on Trista's.

"So you're basically telling me I've spent ten years with a man who made himself the worst man on the planet only to elicit some . . . fetishy response from me?"

"I—"

"No, no—and the reason I didn't, and I never, ever lost it, was because his parents yelled at him his *whole* life! And I made *such* a conscious effort not to—"

Another eruption of laughter. Margo took another piece of Brie and smeared it across the golden surface of a crostini.

"Wow, that's a messed-up cycle, right there!" she guffawed. She looked at Trista, who looked stunned, a frozen smile on her face. "Oh, Trista, it's okay to laugh. I was never going to win this one."

The two of them laughed and laughed until Margo finally cried before laughing again, and another bottle of wine was opened, and the decision to make cake was made.

CHAPTER TWENTY-ONE

MAX

Max thought he'd been through it all, *felt* it all, in his life—big highs, deep lows, and everything in between. But as he was oiling the surprisingly ornate woodwork on the stairwell, finally down to the finishing work, he realized he'd never quite felt the quiet satisfaction of working on a simple task like this. This had to be what meditation felt like for those who were able to sit through that stuff without falling asleep or peeking around.

As he went along and watched the *before* turn to *after,* the grungy blackened lines turning to soft, burnished cherry-wood with layers of life stacked in like tiger stripes, he felt a peace like he'd never felt before. Like the years of wood he was cleaning, the silence around him seemed to layer itself down, from the most recent dings and traumas back to the original structure that built him.

The wood was easier, of course.

But Max wasn't a particularly complicated guy. He wasn't that moody, he wasn't severely damaged by childhood trauma or neglectful parents. His childhood had been fine. Almost everyone he knew would say the same about theirs. But when it had come to choosing a responsible vocation and starting to plan his retirement savings at eighteen, as his father had suggested, Max had resisted. He didn't want a nine-to-five job. He didn't want to have to buy the store brand instead of Kraft.

Majoring in theater had been a no-brainer, once it was time to enter "thirteenth grade." To those who said he was unreasonably lucky, he had to give a nod. It had come pretty easily to him. Opportunities had fallen like autumn leaves in his path.

Now, though—now his perspective was changing. Growing, you might say. He knew he was lucky to have enough money to comfortably cover all his life expenses, but he was also smart enough to know that life liked to change itself at any given moment and the things that were most important were not the things that gave ego gratification or allowed him to buy a shiny new car whenever he wanted. *Stuff* was fleeting.

Which made his time here at the farm that much more treasured. Everything about it was permanent, even if it was showing its age. In fact, the aging itself was beautiful. Comfortable. Yeah, the snakeskins over the windowsills were right out of a horror movie, but they weren't permanent. They didn't affect the good bones.

In short, he was in a place that was a diamond in the rough, almost in the most literal sense, and this was a place he could see polishing and making into a perfect life for himself.

And, sure, it could stop there. He wasn't a kid who needed someone to keep him company.

But, damn, he loved when Margo was there with him.

He loved it because he loved being with her and he loved it because he knew she loved being there. He'd gone through Instagram and Facebook now, seen her pictures over the years, her gardening, her harvests, her small attempts at making the place beautiful while she was trying to maintain a McMansion for a lifestyle aesthetic her husband preferred.

But the Margo he'd known—and he thought he knew her well—was the kind of girl who'd love to wipe away the dust, bring in a pizza, and play cards at the old barnwood table. The Margo he knew would crank Lana Del Rey and ballet around the place, sweeping away cobwebs with every arc of her arm.

The Margo he knew didn't want to sell this place.

And he didn't want her to either, unless it was to him. That was what he really wanted. But if she wasn't willing to do that, he was still fine with making it the place he knew she'd always longed for it to be.

What he couldn't see was them not being there together.

But when the phone rang and he saw her name, he felt like a damn idiot kid with a crush who barely knew how to talk to her.

Act, man, *act*! "Hey, Margo, what's up?"

"Hi, I just made too much chicken salad and thought maybe you could use a sandwich. It's not quite the same as bringing steak and lobster, which you're probably used to, but it's what I've got. Well. And some leftover cake . . ."

"I love chicken salad." I love you. I love you for offering chicken salad. "Yes! Please! I've got some Spiced Sam Adams that should go perfectly with it. And yeah, let us eat cake."

She laughed. "Sounds right. So see you in an hour or so?"

"Great!" He'd have to shower, he smelled like old wood grunge and oil soap. "See you then."

Half an hour later, he felt like an idiot because he'd showered and spent too much time picking a lumberjack-y red flannel shirt, and felt so nervous he pounded four beers and was kind of feeling it by the time she got there.

"Wow, it looks great in here!" she said as she came in with a bowl covered with plastic wrap and a box of Costco croissants perched on top. "How did you do all of this so fast?"

He laughed. "When I looked closer at the floors, I realized it was good wood, so I just went to the Rent-A-Center and got the stuff to sand it down. Pretty easy, since there wasn't a lot of stuff in here that needed to be moved or covered up. It was a lot faster than putting flooring down."

She looked at him and shook her head. "This is so far below your pay grade. But you did an incredible job. Maybe too good. How can I possibly make this worth it for you?"

"You have me staying here for free. That's worth it to me."

She set the food down on the counter. "But the increase in the value of the house, based on this alone, is more than the cost of rent could ever be."

He looked at her. It was probably true. He didn't care about that. "I want this for you."

"What?"

"You seem to have spent a lot of time here, cultivating a garden, cultivating an idea, an aesthetic. Maybe I'm wrong, but it feels like you love it here but"—he splayed his arms—"it's overwhelming for one person."

She looked thoughtful. "I couldn't allocate any money to it because . . . you know. Calvin didn't want to, and I wasn't making enough to justify it. My parents had a joint checking account and trust. My husband and I did not."

Max shrugged. "Maybe for the best in this case. If you'd made it look like *we're* going to make it look, he never would have let you have it in the settlement."

She smiled. Small at first, but it grew. "I'm not sure anyone has ever *we*'d me like that. Backed me up like you do."

"I've never wanted so much for someone else." He frowned and shook his head, hoping she wouldn't see the heat creeping into his cheeks. "I feel stupid saying that, but it's true, you were always so true. Always. You didn't deserve these jerks. You never deserved to be treated the way you were."

Something seemed to flit across her face, some sort of private amusement.

Her eyes gleamed then, suddenly, and she swiped at them with the back of her hand. "Stop, you're going to make me feel sorry for myself and that's such an ugly look."

He took a step toward her. Finally. After all these years, he took a step toward her, into her space. "You have no ugly looks."

She looked up at him and sniffed. "I hate to break it to you, but this"—she gestured at her face—"is real." She gave a slight laugh.

He did not. He reached out and cupped her face in his hands, brushing away her tears with his thumbs. "This," he emphasized, "is beautiful."

And then he kissed her.

Finally, he kissed her.

And she kissed him right back.

It wasn't as if he'd imagined this moment a million times. Sure, back in the day, he'd thought of it. Once or twice. Hoped for it. Admittedly. Wanted it. But he couldn't have imagined, even if he'd tried, just how *right* this would feel. Just what a relief it would be to hold her close. The stresses of work, the pressure to constantly be something he wasn't, all fell away and left him without doubt about where he belonged.

This was home. There was no other way to say it.

It felt like home.

"Max," she murmured against his cheek. "It's been so long. I've wanted this for so long."

"No . . ."

"Yes." She drew back, suddenly looking embarrassed. "You mean no *you* don't?"

He kissed her again. "I mean you pushed me away."

"When?"

He tightened his arms around her and she melted against him, running her nails gently up his back. "It doesn't matter. Ages ago. When you went off with JB." It was hot as hell in this kitchen.

She drew back again with a laugh. "But you *wanted* me to go off with JB. Or, I suppose, anyone but you."

He looked into her eyes and couldn't help but give a laugh. "That's . . . incorrect."

She wiped her forehead with the back of her hand. "But—"

"I was so stupidly hurt when you took up with him. But I didn't have the nerve to tell you so. Not before or during. There wasn't an after while I was still around."

She closed her eyes and leaned into him. "I . . . I tried to tell you how I felt about you. I told you there was someone I was into but I think you knew I meant you and you shoved me right at JB." She shook her head against him. "Of course, it was my own damn fault I went."

"I definitely didn't tell you to get with that clown." He felt like there was steam rising off him like smoke, despite the chill outside.

"You did. Though I can't swear I was all that clear in trying to tell you it was *you* I wanted. I just . . . thought you'd figure it out."

He remembered then. The conversation where he was so sure she was asking his advice on getting the attention of a rock-headed jock. He'd thought he was doing her the favor she wanted when he'd nudged her to go take her chances.

Could she really have been talking about him?

He kissed the top of her head and felt her arms tighten around him. "If you're talking about the conversation I think you're talking about, you are the absolute worst *hinter* ever."

She looked up and pressed her lips to his for a moment before smiling and saying, "That sounds consistent."

"Well, this sucks." He laughed.

She did too. "But who knows what would have happened if we'd gotten together back then? You might have gotten derailed just long enough to not be in whatever magical place at whatever magical time that led you to everything you have. Your career, your fame, your car . . . everything you value. To say nothing of how much pleasure you've brought to so many people."

"It would have been better with you there."

"But then I wouldn't have . . . Kenneth."

He paused. "Kenneth?"

"My divorce attorney." She kissed him again, and they sank

into the kind of heated, urgent fumbling that had been simmering for ten years. Dormant, but never gone.

Minutes passed. Clasped in an almost desperate embrace, awkwardly pulling at their shirts.

"It's cold in here," she said.

"My landlord hasn't had the furnace serviced."

"You probably have a case for inhumane conditions."

He shrugged. "It's not like I couldn't go sit in front of the fireplace."

A light came into her eyes. "Does it work?"

He smiled. "It does now." He kissed her again, and she responded with even more heat than before.

"Light a fire," she said after a moment.

"I hoped I just did."

"You're right."

He winked at her and led her to the front room. In a house with four ancient fireplaces, the stone fireplace in the living room was magnificent, clean, and—now with the flip of a switch—had a roaring fire dancing within.

She laughed. "You hooked that up yourself?"

He nodded. "I have a lot of surprises for you."

She smiled and put her arms around him. "Six months ago, I wouldn't have believed this would be the best year of my life."

He took her hand in his. "And this year is almost over. Wait 'til you see what I have in store for you next year."

MEETING 7–DECEMBER
The Joy of Cooking

CLASSIC GLAZED HAM—Best I've had, will advertise as JOC original.

POPOVERS—Why don't I make these all the time? Delicious! Easy! Gorgeous! Perfect vehicle for honey butter.

RIB EYE STEAK—Expensive but everyone's favorite; make house béarnaise for the side, and baked potato.

Aja looks like she's about to pop—I can't imagine being that tiny and that big at the same time. How does she sleep? Can't imagine being pregnant.

Margo has a boyfriend. Big secret??

January

CHAPTER TWENTY-TWO

AJA

As fate would have it, Aja was telling Michael about the baby when she went into labor. The contractions came on strong and fast, right from the beginning, but she insisted he sign the custody agreement before she would leave and go to the hospital. Perhaps it was unfair, but she knew she'd be sorry later if she didn't.

Fortunately, Margo and Trista were waiting right outside in the car, and Margo still had her notary commission, and stamp, from working for a Realtor three years ago, so as soon as Aja texted them to come in and witness the signing of the document, they were able to both sign and notarize it.

She'd never know if Michael would have fought it or not. All she knew was that *her* intention was to let him be as involved in the baby's life as he was willing to be; she was never going to play games with her child's access to both parents.

She was less sure that he would play as fair, if push for some reason came to shove.

She even offered to let him come with them to the hospital and be in the delivery room, but as soon as the words were out of her mouth, he went pale, and it was obvious he was too squeamish to be there.

Which suited Aja just fine. Their intimacy had been limited to sex. In actual fact, she wasn't that comfortable with him in real-life situations, like, say, giving birth.

As soon as the document was signed, they rushed out the door—Trista yelling over her shoulder that she'd get a copy to him after she filed it—and they hit the road in Margo's Lexus SUV to the hospital.

It was a Saturday evening, mid-January, and for some reason the traffic was hellacious. Where Aja had felt relaxed at first, happily doing her yogic breathing through the initial contractions, as soon as they were sitting in traffic behind blaring red brake lights, not even the New Age flute meditation track she usually loved could calm her down.

"Breathe," Trista said calmly, but Aja noticed Margo's grip on the wheel was tight. "You'll be fine."

"How do you know? Have you ever done this? You've never done this!" She tried to breathe but another cramp gripped her.

"Well, you're going to be fine no matter what," Trista reasoned. "But the hospital is, like, two miles away, so unless you're *really* determined and pushing right now, you're going to make it."

"I should call Lucinda," Aja said.

Margo and Trista looked at each other.

"What?" Aja asked, then took a long breath in through her nose, held it for a moment, then expelled it through her parted lips.

"Nothing," Margo said, "if you want her there, you should *definitely* have her there."

"Right." Aja nodded and took out her phone, then looked back at Margo. "Right?"

Margo nodded, and from the backseat, Trista said, "Right. And if she causes any trouble, we'll have an orderly kick her out."

Aja smiled despite herself and called Lucinda's number. It only rang, no answer. Not even voicemail kicked in.

She hung up and put the phone back in her purse. "I tried."

"There will be plenty of time for her to meet her grandchild," Margo said.

"I know, I just . . ." Aja felt inexplicably emotional. "I don't know why, I thought she should be there. I think it would mean a lot to her."

"Maybe she'll see that you called and figure out why," Trista suggested. "Send me her contact info and I can keep trying while they triage you, if you want."

"Perfect." Aja went to the "share contact" button and sent it to both Margo and Trista.

Just a few minutes later, Margo was tearing into the ER entrance of the hospital. She pulled up out front and told Aja and Trista to go in, she'd park and meet them inside.

The minute she was through the doors, under the bright fluorescent lights, Aja felt relieved. She'd made it this far. She wasn't going to give birth on the roadside in Margo's nice car. That would be unthinkable.

They put her into a wheelchair immediately and took her up to the maternity ward. No sooner was she off the elevator than she locked eyes with Lucinda.

"How did you know?" Aja asked.

"I had a feeling," Lucinda said, with a smile that was completely without artifice. "Then Michael called and told me. He's on his way," she added. "Don't worry, I think he's a waiting room kind of father. He can meet his son after he's been cleaned up."

"Son?"

Lucinda smiled again and gave the smallest wink. "Trust me. I have a feeling."

EPILOGUE

MARGO

W e have a new member," Aja said, though they all knew it. Her relationship with Lucinda Carter was remarkable—the woman was as formal as a statue, and Aja whipped around her like a petal on the wind, and seemed to adore her. "This is Beau's grandmother, Lucinda."

"Hi, Lucinda," Trista said. "Good to see you again." She winked and asked Aja, "So Michael has Beau overnight?"

"Oh no." Aja laughed. "No, no, no, I don't think Michael's going to want an overnight until Beau can completely express his needs in full sentences."

"Why is that?"

"He's terrified of getting it wrong. He went through—what was it?—like *ten* diapers before he got one on right the first time. Lord, I was doing laundry for days, it felt like."

"Cloth diapers." Lucinda shook her head. "I thought we'd seen the last of those."

"Oh, but it's *so* much better for his skin," Aja said. "Do you know that diaper rash can—"

"Stop." Trista held up her hand. "We do *not* need to talk about diaper rash in these meetings. Especially when—" She stopped and went a little pink. "Well, never mind. Lucinda, I see you brought some sort of a pie?"

Lucinda nodded. "It's a strawberry pie. I found out last summer that I *really* like it, so I had my gardener"—she exchanged a look with Aja—"plant some strawberries in my garden, and that's what I used."

Margo's heart swelled. She would never forget that day she and Aja had made the pie. It was the first time she'd really felt comfortable with a friend in as long as she could remember. Even though she hadn't known Aja very well at the time, she was still easier to talk with than the *wives* of Calvin's colleagues she usually met through his work functions. For a long time, those, along with her ex–book club's bimonthly meetings, were the only occasions in which she went out.

"And that was when we started to become friends," Aja said. Then corrected, "Or, maybe, right before we started to become friends."

"Oh, I knew you were a dear right away," Lucinda said. "I had just seen Michael with a different kind of woman prior to that. Business focused, very little fun. You were a shock."

"She was a shock to all of us," Trista said, and gave Aja a wink. "Then she went and had a baby for us so we don't have to listen to our clanging biological clocks. We can all just focus on Beau!"

"To be honest," Lucinda said soberly, "I'm enjoying the fact that Beau has brought out some of the son I remember in Michael. It's been a long time since I've seen him smile the way he does when he watches Michelle and Beau together." She looked down, thoughtful. It was impossible to say what crossed her mind, but then she shook out of it and said, "As I believe he said to you when he came in to meet Beau, you are an unexpected but constant blessing."

Aja's face went pink.

"Did he say that?" Margo asked. "I wanted to get all the deets, but of course I didn't want to be rude . . ."

"You can ask me anything!" Aja looked surprised. "I thought you all were there at the same time but my brain wasn't exactly functioning fully. But he did say that, he did." This time it was Aja who looked thoughtful. "Maybe there *is* fate. It's just not always what you expect it to be."

But sometimes, Margo thought, *it's exactly what you need.* She'd finally gotten used to the two faces of Max Roginski and was able to meld them into one person. Not that she'd ever say that to him—it would be highly disconcerting for him to know she'd ever been daunted by his fame. And now that they shared a bathroom and a shower and a bed and everything else at the farm, she was very used to him as a real human being, day in and day out.

"What about you, Margo?" Trista asked. "What did you bring?"

That snapped her back out of her reverie. "Well, it was kind of tough, since we're going solo without a book this month. With the whole world to think of, I couldn't think of a thing. But then I remembered this chicken salad I had at a bridal shower once and I looked online and found either it or something better. It was kind of an odd recipe, with mayo and sour cream and almonds and pineapple, and tarragon and curry."

"I couldn't stop eating them when I put them on the table," Aja said. "The croissants are perfect with it, I think, because they are so tender they don't overwhelm it."

"Cheater," Margo said. "That watercress soup you brought looks pretty damn good too, but I wouldn't know for sure, since I haven't tried it." She had, though. In fact, she'd dipped her (clean) finger right in.

It was delicious.

"Put it on your channel, then, movie star," Aja said, with a smile. "Then I'll be famous and do a cookbook too!"

Margo's face flushed. She didn't think she'd ever get comfortable with this YouTube fame. Thanks to Max, she had more than two million subscribers now. She liked to think her content was good—in fact, she knew it was—but she also knew that tons of people out there had good contact and it was Max's occasional appearances that brought her numbers up.

He'd just finished filming a special for one of the streaming services about his farmhouse renovation sabbatical, which was sure to call attention to the beautiful kitchen where Margo had taken to filming her content.

A literary agent who had started watching her early on, thanks to his mother's insistence that he check out her friend's daughter's videos, had taken a chance on her and helped her put together a cookbook proposal. The book was due to come out next summer, so she was pretty psyched for tonight's offerings while she still had time to do edits.

They already wanted to add Max's SpaghettiOs alla Vodka, which she'd made the mistake of joking to her editor about. Though it had to be said, a little allspice, a little cream, a dash of vodka. That really raised the profile of SpaghettiOs.

"Okay, Trista," Aja said, her eyes gleaming. She knew something, Margo was just *sure* of it. "And what did *youuuuuu* bring?"

Trista laughed. "Why, Aja. Funny you should ask." She rolled her eyes playfully, then cleared her throat. "Another burned-out lawyer—"

"Brice," Aja said.

"Yes, Brice suggested that maybe his oddball but bighearted stepbrother—"

"Louis," Margo supplied.

Everyone laughed.

"Yes, *Louis* could run a food truck as a satellite to the restaurant. Taking our best quickie-foods out, and bringing customers in once they've tried what we have to offer."

"I can't keep quiet, I saw the Babe's Blue Ox truck on Constitution Avenue the other day," Aja said. "I'm a thousand percent positive he got a parking ticket but I'm also sure the line that wound around practically to the Washington Monument more than paid it."

"True, and true," Trista said. "Louis, I think we all know, is an ace researcher. Ever since he was a kid, he's been wanting some lobster roll he got in Boston at some rando place for lunch. Don't get excited about the punch line," she interrupted herself. "No one has any idea what the place was called, but Louis googled everything from the big bang to cold water lobster versus warm water, and, I gotta admit, he came up with an amazing Lobster Roll. So let's go load up our plates, huh?"

They all went to the food on the bar, oohing and aahing over everything. Monday nights at Babe's Blue Ox were closed for most, but for this group they were the best night of the week.

It turned out to be Lucinda who summed it up the best.

"All my life I have heard the quotes of wise men saying we all become friends when breaking bread together, but until I met this little chicken"—she gave Aja an affectionate pat on the shoulder—"and the rest of you, I didn't fully know what it meant. Now I do." She held up her glass of wine. "Cheers to you all."

ACKNOWLEDGMENTS

Adam Smiarowski, you have kept me going through some really tough times over the past couple of years—there are not words enough to thank you for your unflagging love, kindness, and support.

Thanks to my dear friends and associates who pre-read and proofread and helped me get my ducks in a row, book after book: Paige Harbison, Jack Harbison, Lucinda Denton, Tris Zeigler, and Denise Whitaker.

Thanks to Steve Troha for sage advice, good drinks, and great fun.

Asanté Simons, thank you for all of your help and backup in getting things together for this book, and for the gentle reminders when I run up against a deadline.

Thanks to my cousin Craig Atkins, as well as Jamie, Wyatt, and Parker, for providing some seriously inspiring and delicious vacation days in both Cabo and Newport while I was working on this book.

A million thanks to everyone at Jane Rotrosen Agency for keeping my professional life moving so smoothly and always having the answers. Particular thanks to Donald Cleary for patience in responding to my requests for my 1099s, and other forms, over and over. I swear I try to keep organized, but in a pinch I can never find anything!

Finally, and as always, all the gratitude in the world to my mother, Connie Atkins McShulskis, whose memory fades daily but whose nurturing of the imaginations of three daughters brought three voracious readers and writers into the world.

About the author

About the book

Insights,
Interviews
& More . . .

Meet Beth Harbison

Chandler Schwede

New York Times bestselling author BETH HARBISON started cooking when she was eight years old, thanks to *Betty Crocker's Cook Book for Boys and Girls*. After graduating college, she worked full-time as a private chef in the DC area, and within three years she sold her first cookbook, *The Bread Machine Baker,* to Random House. She published four cookbooks in total before moving on to writing bestselling women's fiction, including the runaway bestseller *Shoe Addicts Anonymous* and *When in Doubt, Add Butter.* ❦

A Chat with Beth Harbison

Q: *How did you come to write* The Cookbook Club?

A: I was actually working on something different, something quite a bit heavier, and during a brainstorming session, one of my agents mentioned her daughter's cookbook book club. Food comes up a lot with me, so the anatomy of that conversation wasn't that weird, but when she said it, a light went off. For one thing, what a *brilliant* idea—a cookbook book club! This is a dream come true for me. It's everything I love in one place. So immediately I started constructing my ideal group in my head and . . . the idea took off from there.

Q: *You collect cookbooks. What are a few of the most interesting cookbooks you own?*

A: My absolute favorite is *Eat, Drink, and Be Chinaberry.* Chinaberry was a catalog of primarily children's books, and it was organized by people who clearly truly, truly loved books. I think that's how they got their following—also a bunch of people who truly loved books. So at some point they decided to do a Junior League–style cookbook and put out a call for recipes, and these book lovers from all over sent in their favorite recipes. The Chinaberry group then tested and tested and voted, and what they ended up with was this odd little mix of unbelievably good recipes, each of which has an interesting story of origin from the person who sent it in. It is my favorite cookbook.

Some of my daily favorites include both of Chrissy Teigen's cookbooks, *Magnolia Table* by Joanna Gaines, and the *Delish* cookbook, as well as everything Mollie Katzen or *America's Test Kitchen* ever produced. To widen my horizons, I put a call out to my own readers for *their* favorites a couple of years ago, and that's when I discovered *Deep Run Roots,* a modern southern cookbook (and a bit of a memoir) by Vivian Howard, with recipes that are earthy, sophisticated, fresh, and delicious; it's really special. I also like to get old collections, like Junior League, school fund-raisers, and so on.

I think anytime people send in their best, most-loved, most-requested recipes, you're going to end up with a winner ▶

of a collection. One of my favorites of those was put out by Ginger Silvers, the food columnist for the *Washington Star* back in the 1970s. She lived in the neighborhood, and my friends and I were so "starstruck" when we saw a recipe contributed by a name we knew. Occasionally, I find an old classic Betty Crocker or *Better Homes and Gardens* sort of cookbook at a yard sale that has the previous owner's notes and even recipes torn from magazines. That is a treasure trove to me.

Q: *What is the most complicated thing you have ever made? What is your biggest cooking disaster?*

A: The most complicated thing that comes to mind was a burger, believe it or not. It involved caramelizing onions in Guinness stout and making a Jameson whiskey sauce. There's blue cheese involved too. It's unbelievably good—I'll try and find it and post it to my website.

Biggest cooking disaster—well, I remember making muffins as a child and thinking "root beer muffins" sounded like a great creation. So I poured pure root beer extract over the muffins when they came out of the oven. I learned a valuable lesson about extract that day. Yet I have not yet figured out what root beer extract could possibly be good for.

Q: *Is there a utensil or appliance you just couldn't do without?*

A: My KitchenAid mixer! I use it all the time, for everything. But at least once a week I use the pasta attachment and make my own pasta noodles from flour, eggs, salt, oil, and water. My grown children come over and beg for my spaghetti as if they were ten years old still. Good knives are imperative. And I use my two-dollar wooden citrus reamer more than you'd think.

Q: *If you could open a restaurant, what would you call it? What kind of food would you serve?*

A: This is a conversation we've had a lot in my house. My late husband's grandfather was a famous DC caterer—he catered to seven presidents! So the name "Harbo's" has been tossed around a lot. But I always like the personal name that implies a lot: Joan's

Diner. Right or wrong, you can come up with a lot of ideas about what you'd find there and what Joan looks like.

If I were to open a place, it would be a breakfast-and-lunch place with lots of buttery comfort food. And mimosas. I'm already sweating how hard it is to get a liquor license, but given my druthers, I'd like to have a place that serves slow scrambled eggs, hollandaise sauce on everything, and champagne with lots of fresh raspberries in it.

Q: Any advice for those who say they "can't cook" or that they are a disaster in the kitchen? Keeping in mind that some people just shouldn't go near a stovetop!

A: Yes—stop being lazy and self-limiting! Follow a recipe, paying attention to the elements. If you're brand-new or think you've failed miserably before, make sure the heat is right (not too hot) and smell and taste every ingredient before using it in order to make sure it hasn't gone bad. Oil that sits on a shelf for too long can go rancid, and you know it from smelling it. If a sauce has separated in a weird way, don't trust it. Check expiration dates. If you're following a recipe from a reliable cookbook, and you're not burning stuff in a screaming hot oven or over an uncontrolled flame, you're going to succeed.

That said, my cooking fails wildly now and then without any obvious reason. I made a bad avocado Brie sandwich the other day and wouldn't previously have thought that was possible. (I think the wrong move involved the mayo substitute I used to mellow the mustard. Ignored my own rule and didn't taste it first because I assumed it was fine.) In the past few weeks, I've also managed to make hummus that was so bad that I had to throw it out. Afterward, I realized I didn't like the tahini. You can't cook a dish you're going to like with an ingredient you don't.

Which reminds me: I don't know who needs to hear this, but never cook with wine you wouldn't drink. You can get drinkable wine as cheap as cooking wine. I keep a box of it in my pantry. If you hate the smell or taste of it in the bottle, you're going to really hate it in your soup or sauce. ❧

Reading Group Guide

1. In what ways do you think Margo uses food as a replacement for facing her deeper emotions?

2. Margo seems shocked at Calvin's actions at the beginning of the novel. Why do you think she didn't see it coming?

3. Trista makes her dream to open a restaurant come true. If money or risk was no object, what would your dream job be?

4. Why do you think Aja is attracted to Michael? Are her feelings understandable given her background?

5. In what ways would Lucinda perhaps be different if her life had been different? Or was she always so conservative?

6. While this is a novel about women and female friendship, how do the men in the novel change from the beginning to the end—or do they change at all?

7. Food and friendship and family go together. What are some of the food traditions you have? Are they holiday traditions? Super Bowl traditions? Seasonal traditions?

8. Many people dream of opening a restaurant, which Trista does. And many others dream of renovating an old house, as Margo does. What is it about owning a restaurant or fixing up an old house that captures the imagination of so many?

9. Are there cookbooks that you use all the time? What is it about cookbooks that is so appealing? What is the kookiest or funniest cookbook you've ever seen?

10. If you are a cook, talk about the biggest cooking disaster you ever had!

Bonus: for your book club, everyone makes a recipe from the book! ∿

Recipes

<u>SNACKS</u>

Stuffed Mushrooms

This is a recipe I only recently adapted from Eat, Drink, and Be Chinaberry, *because I'm just getting into mushrooms. The culinary kind. I wasted a lot of time thinking I wasn't a mushroom person. Anyway, this can be prepared right up to the cooking point a day in advance if you prefer—just make sure you cover it well with plastic wrap before refrigerating, so everything doesn't dry out.*

- 25 cremini or baby bella mushrooms (or whatever your favorite is)
- ⅓ cup crumbled cooked bacon
- ½ small sweet onion, very finely chopped (about ¼ cup)
- 4 scallions, sliced from white through light green parts
- 1 8-ounce package cream cheese, room temperature
- ½ cup shredded cheddar cheese

1. Heat oven to 350°F.

2. Wash mushrooms and remove the stems, but only discard the dried bottom of the stems (the first ⅛ inch, approximately). Dice the rest of the stems and add them during step 4.

3. Spray a cookie sheet with nonstick spray and put the mushroom caps down on it, bottom side up.

4. Mix remaining ingredients and spoon an even amount into each mushroom cap.

5. Bake for 15 minutes, then serve.

Tomato Pesto Dip

This recipe is based on an old Disney World recipe I got when I took my then three-year-old on a "date" to Tony's Town Square Italian restaurant. It was so good I asked for the recipe—incredibly, they gave it to me!—and have been building things around it ever since.

- 2 tablespoons chopped fresh basil (or 2 teaspoons dried)
- 2 tablespoons chopped fresh Italian parsley (or 2 teaspoons dried)
- 2–4 (or more) large garlic cloves, chopped, to taste
- 2 ounces pine nuts or chopped walnuts
- ½ small white onion, diced
- 4 ounces sundried tomatoes in oil
- ⅓ cup grated Parmesan
- ¼ cup balsamic vinegar
- ½ cup olive oil
- 1 tablespoon tomato paste
- 3 ounces peeled and chopped tomatoes
- ¼ cup good red wine (you're not cooking it, so use one that's drink-worthy)

1. Put basil, parsley, garlic, nuts, onion, and sundried tomatoes into the bowl of a food processor and process for 10 seconds to incorporate. Add remaining ingredients and pulse until just incorporated but not liquefied.

2. Enjoy with toasted baguette slices, pita chips, or Ravioli Chips (see page 10). ▶

Ravioli Chips

These are addictive. And too easy. And you won't find the recipe in any diet cookbook. But, man, this is good. Your guests will love them . . . if you don't eat them all before everyone arrives.

- 20+ small-to-medium cheese ravioli
- ½ cup finely grated Parmesan and/or Romano cheese
- 2 tablespoons panko bread crumbs
- Italian seasoning
- Red pepper flakes, optional
- 1 egg, lightly beaten with 2 tablespoons water
- Vegetable oil, for frying

1. Check the ravioli package for al dente cooking instructions and cook one minute short of that. You want them cooked but *really* al dente.

2. While they're cooking, set out a plate and onto it mix Parmesan with panko and season with Italian seasoning and red pepper flakes, if you want a little heat.

3. Put the egg and water in a bowl.

4. Heat ½ inch of vegetable oil in a large skillet over medium-high heat. You're looking for about 250°F to 275°F.

5. When the pasta is cooked, drain it, quickly tossing it back into the pot with some cooking water to keep it warm while you're working.

6. Working quickly, dunk cooked ravioli into egg mix, then coat in cheese mix and fry for 1 to 2 minutes per side to reach a warm golden brown. Transfer them to paper towels to drain excess oil as you go.

7. Serve warm, with marinara sauce for dip. Tomato Pesto Dip (see page 9) is also a good accompaniment.

Curried Deviled Eggs

These are just so good, despite their simplicity. If you're not a fan of curry, you can replace that with any favorite seasoning—my son prefers Lawry's Seasoned Salt. Go figure. But I like curry and have been known to taste as I go and add up to 2 teaspoons of it, but better to underseason and keep going than to overseason and throw the whole lot out.

- 1 dozen extra-large eggs
- ⅔ cup mayonnaise
- 2 teaspoons champagne or white wine vinegar (*not* distilled white)
- 2–3 teaspoons Dijon mustard, to taste (some Dijon is more pungent than others)
- 2 teaspoons dried tarragon
- Pinch of cayenne
- 1 teaspoon curry powder
- Salt and pepper, to taste
- Smoked paprika

1. In a pan, cover the eggs with cold water and bring to boil. Then place the lid on the pan and turn off the heat, letting the eggs sit for 12 minutes before rinsing in cold water. Once the eggs are cool, peel and cut each one in half widthwise (then you just make a flat surface on the bottom by cutting a small slice).

2. Combine yolks and remaining ingredients, except paprika, gently and pipe into halved egg whites. Sprinkle with paprika to top. (Weird tip: hold your hand high over the eggs while sprinkling the paprika—it gives you more control and fewer clumps.)

3. Cover with plastic wrap and chill until ready to serve. ▶

Creamy Margarita Pops

Yes, I'm going to go ahead and call this an appetizer because whenever I serve it as one it's very popular and people tend to forget about food in favor of more pops. Seriously, I'm not including them as "drinks" per se, because they require attention, concentration. They aren't casual nibbles.

- 3 pounds, or about 26, fresh limes, squeezed, or about 2 cups of lime juice
- ¾ cup silver tequila
- 1 cup water
- 1 14-ounce can sweetened condensed milk
- Margarita or kosher salt for the rims
- 10 3-ounce paper cups
- 10 Popsicle sticks

1. Mix lime juice, tequila, water, and sweetened condensed milk in a blender to thoroughly incorporate.

2. Set out a plate of salt and a plate of water and rim about half of the cups (unless you know all your guests are going to be wanting salt or not wanting salt) by dipping the cup rim quickly in the water, then quickly in the salt. Turn right side up and pour the mixture evenly into the cups.

3. Freeze for about an hour to thicken enough to put the sticks in and have them stay upright. Then freeze at least overnight.

4. Serve and bask in the praise. (These would obviously be good with the Layered Fiesta Dip, see page 19, or even just chips and salsa.)

Pesto Torta

This is a beautiful presentation for company and also a good excuse to make Tomato Pesto Dip (see page 9), which you can spend the rest of your week using as a pasta sauce, a cracker dip, or even just for dipping your finger in like an animal in the middle of the night. It's good, but it's garlicky, so remember that before a date!

- 2 8-ounce packages cream cheese, room temperature
- ½ cup sour cream
- ¼ cup butter, softened
- 1 cup shredded Parmesan
- 1 cup fresh pesto (Tomato Pesto Dip recipe would be great here)
- ½ cup chopped pistachio meats (optional)
- 8 sundried tomatoes in oil, chopped (or cut with scissors)

1. Line a flat round bowl with plastic wrap (two pieces, going in opposite directions to cover the whole space)—don't worry about being neat; this is only so you can get the torta out in one piece. It's basically a mold for the torte. (Working with plastic wrap is a nightmare, but it's worth it.)

2. Combine the cream cheese, sour cream, butter, and Parmesan in a bowl. And combine the pesto, with or without optional pistachios, in a separate bowl.

3. Now you build: set sundried tomatoes evenly in the bottom of your dish (it will be the top in the end), top with all of the cream cheese mixture, then with the pesto (with or without pistachios). You *could* make another layer here with charcuterie meat, but I'm no expert on meats, so you'd have to wing it with your favorite, sliced into matchsticks for easy spreading.

4. Fold the plastic wrap over the top, press *gently*, and refrigerate overnight or until ready to serve (at least 6 hours). When ready, uncover the top, turn the whole thing upside down onto a serving platter, and carefully set down. Remove plastic wrap and serve with sliced crostini. ▶

Chicken Pot Pie Fritters

You can argue that these are cheat-y, since they are, and you are welcome to get down off that Clydesdale and make your own roux-into-cream-soup and cook your own chicken breasts. But if you want a really fast comfort food snack that makes everyone think you're a culinary genius, look no further! These are pretty substantial, so you really only need to have one or two per person, tops. This recipe makes 8, so adjust accordingly.

- 2 teaspoons butter
- 1 small yellow onion, peeled and chopped
- Pinch of salt
- 1 pound rotisserie chicken breast meat, shredded
- 1 10.5-ounce can cream of chicken soup
- ¾ cup frozen peas and carrots
- Salt and pepper, to taste
- 1 package crescent rolls

Okay, so the onion really adds something to this, but if you're in a hurry or you hate onion, you can *skip it, but I wouldn't.*

1. Just put 2 teaspoons of butter into a saucepan with the chopped onion and a pinch of salt and cook over medium heat until translucent (about 8 minutes).

2. Add chicken, soup, frozen vegetables, and ½ cup of water, and stir. Season to taste. This is the bulk of your dish, so you want it as tasty as possible—if you have a favorite seasoning that you're just dying to add, do it!

3. Heat oven to 375°F.

4. Spray a muffin tin with nonstick spray and stretch one crescent roll into a muffin cup, then fill with ⅛ of the soup mixture and pinch the roll closed with your fingers. If you find the odd shape of the crescent rolls hard to work with, you can lay them out and pinch all the seals and cut the dough into squares if you prefer. That's what I do, but it just sounds like so much work for such an otherwise easy recipe.

5. Bake for 12 to 15 minutes or until golden brown on top. Serve immediately.

Corn Fritters

Urbana, Maryland—once my home—was a sleepy little farm town in the middle of Civil War battlefields and sprawling farms and cornfields. The Peter Pan Inn opened there in 1926 and ran for more than sixty years, a huge white historical house, with patio gardens surrounded by wrought iron fences and roaming peacocks acting as mobile decor. The place was hugely popular even in my childhood in the 1970s and 1980s, and we used to drive up from Potomac, about twenty-five miles, for a special night out at the Peter Pan.

It closed in the mid-1980s and was slowly dismantled to the sad, unoccupied shell it is today. But I still have a drink swizzler and an old matchbook bearing its name, and memories of arriving cranky and hungry and leaving happy and full. The food was good old country fare—pot roast, ham steaks, shrimp, fried chicken, and corn fritters. Always corn fritters. Somewhere along the way, some lucky soul got the recipe, and here it is, preserved for generations to come.

- 1¼ cups all-purpose flour
- ½ teaspoon salt
- 3 tablespoons sugar
- 1½ teaspoons baking powder
- 1 egg, lightly beaten
- ½ cup whole milk
- 1 cup whole corn kernels, drained
- Vegetable oil, for frying
- Powdered sugar, for garnish

1. Sift all the dry ingredients together in one bowl; mix the wet ingredients and the corn in a separate one. Pour the dry ingredients into the wet and fold gently with a wooden spoon or spatula. Do not overmix—it's okay if there are some lumps!

2. Heat vegetable oil—with a little bacon fat if you have any (I always have it in my fridge)—to 275°F for frying. When it reaches temperature, drop spoonfuls of the fritter batter in and fry for about 3 minutes, until golden brown.

3. Lift out with tongs or a spider skimmer and let cool on paper towels. Sprinkle lightly with powdered sugar before serving. ▶

Carolyn Clemens's Spinach Artichoke Dip

Carolyn has been a friend for more than twenty-five years, and simply put, she is the best cook I know. We used to live across the street from each other, and every once in a while the doorbell would ring and one of her four boys would be standing there with a plate of something delicious she had just whipped up—cookies from the oven, cheesy biscuits, or, one of my favorites, warm latkes with a dollop of sour cream and applesauce, ready to eat! So for many years my family has known, if Carolyn made it, it's going to be great. Even if it's something you think you've had a million times.

This is her base recipe. The ingredients she calls her "constants." Now and then she might add something on a whim, but this is her Spinach Artichoke Dip, and we're all lucky to have it.

- 1 10-ounce package frozen chopped spinach, thawed
- 1 14-ounce can artichokes, chopped small
- 1 8-ounce package cream cheese, room temperature
- 2 or 3 onions, chopped and sautéed in butter then cooled
- ¼ cup mayonnaise
- Cheese (I think it's important to just quote her on the cheese amount and selection: "I almost always add two or more cups of chopped Swiss cheese, less if I've got Gruyère too. Some Parm, some sharp cheddar, blue cheese crumbles if I have them, some heavy cream if I have it.")
- Salt and pepper, to taste
- Optional: pinch or two of red pepper flakes, garlic powder, onion powder

1. Heat oven to 350°F.

2. Squeeze the water out of the spinach. All of the water—use a potato ricer if you need to.

3. Mix everything together and dump it into an oven-to-table dish. This is what you'll serve it in, so pick a pretty one.

4. Bake for 20 minutes, then serve with pita chips or crudités.

Black Pepper Gruyère Cheese Puffs

Gruyère is my favorite cheese, I think. It's close, between that, Morbier, and thin slices of real Parmigiano Reggiano. Fortunately, this recipe has two out of three.

- 1½ cups whole milk
- 1 stick butter
- 2 to 3 teaspoons kosher salt (3 if using a very coarse kosher salt, like Morton's)
- 1 teaspoon freshly ground or cracked black pepper
- 1½ cups all-purpose flour
- 5 large eggs, lightly beaten
- 1 cup shredded Gruyère, divided (keep 3 tablespoons aside)
- ½ cup grated Parmesan cheese

1. Heat oven to 375°F and line two baking sheets with parchment paper.

2. Put milk, butter, salt, and pepper into a saucepan and cook over medium heat and bring to a slow boil. Reduce heat to low and whisk in the flour, stirring constantly to thicken the mixture and eliminate lumps. It will thicken quickly and you'll need to trade the whisk for a wooden spoon.

3. Cook for 3 to 5 minutes over low heat, making sure not to burn—the dough will keep thickening and become a ball that isn't sticking to the bottom anymore.

4. Remove from heat and transfer to a stand mixer, or get your muscles ready with a bowl and wooden spoon. Stir in the eggs, one at a time, then add the shredded Gruyère (minus the 3 tablespoons of Gruyère that you set aside) and the Parmesan.

5. Drop about one tablespoon at a time onto the parchment paper, as if you were making drop biscuits. Sprinkle all with the remaining Gruyère and bake for 30 minutes, or until golden brown.

6. Serve warm or at room temperature—they're not as flavorful cold. ▶

Periyali's Almond Skordalia
(Potato, Almond, and Garlic) Dip

I first had this at the Greek restaurant Periyali, in New York City. What a lovely, intimate, friendly little place. I've been back many times since then. But that first time, I was at a business lunch and my boss wanted me to try this. She was a major foodie in a major food town, so even though this didn't sound like "my kind of thing," I trusted her and tried it. It was love at first bite.

- 1 small all-purpose potato, peeled
- 5 slices dense home-style white bread, crusts removed
- ½ cup whole blanched almonds, coarsely chopped
- 2 or 3 large garlic cloves, pressed or smashed with the side of a knife
- 3 tablespoons lemon juice
- 3 tablespoons white-wine vinegar (not distilled white)
- 2 tablespoons extra-virgin olive oil
- ¾ teaspoon salt
- ½ teaspoon sugar
- 1 16-ounce can large butter beans

1. Boil the peeled potato for 20 to 25 minutes, until it yields when pierced by a fork.

2. Toast the bread in a 300°F oven for 20 minutes, then put it into a bowl of clean water to soak. Squeeze out the excess water with your hands and set aside.

3. Put the almonds, garlic, and potato into the bowl of a food processor and process until smooth, then add the bread (you wait until the end so the bread doesn't get too gummy).

4. Combine the lemon juice, vinegar, olive oil, salt, and sugar in a bowl and add that mixture a bit at a time to the processor bowl, pulsing between additions. It should be quite smooth; if it's not, add a little more olive oil.

5. Spoon mixture into a serving bowl, cover, and let rest for an hour or more so the flavors can meld.

6. Serve on a plate with large butter beans—drag the beans through the skordalia with your fork to eat. No bread or crackers necessary!

Layered Fiesta Dip

There isn't much to say about this that you can't guess from the name and the ingredients. But don't let that fool you—this is the best recipe you'll find for this layered dip, and though I list the avocados as optional, around these parts they are necessary.

- 1 cup sour cream (not light)
- 4 ounces cream cheese
- 1 16-ounce can refried beans
- ¾ cup salsa
- 1 tablespoon taco seasoning
- 4 Campari tomatoes, sliced
- 2 cups grated Monterey Jack cheese
- Sliced avocado, optional (dip slices in lime juice to prevent browning)

1. Heat oven to 350°F.

2. Mix everything but the tomato slices and grated Monterey Jack (and avocado, if using) in a bowl, or in your mixer with the paddle attachment. Mix to incorporate, not to whip.

3. Spray a baking dish with nonstick spray and spread half the bean mix across the bottom. Sprinkle with 1 cup of Monterey Jack cheese, top with tomato slices, then add another layer of the bean mix. Top with remainder of grated cheese and bake for 20 minutes.

4. Add avocado slices, if using, just prior to serving with tortilla chips. ▶

The Very Best Sweet Hot Sauce

This is my exact recipe, the one that I like best. But it's totally flexible—you can use 2 pounds of whatever chilis you like, and if you prefer a very mild sauce, include a sweet bell pepper in that weight. If you hate garlic, leave it out entirely. If you're just meh about it, at least put in one or two cloves to round the flavors here.

- 1 lemon or lime, cleaned and dried
- 3 tablespoons raw sugar
- 1 pound fresno peppers (½ roasted)
- 2 poblano peppers, roasted
- 2 Italian sweet hot peppers, roasted
- 6 cherry chili peppers
- 1 jalapeño pepper, roasted
- ½ to ¾ pound pineapple, diced (I prefer more)
- 2 sweet Maui onions, peeled and rough chopped
- 8 cloves garlic, peeled and rough chopped
- 2 Compari tomatoes
- 4 cups distilled white vinegar
- 1 ripe mango, peeled and sliced
- ½ cup cider vinegar
- ¼ to ½ cup honey or maple syrup, to taste
- Salt and pepper, to taste
- 1 teaspoon Worcestershire sauce
- 2 teaspoons curry powder
- ½ teaspoon allspice

1. Peel the zest off the lemon or lime, avoiding the white pith as much as possible. Put the zest into a small Ziploc with 1 tablespoon of sugar and seal. Leave for 8 to 24 hours. The sugar draws the oils out of the zest.

2. Meanwhile prepare your peppers, pineapple, onion, garlic, and tomato by chopping them all roughly and putting them into a bowl. Sprinkle a teaspoon of salt over the mixture. Add 4 cups distilled white vinegar, cover, and leave to sit those same 8 to 24 hours.

3. Juice the lemon/lime you zested and put the juice and zest into a pan with 2 tablespoons sugar. Cook gently over medium heat, never boiling, until the sugar and juice become clear, just about 5 minutes. Remove from heat, cover, and let cool.

4. Combine the mango and the pepper mix in a pot and heat for 15 minutes on medium heat. Cool to room temperature and puree in a blender, then strain through a fine mesh sieve. I like to strain it into a large work bowl, clean the pot, and return the mixture to it.

5. Add cider vinegar and honey (or maple syrup) to the mango and pepper mixture, then cook down to a slightly thicker consistency. Remove from heat and add citrus zest and the sugar syrup with them. Stir well and let sit for 1 day (or longer, depending on how citrus-forward you want it).

6. At the end of that time, heat gently for the last time, add Worcestershire and seasonings, to taste. Then cool, strain, and bottle. Keep in the fridge. ▶

<u>DRINKS</u>

Autumn

Apple Oat Vodka Creams

This is based on a recipe for Honey Oat vodka from Blue Hill at Stone Barns in New York, a restaurant I have not yet been to, but I have friends who went and raved about everything from the food to the air. So when a variation of this recipe (originally made by mixologist Philippe Gouze) appeared in the Washington Post, *I was all about trying it. I have adapted it to accommodate more ordinary vodka than they use, and added apples for an extra sweet, autumnal flair.*

- 1 liter of good corn vodka, like Tito's (about 4 cups)
- 2 cups rolled oats (preferably organic, always, and not quick-cooking ones)
- 1 cup honey
- 1 apple (I prefer a sweet red), sliced (no seeds or stem)

1. Combine everything in a large jar with a lid and shake well. Refrigerate and shake every day for a week.

2. After a week, filter three times through cheesecloth and pour into a new, clean vessel. Keep in fridge until gone.

3. Serve as shots or combine 1:1 with half-and-half and serve over ice. Garnish with a slice of apple.

Winter

Italian Chocolate

Amaro Averna is an Italian digestif, made from a secret infusion of Mediterranean herbs, spices, and fruits. It has been a traditional drink in Sicily, where it is made, since Salvatore Averna invented it in 1868.

So while this recipe is deceptively simple, the ingredients are doing the heavy lifting, bringing depth and complexity to this warming winter treat, over ice or in a cup of coffee.

- 2 ounces Amaro Averna
- 4 ounces Godiva white chocolate liqueur
- 8 dashes chocolate bitters
- Cocoa powder, for garnish

1. For each drink, shake ½ ounce Amaro Averna, 1 ounce Godiva liqueur, and 2 dashes of chocolate bitters together, then pour over ice and sprinkle lightly with cocoa powder. ▶

Spring

Flower Girl

For a long time, Crème de Violette was impossible to get in the United States, but since 2007 it has been back, and you shouldn't have too much trouble finding it. And what better way to celebrate the new buds of spring than with a sip of violet?

If you or your guests have seasonal allergies, skip the baby's breath garnish, though it is spectacularly beautiful posing in a drink.

- 4 ounces Crème de Violette
- 1 ounce lemon juice
- Brut champagne, cava, or prosecco
- 4 sprigs baby's breath (rinsed!), for garnish

1. Pour 1 ounce of Crème de Violette into each of four champagne flutes. Then add a quarter ounce of lemon juice and top with bubbly.

2. Add your garnish and serve!

Summer

The Babe

Passion tea lemonade—half lemonade, half brewed Tazo Passion tea—is one of my favorite summer staples, so it's nice to have these teabags on hand all summer, if not all year. If you need to, however, you could substitute with any strong, fruity herbal tea.

The lemon oleo is worth making because the saved rinds add a citrusy zest to any food or drink, and they're one of the ingredients in my Very Best Sweet Hot Sauce (see page 20).

- ½ cup lemon oleo saccharum (recipe below)
- 10 lemons, washed and dried
- 1½ cups plus 2 tablespoons sugar
- 1 cup brewed Tazo Passion tea
- 6 ounces vodka
- 4 sprigs of mint, washed (even if it's from your garden)
- Club soda or tonic

1. Start by making the oleo: Carefully peel the zest off all the lemons. Put your favorite playlist on, as it's going to take a little while. Try to avoid the pith as much as you can—it's bitter. Drop the zest into a Ziploc and toss with the 2 tablespoons of sugar and allow to sit overnight—the sugar draws the delicious lemon oil out of the zest.

2. Save those lemons—you need to juice them all the next day and strain the juice into a nonreactive pan. Add 1½ cups of sugar to the lemon juice and the zests and cook over medium heat until the liquid is thick and clear. Cover and turn off the heat. After 10 minutes, strain the liquid and set aside for drinks. Put the zest back into the bag for drinks or hot sauce purposes.

3. To make the drinks: Put ¼ cup of tea into each of 4 glasses. Stir 1½ ounces vodka into each, along with 2 tablespoons of oleo. Spank the mint—yes, literally—to bring out the natural oils and flavor. Don't beat it senseless—that is ▶

Recipes *(continued)*

actually counterproductive; you're just trying to express the oils, not shred it all. Compare the spanked and unspanked sprigs and you'll notice how much fuller the mint scent is on the spanked ones. Drop one mint sprig into each glass, stir gently, then top with club soda or tonic. Serve. ⌒

Discover great authors, exclusive offers, and more at hc.com.